THE BREAK IN THE LINE

THE BREAK
IN THE LINE

*

BERKELY MATHER

THE
COMPANION BOOK CLUB
LONDON AND SYDNEY

*Made and printed in Great Britain
for the Companion Book Club
by Odhams (Watford) Ltd.*
SBN/S. 60077144X
SBN/D. 600871444
8.71

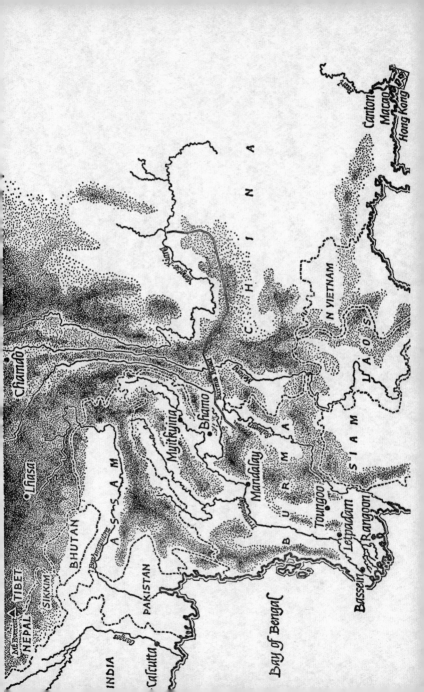

Chapter One

THERE WAS NO MOON THAT NIGHT, and a high mist was blanketing the stars, so that sea and sky were one uniform blackness, relieved only by the reflected glow from Hong Kong's million neon signs, twenty miles away to the southeast. Here there were fourteen pinpoints of light; a smoky hurricane lamp on each of the twelve junks and the two brighter anchor lights on the Fisheries Patrol launch. If you watched any one of them for more than a few moments it appeared to be moving ahead, but that was only an illusion caused by the strong current of the Pearl River bringing flotsam downstream and breaking the wriggling reflections in the water.

Kam Foo said, 'When I was a kid the fisher types always used paper lanterns instead of these stinking tin things. Bloody pretty.' It worried me a little because Kam Foo always got terribly English when he was jumpy. But let's be honest. I was jumpy too.

Our lamp was hanging in the junk's main shrouds, with another one, alight but obscured by a black cloth cylinder, on the mast of the longboat which was anchored alongside. The cylinder was attached to a bamboo fishing-rod which projected out over the rail of the junk. I looked at my watch for the tenth time in the last hour. It still wanted two minutes to switch time, and I had to fight down the temptation to jump the gun.

I counted one hundred and twenty, then grunted to Kam Foo and climbed on to the rail and raised the glass of the hurricane lamp in the shrouds. He took hold of the bamboo pole and waited. I said, 'One—two—three—NOW!' and blew out the guttering flame. Simultaneously Kam Foo whisked away the cloth cylinder from the masthead lamp of the longboat, and we both turned and watched the patrol launch. They would have their glasses on us. If the switch was apparent, they would flash us—and the thing would be postponed until tomorrow night. I found myself hoping for the flash, even though that would mean another crawling twenty-four hours on this filthy junk with the tension building up again. But there was no flash, and after five minutes Kam Foo started to whistle a Viennese waltz very softly. He whistled well—again, when he was nervous.

Kennelly was sleeping on a padded cotton quilt on the poop, his straw coolie hat over his face. He swore, got up and followed me down below when I roused him. The cabin was cramped and there was only about five feet headroom, but it was blacked-out and there was a good strong electric light here that switched off when the door was opened. The place was filthy and it was cluttered with odds and ends of gear—trawl-boards, a bundled purse-seine net and three big packing cases. He knelt and lifted a section of the deck planking and fished out an oiled-silk portfolio of Admiralty charts.

He was a small, lean man, dressed like the rest of us in fish-stinking blue dungarees. He couldn't have passed in daylight for a Chinese—I've yet to meet the pure European who could—but that didn't matter, because in the five years he had commanded the *Hong-mei-Sha*, which means in English 'The Fragrant Flower of the Ocean,' he had never been seen above deck between the hours of dawn and sunset. Chan Lee took over in daylight, with Kennelly conning her from below by means of the tell-tale compass and a weather eye cocked from time to time at one of the dozen strategically bored spyholes in the cabin, and a blistering stream of invective in perfect Cantonese or Hakka as the occasion demanded.

He unrolled and spread the charts and looked up at me inquiringly, but I wanted Kam Foo in on this so I went to the door and opened it. Kennelly grunted irritably as the lights went out.

'We've got exactly six hours of darkness left before getting back to this anchorage,' he said. 'It had *better* be close.'

Kam Foo had been waiting outside. He came in and stood blinking as I closed the door and the lights came on again.

I went across and showed Kennelly the spot I wanted on the chart. It was the other side of the estuary, about fifteen miles inside Chinese territorial waters.

'There's a fishing village here,' I began, 'and five miles further on, a creek——'

But Kennelly was swearing again. 'And a three-knot current against us the whole way,' he said wearily. 'Two hours on full engines, and about an hour and a half back— then we've got to allow time for you bloody soldiers to lose yourselves ashore. Who timed it for you? The Army?'

He straightened and pushed past us and went out on deck and, following him, I heard him telling Chan Lee to cut the cable and to pick up the anchor from the longboat, which was sharing it, when we came back. Then we returned to the cabin while he worked things out properly and put her on course, with the big silent electric submarine engine whispering and juddering slightly below us.

It wasn't as bad as he had made out. I reckoned an hour and a half there and an hour back, and, with luck, Kam Foo and I could be through our business and back on board in half an hour. We helped him to move the packing cases and trawl-boards, uncovering the radar, echo-sounder and gyro compass that lived beneath them, then we left him. Kennelly, past master in the art of blind navigation and possessed of the instincts of an albatross, worked better on his own.

9

I leaned on the rail with Kam Foo and watched the phosphorescent wake slipping past. Behind us the dim lights of the anchored fishing fleet, our spurious one among them, were being lost in the mist. Twelve had arrived at sunset in this farthest corner of British territorial waters to wait for the prime garoupa coming in on the flood tide at dawn to feed on the small fry brought downriver, and twelve, to anybody interested enough to watch from the Chinese-held mainland, were still there. And twelve, we hoped, would be back there at daylight, ready to up-anchor and hightail it home to the markets of Victoria and Kowloon with full fish-holds.

We, of course, would have no fish, but that didn't matter. We would just be one of four hundred fishing junks puttering back to harbour on smelly diesels—ours doing dual duty by recharging the batteries that drove our motors—and we'd peel off and make for our quiet, secluded anchorage in Clearwater Bay, just another unremarkable microcosm among the teeming traffic of this vast port, as noticeable as a taxi in Piccadilly in the rush hours; and mid-morning should, with a little bit of luck, find Kennelly in his not too flourishing import/export agency in De Voeux Road, Captain Kam Foo drilling his Locally Enlisted Personnel at Limun Barracks, and me, James Wainwright, back at the ledgers of the Hong Kong and Southern China Bank. Yes, that's what I did as a cover job, God help me.

Kam Foo said. 'When you're browned off with spitting in the water, old boy, you might tell us the score?' There was no umbrage there at my keeping him in the dark up to now. He was new in the business but he'd learnt that much. Only the man in charge of the operation was fully briefed, and he passed down just as much, or little, as was absolutely necessary for his subordinates to know, and he did it as late as possible. The less you know and the later you know it, the less chance there is of a leak—by accident or design. You might think from this that we didn't altogether trust each other. And you'd be goddam right. We didn't.

I said, 'You saw the spot on the chart. It's a pick-up and a squeeze-pidgin.'

'What's a squeeze-pidgin?'

I stared at him. 'Are you pulling my leg?'

'Honest to God, it's a new one on me.'

I sighed. I suppose I should have been neither surprised nor angry. He had been born in Hampstead and educated expensively at a Broadstairs prep school, Wellington and Sandhurst. He had learned, at his grandfather's knee and the School of Oriental Languages, Bloomsbury, classical Mandarin, which he spoke, read and pen-painted perfectly, but he knew less Cantonese, Hakka and Hong Kong gutter pidgin than I did.

'A bribe,' I explained. 'Something you *squeeze* out of somebody.'

'Expressive,' he said. 'I like that. Who's squeezing who?'

'We're paying off a bent Communist official,' I said. 'Bent means——'

'Corrupt,' he supplied. 'Don't worry about my English slang. It's only the local brand that throws me.'

'The pick-up will be giving three flashes on an infra-red torch—repeated every ten minutes between midnight and one o'clock. If he doesn't, we come back tomorrow at the same time. No joy tomorrow—we give up and go home.'

'Who is he?'

'A guy who will answer "Charing Cross" when I say "running water". I know no more than that.'

'A European,' he said, and it was a statement rather than a question. 'Bound to be.'

'What makes you think so?' I asked.

'They wouldn't give a Chinese, even an educated one, a password with two "r" sounds in it. I'm the only Pong I know who wouldn't say "Charling Closs".'

'Clever fellow,' I said dryly. 'We have a furbler, of course. A furbler is——'

'Something you tell the Opposition in case you get gathered in and leaned on a bit heavily,' he said promptly.

I took a deep breath. 'Dead right,' I told him. 'In that unhappy event we tell the Opposition that the answer we were expecting was "Tai Mo Shan". And now, for Christ's sake, will you stop being bright and intuitive and let me get on with the briefing.'

'Sorry,' he said, but didn't mean it.

'When we pick up the flashes, you and I paddle ashore in the inflatable dinghy. We'll be on the end of a line. The line will be on a high-speed winch back here on the junk. You'll paddle on the way in, I'll be covering with the burp gun. If everything is all right, two men—and two men only—come down to the boat, with their hands on their heads. We exchange the words, I toss the squeeze ashore, one man comes forward and gets in with us, we give two flashes on our infra-red torch and they start winding us back. Any questions?'

'If everything *isn't* all right——'

'If more than two men come forward or we're rushed out of the darkness, I cut loose with the gun and they wind us in *really* fast on the winch. The line is attached to our safety-harness, not the dinghy. It will yank us clean out into the water, in which case you lie stiff and hold your breath——'

'I've done the course,' he said shortly, and added, 'You're unhappy about this, aren't you? About my being with you, I mean.'

'No more than I'd be with any other first-timer,' I told him. 'Or tenth-timer, if it comes to that. Nothing personal. Put it down to nerves.'

'But you don't altogether trust me?'

'I've known two guys in this business who altogether trusted other people,' I said. 'One was a queer; I put flowers on the grave of the other every tenth of July, when I happen to remember it. I'm not queer, and I'm still alive. Touch wood.'

'God, what a horrible racket this is,' he said.

'Why, then, did you come into it? Nobody has his arm twisted.'

'Survival. I'm of the fourth Hong Kong-born generation. Technically I'm as British as you. What would be ahead of people like us if the real Chinese took over?'

'Your old man saw it coming thirty years ago, so I'm told, and got out to England while the going was good—with his dough. You should worry.'

'*Technically* British. Underneath I'm still Chinese, and family feeling is strong in us. There are a hell of a lot of my family still out here—both sides of the line.'

'Some of whom——' I began, then broke off and felt for my infra-red glasses and put them on.

'Put your blinkers on so you'll be adjusted when we get up there,' I told him.

'Some of whom have made a deal and gone over? Is that what you were going to say?'

'Forget it,' I said.

'But that's really the reason why I'm not fully trusted?' he persisted.

'Listen, Foo,' I said. 'You know exactly as much about this mission as I know myself.'

'But you only told me now, when it would be impossible for me to leak anything. When, if the crap hits the fan, I'd stop some of it myself.'

'For God's sake,' I told him wearily. 'I was only briefed myself a few minutes before we sailed. You heard me tell the skipper the pick-up point within the last half-hour. Until then he hadn't the faintest idea what his task was. The skipper of the Fisheries Patrol launch knows nothing either. He was merely told to watch our lights and if he detected anything in the nature of a switch, or if he guessed we were slipping our cable, he was to flash us. You probably think that I'm holding out on the identity of the pick-up. Actually I'm not. I don't know who it is and I don't want to know—but if I *did* know, I still wouldn't tell you. Can't you see the reason for it all?'

'Yes,' he said sulkily. 'They told us all about it on the course. Top secret—burn before reading—knock twice and ask for Alice. I say it's confusing and unnecessary. At Sandhurst and in the regiment I was taught that the pre-requisite for any action was mutual trust and confidence—and respect —between the officer and the men. I think I achieved that, even in the British regiment I was first posted to, where I was a bloody Chink and I used to hear *sotto voce* jokes about chop suey and laundries, and my nickname was Hoo Flung Dung.'

'Ah! So that's what's behind it all?' I said. 'Good. Ring the Race Relations Board when we get back, and complain about discrimination. Listen, you bloody twit, I don't give a damn whether you're black, white, yellow, brindle or khaki, I still wouldn't tell you a word more than I had to, any more than I'd want to know myself—for the starkly simple reason that the less one knows the less one can give away under torture or brainwashing. And finally, don't ever compare this game with soldiering. They haven't a single point of similarity. We don't shield our fallen comrades with our own bodies. We don't pick up our wounded or bury our dead. If two get into a clamp and there's a way out for one, he takes it—without a backward glance or a flicker of remorse —and he assumes that the bloke who gets left is going to talk, so he acts accordingly and changes the whole plan, even if it means leaving his own brother in the lurch.'

Kam Foo sighed. 'Yes, we had that on the course too— "idealism is a greater hazard than treachery," or as the Gaffer used to put it, "well-meaning heroes have buggered more missions than two-timing bastards working for a double pay-cheque." I suppose one has to accept that in the long run, but one doesn't have to *like* it.'

'One accepts or quits. The option is there—at least in the early stages.'

'You never thought of quitting?'

'Several times, but in the end I *didn't* have the option. I was fired as incompetent.'

'But you're back—so you must like it.'

'Whether I like it or not doesn't enter into it. It was a straight case of wounded vanity. They were temporarily stuck for someone to do a very simple and very dirty little job, so I was invited in again, on probation sort of. This time I didn't make a nonsense of it.'

'What was the job?'

'That doesn't enter into it either, and if you'd been longer in the game you wouldn't ask. Still, there's no harm in telling you. I had to stick a knife in one of theirs, and plant the knife on one of our own, who was duly executed for it. I won't tell you how or when or you'd be able to check on it.'

There was silence for a long minute, then Kam Foo said, 'As you remarked yourself, very dirty.'

'Taken out of context, no doubt. But it was also logical. Theirs was a very dangerous number indeed. Ours was doubling for the other side. Their removal meant that a round half-dozen of ours were still on the board. The point I'm trying to make, though, is that I didn't know the ins and outs of it beforehand. They didn't give me any moral justification or pragmatic considerations for it in advance. That came afterwards, as incidentally as I'm telling you now. Then it was just two clients to be done. Their names and addresses, a knife and a pair of rubber gloves. Get on with it—in the full knowledge that I was completely expendable, and if I'd been caught on the job, I'd have been taking the eight o'clock walk myself.'

15

Kam Foo said, 'Er—yukk!' and spat in the water. I was worried about him.

I walked about the deck stumbling over dunnage. Infrareds are peculiar things. They completely black you out for ten minutes or so, then you start seeing things 'as in a glass, darkly' but more distinctly on a thoroughly pitch-black night than with the naked eye, and the beam of the special torch that goes with them, which is completely invisible under normal conditions, comes up through their lenses with crystal clarity.

Kennelly was giving the winch a trial spin. It went round at a hell of a rate and was capable of pulling a quarter of a ton through water at over fifty miles an hour, stopping dead at intervals to avoid dragging the man on the end under and drowning him. I'd had a test run on it. I hoped we wouldn't be using it tonight.

Kennelly tossed me the two safety-harnesses we would be wearing and helped me into mine. He looked around in the darkness for Kam Foo, swearing impatiently, and then someone called softly from the poop for him in Hakka. He left me and ran silently in his rubber shoes along the deck and up the short ladder.

Everything was silent. There was the slightest vibration, that was more a pulse, from the electric motors, but no noise other than the murmur of the wash and the faint clacking sound made by the revolving radar scanner that after dark was mounted on the top of the mast. It was weird and unnerving.

Kam Foo was still leaning over the rail. I helped him into his harness and was about to suggest going into the cabin for a smoke, when Kennelly loomed up behind us.

He said in a low voice, 'We're bang opposite the spot according to my reckoning, about three-quarters of a mile offshore.'

'How close can you get in?' I asked.

'Three hundred yards. That will leave me four feet under my keel. How does that suit you?'

'All right by me. What about winch tolerance?'

'Nothing that need worry you. There's over a mile of line in the reel.'

'All right then.' I looked at the luminous face of my watch. It wanted five minutes to midnight. 'We'll start looking in now. How's she pointing?'

'Dead for the beach. I'll cut her back to bare steerage way. You watch over the bows.'

Kam Foo went forward, while I slipped into the cabin for the squeeze. It was a two-pound brick of pure heroin, wrapped and sewn in oiled silk. Time was when squeeze currency was gold, but heroin, weight for weight, is worth exactly a hundred times more smuggled back into Hong Kong, where the lousy stuff was made—from raw opium in turn smuggled in from the Burma-Thai border country. Very few, if any, of the Communists were hooked on it themselves—it would have made things much easier for us if they had been— but they loved the Scotch, fountain pens, wrist-watches and canned food it bought them, both for their own sake and as currency among the higher echelons of the Comrades; and if it still further debauched the hated Capitalist-Imperialists, so much the better. John Chinaman, whatever his politics, was ever a grafter, and I never met a Communist official yet who couldn't be bought with a hunk of horse, providing it was big enough. But if you were caught with it the wrong side of the border, your head came clean off at the neck and went up on a pole along the International Boundary; it still didn't deter the runners.

We saw the first flashes at three minutes past twelve, right smack over the bowsprit. Kennelly dived back to his controls, leaving two of the crew to get the inflatable over the side and latch us on to the end of the line. There was a bit of trouble here. The line itself was a very fine wire rope of immense tensile strength. It ended in a spring clip that was intended to fit to a ring in the back of the harness, but tonight there were two of us and at the last minute they couldn't find the link-strap that was supposed to hitch us together, so they had to make do with a piece of rope.

We pushed off. Kam Foo wasn't awfully good with the paddle, and there was rather more splashing than I liked. Still, it was only a matter of yards, and the pick-up knew his stuff and kept giving us the flashes at regular intervals and so we managed to keep on course. We inched slowly in to the beach.

Chapter Two

THE CURRENT was unexpectedly strong here and it was sweeping us away to the left, so that getting across that last couple of hundred yards was a matter of clawing our way crabwise. I crouched over the rubber whaleback of the dinghy straining my eyes towards the lighter smudge of the wide beach, the Sterling cocked and my thumb on the safety-catch. Behind me I could hear Kam Foo swearing in a rumbling undertone as he tried to hold us against the side-sweep, and making too much noise about it.

I said over my shoulder, 'Closer, closer! Get her in until you can touch bottom, then dig your paddle into the sand and hold her.' He grunted angrily that that was what he was trying to do. But it was no good. I could feel her fabric bottom grating on the sand, but the current was pushing her buoyant stern round and plucking us off into deep water, so that in the end I stood up and stepped out knee-deep and held her by means of the rope link between his harness and mine.

I saw them then—two shadowy figures emerging from the shelter of a tumbled pile of rocks. I couldn't see if their hands were on their heads—I couldn't make out any details whatsoever. They were just two very slowly moving blurs coming towards us, but I had no doubts about them. I let them close the distance to about half, then I called softly, 'Running Water', but there was no answer immediately. They stopped uncertainly and I was about to call again, louder, when Kam Foo yelled, 'Look out! To the right!'

There was a line of them, rising silently from behind a ridge in the sand that until now had appeared flat beach. I shoved the safety-catch off and pressed the trigger, spraying from left to right, and above the chatter of my own gun I heard the answering blast, and a ripple of pin-points showed dimly through my goggles, and then my magazine was empty.

I dropped flat in the water and almost immediately felt a terrific pull on my harness and I spun like a hooked minnow on a fishing line. I tried to gulp a breath before going under, but I was too late. All I got was a mouthful of water and sand, and I panicked and tried to fight my way to the surface, choking and blinded. The intervening slack of the wire was pulling me under and my mouth was open and more water was being forced down my throat. Then I remember a jerk, and the pressure eased and I broke surface for a brief second.

I'd been on this thing before, but only under practice conditions when I was prepared for it and was ready with the drill. This was altogether different and it had caught me flat-footed. I spat out water and waited for the next pull, because I imagined that this must be the automatic ten-second rest the winch gave the man on the end to save him from drowning. But there was no second pull. I was floating free and there was a sustained rattle of burp guns from the beach.

I looked round for Kam Foo but couldn't see him, so I fumbled for the rope link, and realized as I felt its slackness that it had snapped under the strain of that terrific initial shock. I wondered whether his half remained fast to the wire, but not for long, because they were really cutting loose with their guns ashore and I could hear the bullets whistling overhead and plopping in the water around me. I don't suppose for one moment that they could see me, because I was a good fifty yards offshore and was drifting rapidly with the current, but when a lot of people are brewing up a fairly small area there is always the chance of stopping the odd one, so I dived and swam underwater, breaking surface only for air and to try and maintain direction. I had a crazy idea of making the junk under my own steam and I kept swimming desperately for a long time after I had realized the complete futility of it. I was being swept downstream very much faster than I was making distance forward, and of course I couldn't see her. I'd lost my glasses, so that even if Kennelly was giving an occasion blip on his infra-red light it wouldn't have helped me, but I still kept on porpoising pathetically.

I hit Kam Foo the fourth or fifth time I came up. It scared us both and we struck out blindly at each other until recognition came and we settled into futile cursing.

He gasped, 'The junk? Will it wait for us?' But before I could answer we were caught in the full glare of a searchlight, so we went down again, fast. When we came up the light had swept on and we heard the thump of a diesel engine in the distance.

'One of their armed scows,' I said. 'There's your answer. The junk will be hightailing it to hell downriver now.' And even as I spoke, the light picked her up, going flat out and sending up a huge bow wave.

It was only a flash, because she jinked out of the beam immediately, and the light stabbed around impotently for a minute or so before picking her up again. But this time they held her even though she was zigzagging wildly.

The guns opened up then, a pom-pom from the scow and something much heavier from the shore. Twin 105 millimetres I should have put them at at a guess, and whoever was handling them knew their job, because they had her straddled at their third salvo and I think it was the fourth that actually got her. One minute she was going hell for leather, the next she was just a sheet of flame. They must have hit the fairly heavy load of Bofors ammunition she carried, and then the fuel in her large tanks took over. She hadn't a chance.

21

The scow kept the light on her until they had closed right in and didn't need it any more, because she was a torch lighting up the whole sea and shoreline. They circled round her, hoping no doubt for the odd survivor, but they obviously saw none, because they withdrew and made off after the one circuit. There was nothing solid left; just patches of fuel oil burning on the surface. I suppose the whole thing took about four minutes.

Kam Foo said in a flat voice, 'I was cursing them for cowards for leaving us. I don't feel angry any more. Just sick—and very, very sorry.'

'Why cowards?' I asked. 'I told you, didn't I? You don't wait for lame dogs. We're two men. He had thirty aboard, and a couple of hundred thousand quids' worth of valuable equipment. An armed vessel in their territorial waters? Use your sense, Kam Foo, will you?'

We were still drifting fast. So fast that we hardly needed to swim to stay above surface, and the water was like a tepid bath.

'So what do we do now?' Kam Foo asked, breaking a long silence.

'Just what we're doing,' I told him. 'Keep going down-river until it's light enough to see the shore, then climb out and hide up somewhere.'

'And then?'

'Stick to that for the moment. Can you see anything at all to our right?'

'Not a damned thing.'

'We'd better edge in that way. Our greatest danger is of being swept out into the middle. The estuary is all of thirty miles wide here.'

'Where's "here"?'

'I reckon from what I remember of the chart, about fifty miles north of Macao. At least we're travelling in the right direction.'

We lapsed into silence after that, and I found myself almost dropping off into something between a sleep and a torpor, but I snapped out of it quickly when I realized once that we had drifted apart. I splashed and yelled, and he answered me from some yards away. After that we linked ourselves together with the tail of the broken rope.

Then we overtook a twisted mass of bamboo floating downstream, and things were easier. All we had to do was to rest out bellies on it and give the occasional kick. But the thought of drifting out into the middle was worrying me the whole time, and first light did nothing to help when it came, because there was a heavy mist that cut the visibility to a few yards. And I was thirsty. I tried the water, but although it wasn't quite sea-salt, it wasn't far off it. It was brackish and horrible and the colour of coffee—coffee with curdled milk in it.

My watch was still going, although there were times when I doubted it as the crawling minutes ticked by, and it was something after nine o'clock before the mist lifted, suddenly and dramatically, as it does in those parts.

I saw then that my worries hadn't been groundless. The shore was the thinnest thread away to our right. Admittedly our horizon down at water level was probably only a mile or so away, but it was still going to be a hell of a swim across current.

I prefer not to think of it. It was sheer grinding, frightening misery. For a couple of hours we just kicked along on the bamboo, but the stuff was balky and seemed to be possessed of a will of its own and kept taking us more and more to the left, so finally we left it and started to swim. We made faster time that way, but tired quicker, and the thirst got worse.

Twice big sea-going junks, one sail one diesel, swept down past us, and each time Kam Foo and I looked at each other. Should we yell? Had either given the slightest nod we'd have

23

done it. Maybe we'd have got away with it. The peasants and fisherfolk don't like officials whatever their politics, and they're usually open to a deal if they're not too frightened—but there was always the chance of an earnest Comrade being aboard with an armband, *The Thoughts of Chairman Mao* and a gun.

We made it at about four in the afternoon, which meant we'd been in the water for sixteen hours. There was a little rocky promontory jutting out at this point, and a vagary of the current helped us over the last couple of miles.

There was a tiny shingle beach on the downriver side of the promontory, which was lucky for us, because neither of us could have coped with a climb over the rocks. We just dragged ourselves out on to it and lay gasping like two grassed trouts.

I woke as the sun was going down, and looking at my watch I saw I had slept for three and a half hours, on my face the whole time, because the back of my clothes had dried out but I was still soggy in front. I looked round for Kam Foo, but he was not there. I sat up and stretched, and felt that someone had done it for me already, on a rack. I was aching in every limb and my mouth and throat were like a lime-kiln. I took stock of myself. I still had my tussah pants, jacket and cotton singlet, but I had lost my hat and one shoe —and both losses were serious. My pockets yielded a sickening mess that had once been a packet of cheap local cigarettes and a box of matches, but no money. It wouldn't have been any use if I had been carrying any, because the peasants this side of the line won't take it as bribe money any more. Possession of Hong Kong currency is a serious 'deviation'.

I heard a slight noise behind me and, turning, I saw Kam Foo climbing down the rocks towards me. He grinned wryly and asked me if I felt like a swim. I answered him obscenely.

'It's that or nothing,' he said. 'Come and look.' I followed him up over the rocks to the top, hobbling painfully on my bare foot, and then I saw what he meant. We were on an island. A lousy little handful of rocks sticking up out of the water and a good half mile from the mainland. I became obscene again and asked him if he'd thought of looking for drinking water.

'Not a drop, old boy,' he answered. 'Except the river, and that's even saltier here.'

I sat on a rock and gloomed across the channel that separated us. At least it appeared to be a backwater with little or no current. The other side we could see a small village, half hidden by a fold in the ground, and along the shore, a few feet above the waterline, were serried rows of rice paddies, their brilliant green making the only splash of colour against the barren, lunar desolation of this bloodiest of all bloody parts of the China coastline. Women were wending their way back to the village in a straggling line, and small boys were driving water buffaloes along the bank. I could see the thin smoke of cooking fires and it made me think of food and, more immediately, of something, anything, to drink.

I said, 'Come on,' and stood up.

'Wouldn't it be better to wait for full darkness?' he asked.

'I want to see where the hell we're going this time,' I told him. 'There doesn't appear to be much current in the middle there, but you never know—and we'll find ourselves out in the estuary again. The way I'm feeling now it'll take us a good hour to make it anyhow, and it will be dark by then.'

I took off my three garments and rolled them into a tight bundle and tied them on top of my head with the rope from the safety-harness. Kam Foo watched me with some embarrassment. Wellington and Sandhurst notwithstanding, he was still Chinese enough to be prissy about the naked form unadorned, even with the same sex.

'You please yourself,' I said, 'but I'm sleeping dry tonight.'

He hesitated for a moment, then retired modestly behind

a rock and did likewise, and we waded out like twin Aphrodites in reverse. It felt cold now, and the water was like yesterday's pea soup, brown and green and scummy. It wasn't by normal standards a hard swim, but even so my estimate of an hour was over-optimistic by another fifteen minutes, and I was pooped when we got to the other side. To make matters worse we hit mud—deep, slimy and clinging, and it took us almost as long to slough through it to the hard foreshore, and, as if that wasn't enough, there were leeches there by the thousand. I had over a dozen fastened to my legs below the knees, and Kam Foo had as many. With a lighted cigarette or a handful of salt they are no problem. Touch them with either and they back out in reverse, but if you just pull them off you're likely to leave the heads there, and that can be serious. However, we picked them off as carefully as we could, then dressed and climbed over the bund to the rice paddies. Normally there is water in them, but the crop was too far advanced now, and the earth was hard and dry.

We sighed and turned towards the village by common consent. Neither of us was talking much, because our throats were too dry, but I croaked to Kam Foo that he'd have to do the best he could with his classical Chinese and go in by himself and try and do business with one of our watches.

'I can't be seen myself, naturally,' I told him, trying to sound cheerful. 'Tell 'em you're a bloody poet from the north, but the Comrades don't appreciate your stuff down this end. Just ask for some grub, and see what you can do about a hat for me—one of those big cartwheel things that will come down over my face—and if you can knock off a left shoe from somewhere I'll put preserved ginger and lacquered ducks on your grandfather's grave every Chinese New Year.'

'The vicar wouldn't like it,' he said gravely. 'The old boy's buried in Hampstead.'

26

I sat on the bund and watched him fade into the darkness, and tried not to think of iced lager, medium-rare steak, clean pyjamas and decadently soft beds.

I could see a few dim lights in the village, but there was no noise, and that cheered me a little. When there's a visiting committee of the Comrades in residence they invariably round the locals up for culture sessions at the end of the working day. It used to be long and prosy lectures on the straight Marx-Lenin ticket at one time. Now it's Chairman Mao and quavering, high-pitched songs about beautiful tractors and the glories of collectivism. No culture meant no Comrades, or so I hoped.

He was away two crawling hours, and I sat there cursing the Chinese concept of time, imagining him holed up comfortably in some hut eating and drinking his head off. But I forgave him everything when he returned. He'd done all right. The first, and biggest hut he had come to was the village school and, although the authorities had closed it down in favour of a Camp of Youth Enlightenment some six miles away, the old schoolmaster still haunted the place like a sad ghost. He was by way of being a bush classicist and had sat happily swapping hunks of Lao-tse with Kam Foo for the first hour and a half before, without a single question, giving him just what he asked for, food, an earthenware jar of water, a Hakka hat and a pair of sandals.

'I'd had the foresight to leave my own outside,' Kam Foo explained, 'and I told him I'd lost them.'

'Smart feller,' I said through a mouthful of boiled rice and dried fish. 'How did the out-of-work-poet yarn go down?'

'I didn't need to tell him that,' he said. 'I didn't need to tell him anything, except what I wanted, and he gave it to me without so much as a lifted eyebrow. This rice that you and I are eating is probably the best part of a week's ration for him.'

'Nerts,' I said. 'They grow the damned stuff round here.'

'Yes, and have to hand the lot over to the Party pool, and draw their own ration back once a month. If they're under their norm the ration is cut pro rata. The same applies to the fish.'

'What are you trying to do?' I asked, scooping in the bottom of the bowl for the last grains. 'Put me off it? It would be easier to make an Armenian carpet-seller drop his bag. You're in the wrong business, boy. When we get back, *if* we get back, you want to quit and get a job with Oxfam or somebody.'

'I wonder how much of your toughness and cynicism is real—how much phoney?' he said.

'You go back and con another bowl of rice out of him and I'll show you,' I told him. 'All right, Confucius, did you happen to find out anything useful?'

'I think so. A patrol of People's Police came through this morning. They said that a large Capitalist-Imperialist battleship had been attempting to land spies ten miles up-river last night, but they sank it with gunfire.'

'Only ten miles?' I groaned. 'I felt we'd swum fifty.'

'There are the usual warnings out. Rewards for the vigilant who report unusual activity along the coast, and merry bloody hell for those who don't.'

'That means we're still about forty miles north of Macao,' I mused. 'Speaking strictly from memory of the maps, there's a road of sorts between Macao and Canton. The question is, which would be better? To walk it, marching at night and hiding up in daylight, or pinch a sampan and paddle down?'

'I'd be all against the latter,' he put in quickly.

'Yes, yes, yes,' I said wearily. 'We'd probably be robbing a fisherman of his means of livelihood. Let's skip the ethics for the moment and look at things objectively, shall we?'

'I wasn't thinking of that,' he said. 'It was just something that the old chap told me.'

'What?'

'There's a collective fine and a stiff sentence for the village elders if a boat is stolen and not reported immediately to the police, so now they have watchmen on them, and the paddles and sails are collected up into one place at night.'

'You mean you discussed it with him?' I asked sharply.

'I didn't. He told me quite incidentally. Apparently a couple of their young men decided to light out for Hong Kong a few weeks ago. They were captured half-way across, brought back here and beheaded in the village square. They're really on the ball boatwise now, apparently.'

'I take your point,' I said. 'That means walking. Forty miles or thereabouts. I believe there are some rivers running into the estuary. That means bridges. Bridges are usually guarded—so we swim when we come to them. We'd be lucky if we made ten miles a night.' I stood up and tried the sandals tentatively. They were made from pieces of old motor-tyre, worn but serviceable, and they fastened with adjustable thongs —comfortable enough, but not designed for fast walking. 'All right,' I said. 'Now to find the bloody road.'

And it wasn't easy. The only path from the rice paddies lay smack through the centre of the village, but there was nothing else for it. Fortunately the average Chinese peasant is too tired to bother much about what goes on outside once he gets back to his hut at nightfall, so although the village dogs, smelling strangers, set up a racket, we passed through without bumping into anybody.

The path led down to a creek where several fishing sampans were pulled up on to the mud. I looked at them longingly, but then we saw a lantern moving along the bund between us and them and heard a man singing in a high, plaintive monotone to keep himself company, so we dived into the shadows and kept going. And after a while the path petered out among the paddies, so we had to go back to find the turn-off that we had apparently missed, and I started to panic, because the mist had come up again and I couldn't see the stars and I had lost all sense of direction.

But eventually we came to what no doubt would laughingly have been called a road in these parts—just a wide swathe of ankle-deep dust that in the rainy season would be even deeper mud, and to resolve any doubts we may have had, there was a bus shelter here—a tiny mud hut thatched with straw and surmounted by a dragon to deter evil spirits, who notoriously used public transport, from alighting here and finding their way to the village.

'South is left,' I said. 'Unless you've got any strong views to the contrary.'

'Then we go right,' he said positively. 'Walk a few miles and turn about.'

'What the hell for?' I asked, startled.

'To confuse following road devils.' He chuckled. 'Lucky for you I was born in Hampstead or I'd insist on it.'

'Comical bugger,' I grunted. 'Let's see how the wit will be holding up at the end of forty miles.'

Chapter Three

WE PADDED ON for seven hours. Kam Foo went all military and insisted on fifty minutes' walking, ten resting, and reckoned that we were covering three miles in the hour, which meant that we had come twenty-one miles. Personally I very much doubted it. I'd have put it at nearer fourteen, and that certainly wasn't distance made good to the objective either, because the road twisted and turned round the contours of the low hills that ran parallel to the river. There were no bridges in that first march, only fords, and the streams were merely trickles in each case, but fortunately the water was cool, clean and drinkable.

We were out of the paddy-growing area here, and the road was just a dusty ribbon traversing a rocky plateau, inhospitable enough in all conscience, but with plenty of cover. We stopped at a stream as the sun was coming up over the eastern horizon and moved off the road for a couple of hundred yards, and found a cranny among the rocks.

The ground fell away sharply to the front, affording us a clear view of the road for a good mile either way. We were fairly close to the shore. The morning mist was lying low, and over it, a possible fifty miles away in the east, I thought I could make out the faint blue outline of the high hills that enclose the Kowloon peninsula, with the Peak of Hong Kong island an isolated needlepoint to the south of it.

And then Kam Foo rose to heights sublime. I hadn't noticed in the darkness that he had been carrying a bundle. It was a couple of pounds of cold boiled rice and *kanji* that

31

he had moulded into a ball and wrapped in his large and grubby handkerchief the night before. We ate sparingly and saved the bulk of it for an evening meal, then stretched out between the rocks and slept.

Passing trucks woke us several times during the long day. Those going south carried rice in matting sacks. Travelling north they were laden with boxes and crates, and all of them had an armed escort of three or four People's Guards perched high on their loads. One stopped just below us and the driver and troops got down and drank from the stream. They had a yellow Chow dog with them and the damned thing started to fossick among the rocks, coming up to within a few yards of us. It got our scent and stood sniffing and growling, with raised hackles. Then it started to bark, and kept it up for minutes on end.

Peering down through the rocks we saw the troops looking up towards our position, idly at first, but then, as the barking grew in pitch and volume, with more than a comfortable interest. A well-pitched rock would have sent it packing, but of course that was out of the question, so we just lay there and sweated. The troops started to climb back on to the truck, whistling and calling to the dog, but it was thoroughly steamed up by now and had come nearer and seen us. Its barks grew louder and more urgent.

One of the troops jumped down from the truck and started to climb the slope towards us, cursing and yelling at the dog. We were in a hollow and there was no bolthole behind us, and this fellow was carrying a burp gun. Things looked very hairy indeed. Kam Foo, on his own, might conceivably have got away with it as a harmless peasant taking a siesta, but I, as a European, had a snowball in hell's chance. We would both be hauled in willy-nilly now. I felt sick and angry. Fifty miles of road and they, and we, had to choose this exact spot to stop at.

But at the last possible moment the soldier stopped and

32

picked up a chunk of rock. He whizzed it at the dog and caught it in the ribs. It wheeled and streaked off back to the truck, pen-and-inking in the minor key. I love dogs, but my heart warmed to the soldier and his beautifully accurate aim. They scrambled aboard and the truck lurched off on its way, and we breathed again.

We ate again at nightfall, then set out once more on our trek. Things were not so easy this time, though. Villages were more frequent, usually straddled across the road, which meant that we had to make several wide detours, and morning found us without breakfast smack in the middle of densely cultivated paddy between two of them and, at even the most optimistic estimate, I didn't consider that we had made good ten miles.

We turned off the road and tight-roped along bunds that ran through the shoulder-high paddy. We would have been safe enough in the middle of the wretched stuff, but they had had more rain in this area and the dense green stalks were growing in about six inches of liquid mud. We couldn't camp on the bunds because we knew that villagers used them as footpaths through the cultivation, so we just had to press on and on until we came out of it the other side. This time we had turned left, towards the estuary, and we found ourselves on the rocky foreshore. There was plenty of cover here, but no drinking water.

God, what a horrible day that was. Our thirst increased as the sun mounted, until by midday it was intolerable. We went back into the paddy and tried to sponge a few drops out of the mud with our handkerchiefs, but the amount we got wasn't enough to moisten our tongues. We tried the estuary water then, but here, twenty miles nearer to the open sea, it was pure brine.

Then, to make matters worse, some women who had been working in the paddy came down on to the narrow beach a bare ten yards from where we lay among the rocks, and sat and ate their midday rice and drank from earthenware pots.

One of them had the biggest, juiciest melon I have ever seen, and when they hacked it into pieces and ate it I thought I'd go mad. If they had been paid to add to our torment they couldn't have done a better job. A couple of them were young and pretty and, safe from male observation as they thought themselves, they stripped off and went in for a bathe—and I wasn't even interested. It was just that bloody melon that had me hooked. I'd have swapped the whole of Brigitte Bardot for just one slice of it. We crept out after they had gone and gathered up the rind, but they had already done a pretty thorough job on it and there was little of the flesh left that wasn't acid and inedible.

We had a bathe ourselves when darkness had fallen, and it helped a little, then we set off through the paddy—and naturally got lost again. Coming this way in daylight was one thing; groping along those bunds in pitch darkness was another. They weren't laid out symmetrically and I felt that often we wandered in circles, ever and anon slipping into the mud.

But eventually we made it, and hit the road on the southern side of the second village at a spot where the paddy ended on the brink of a sheer drop. It wasn't a long drop, perhaps six to ten feet before it ended in the ditch at the side of the road.

We started to lower ourselves down, and just at that moment a truck came round the next bend, coasting in neutral to save gas as the economical Chinese always do on even the slightest slope, and caught us full in its headlights. The proper procedure would have been to freeze on the spot, and maybe they would have swept by without noticing us, but we had gone too far for that. We just had to drop and dash across the road in front of it and dive into the paddy the other side. Kam Foo made it without damage, but I felt an agonizing stab in my right foot as I landed. I still ran, however, and kept hard on his tail.

The truck stopped, and we dropped flat and lay in the mud in the middle of the first paddy. I could hear men arguing in Cantonese. One wanted to give the paddy a few bursts with his burp gun. Another keen type thought it proper to chase us. Finally a much wiser old sweat said what the hell? Probably some young buck tomcatting around with one of the village girls. More power to his elbow—or words to that effect.

Then the truck started up and went on its way. Kam Foo had got the general drift of the exchange and I heard him chuckle softly and murmur, 'Confucius he say, man taking girl into paddy very soon have piece on earth.'

But I wasn't feeling humorous, because my foot was giving me hell. I limped out of the mud and sat on the bund to examine it by touch. I wiped the mud off with my sleeve, but the wetness persisted, and it was warm. I was streaming blood from a jagged wound in the soft part of my sole. I'd obviously landed on something sharp because there was a hole in my rubber sandal that corresponded with it.

We bound it up with Kam Foo's handkerchief and strips of my singlet and I limped back to the road. There was an irrigation ditch running alongside it here, and fortunately it was too dark to see what the water looked like, so we knelt and lapped like dogs until I thought I would burst. The pain in my foot settled to a dull ache after the first mile or so, but of course it slowed me up considerably and I don't suppose we covered more than seven or eight miles that night.

We halted well short of dawn and searched around for a hide-up close to water, and here, at least, we were lucky. The road ran round the edge of a small lake, and tall reeds grew on the banks and in the shallows.

We moved some hundred yards from the road and bur-rowed into the reeds, and when it was light I had a look at my foot. It was an ugly cut and it had bled a lot, but it could have been worse, and attending to it kept my thoughts off food for a time. I washed it and bound it up again and hoped for the best. Then I slept.

It was the sound of music that woke me. The sun was high overhead, and somewhere not far off it seemed as if fifty pigs were having their throats slit in concert. I sat up and saw Kam Foo's legs sticking out of the reeds. He was lying on his belly and peering at a procession that was slowly wending its way towards us. The band was in front—a collection of drums, gongs and bamboo flutes. Behind them a couple of dozen types in flowing white robes were beating their breasts and baying at the sky in a sustained falsetto.

Kam Foo turned as I moved and grinned at me. He wasn't being heartless. Hampstead-born or not, he still knew that nobody looks sad at a Chinese funeral except the guys who are paid to do just that. I settled down beside him and watched.

Behind the professional mourners came the coffin—a huge carved teak affair borne shoulder-high by the near relatives; then there were a few white-shrouded and veiled women, and after them tables carried aloft by the rest of the family. Kids, a hundred or more, brought up the rear, beating more gongs and setting off strings of firecrackers to scare off the devils. But it was the tables that interested me. They would be, I knew, piled with whole roast piglets, ducks, bowls of rice and stone jars of villainous rice spirit. A lot of it would be fake, of course—*papier-mâché* mock-ups—but that supplied by the near relatives would be real. The coffin would be left in the open somewhere, usually on the side of a hill sloping to the south, and the banquet would be piled up around it. In three days the cortège would return. If the real food had disappeared—a pretty certain bet in this land of kite-hawks, vultures and wild dogs—that would be a sign that the soul of the deceased had eaten and departed on its journey into

36

the next world. The body would be lifted out and laid on the bare earth then, and the coffin thriftily taken back to the village in readiness for the next funeral. A year later the family would collect the bare, whitened bones and pack them in a large porcelain jar which would then be placed in the ancestors' garden just outside the village, where it would be garlanded and propitiated with gifts of food every New Year thereafter.

The procession filed past within a few feet of us. The dead man was obviously someone of importance, because there were a lot of tables following the coffin, and I guessed that a big proportion of the food would be real. We watched them disappear over the plain, our tortured bellies rumbling in duet, then there was a long creeping wait of a couple of hours before they came back again.

Common sense told us that it would be better to wait until sundown, but by mid-afternoon we could stand it no longer, so we came out of the reeds and slunk across the plain like a pair of jackals. My foot had stiffened and I was limping badly, but it didn't slow me up any over the last half mile.

We saw the dogs while we were still some distance off—a dozen or so of them, lean, yellow and scabrous, sitting in a silent circle waiting for the sacrificial fires that ringed the offerings to die down before closing in. They build a lot of these fires for just this very purpose, and reinforce them with firecrackers tied to lengths of smouldering rope, to hold the dogs and birds off until the spirit of the dead man has had time to emerge and eat his fill at his leisure. A bunch of the crackers went off in a fusillade just as we came up to the outer ring, and I nearly jumped out of my skin.

We took a whole roast sucking-pig, a couple of ducks and Kam Foo's knotted singlet full of boiled rice, and withdrew to the lake again. Ghouls? Grave robbers? Maybe—but any finer feelings we may have had on the matter were more than offset by the knowledge that if a scrap of anything edible

37

was found when the mourners returned, it would have meant that the food was so lousy that even a ghost wouldn't eat it, and that would have been a serious loss of face for the relatives. We couldn't have that at any price!

We sat in the reeds and gorged ourselves to the point of nausea, then slept until after sundown. Our food problems were solved now. That which we were carrying would last us three days, by which time we should have reached Macao. But my foot was getting worse. It was badly swollen and the wound was inflamed, and it hurt like hell when I put my weight on it.

But we slogged on, that night and the next, and we came at last to the end of the road. We arrived at midnight, and I was in a burning fever and, I believe, in a slight delirium because the shadows at the side of the road were taking on weird shapes that appeared to be moving with us.

The road ended abruptly at a village—just a huddle of huts with a fishing jetty jutting out into the sea, and junks and sampans were pulled up on to the mud.

Kam Foo said, 'What now?' and I made an effort to gather my wandering wits.

'Macao itself is not on the mainland,' I told him. 'It's on an island about three-quarters of a mile off-shore. You can't see it, but it's dead in front of us.'

'Like Hong Kong in other words?'

'Not quite. The whole of Hong Kong island is British— as is Kowloon and the strip of mainland facing it. Here the mainland is Chinese and so is the island. The Portuguese only hold the tip of the peninsula to the south.'

'So we're still a long way off, and there's a bloody lot of water to cross?' He sounded dismayed, and I was correspondingly irritated. I grunted sourly and led him round the outskirts of the village to the muddy beach.

It was a long and nasty swim—the worst yet. My foot was giving me hell and I kept getting cramps, and I lost all sense of direction after a time, because there were no lights in the village on the mainland, or on the unseen island ahead of us. But Kam Foo was there alongside me the whole time, encouraging me with a quiet word or a touch on the shoulder when I showed signs of flagging or, worse, panicking, as I did very badly about half-way across.

We crawled out on to the mud the other side and lay panting and gasping for a long time before dragging ourselves on. We bickered a lot about direction, I remember— or, to be fair, he was quietly determined on the route while I bitched and snarled at him. Our way lay south but we couldn't agree on where south was, because, as usual, the mist hid the stars and there was no moon.

Theoretically all we had to do was to walk away from the beach and keep going, with the channel at our backs, but it just didn't work out that way. As far as the sea was concerned, two hundred yards away from it, in the rugged hills, scrub and dried water-courses that covered the whole island, and one could be in the middle of the Gobi Desert for all the help it was. There was, I knew, a road running from the landing-place to the ruined wall and archway that marked the entrance to Portuguese territory, but we wished by common consent to avoid that. Roads are dangerous to people on the run near frontiers.

But then finally, when we had reached the very depth of misery and frustration, we saw from the top of a hill the lights of Macao in the distance. The city is nowhere near the size of its brasher sister Hong Kong, or nearly as brightly illuminated, but it was still an unmistakable beacon in that black velvet night, with the lighthouse at Fort Guia flashing high above it.

All sanity departed then and I started to run, and fell into a ravine—and that was it. I tried to get up, shaking off Kam Foo's helping hand, but the whole damned leg just buckled under me.

I said, 'You know the rules. Push on and go to the British Consulate. You'll find it on the Praia Grande—that's the big waterfront boulevard that runs the whole length of the town. Get Barry on the telephone and tell him what's happened.'

'And what will you do?' he asked.

'Come on in my own time. If I get caught short by daylight I'll hide up somewhere and have a shot at crossing after dark.'

'Fine,' he agreed, 'but let's get you out of this gully and on to level ground first.'

He heaved me to my feet and got my arm across his shoulders and somehow we scrambled out, but when we got to the top he wouldn't let me go. I cursed him in heaps and tried to make it an order, but it was no good. He just lugged me on in silence.

I wasn't being heroic. I knew I couldn't make it, and this way we were both going to finish in the bag. Had the position been reversed I would have left him without a moment's hesitation, and he knew it. But he still stuck with me, and when I finally lay down for keeps, he hoisted me over his shoulder in a fireman's lift, although I was a good thirty pounds heavier, and staggered on.

I must have passed out then, because the next thing I remember with any clarity was his slapping my face hard and telling me for Christ's sake to stop singing. It was still dark where we were, but the sky to the east was lightening. We were in a clump of undergrowth, and in front of us was a stretch of open ground and I could make out a long squat building with lights in some of its windows.

He whispered, 'I think this is it. There's a guard post the other side of that building. They changed a few minutes ago.'

It took me a long time to get things into focus, but eventually, as it got lighter, I recognized a section of the crumbling wall that flanks the Port do Cerco, which is the gateway to Macao proper.

'This is it,' I told him. 'Though how the hell you made it with me on your back I'll never know.'

'How's your foot?' he asked. I stood up and tried it tentatively. I had to bite back a yell of sheer agony, but at least it held me.

'I can manage at a crawl,' I said. 'We'd better separate. It will double our chances.' But he still wouldn't listen, so we moved sideways through the undergrowth, leaving the archway to our left. I had never been this side before, although I had been up to the gate from the other. Portuguese territory began at the wall, but I knew the People's Guard would have no hesitation in chasing a fugitive and dragging him back if they saw him actually crossing, so safety was still chimerical until we could lose ourselves in the shadows well the other side.

But we made it through a gap in the masonry and found ourselves at the top of the Praia and then, as a supreme anti-climax, we stumbled into a parked rickshaw, with the coolie sleeping beside it. I've always had a peculiar antipathy to turning a fellow man into a horse, but I climbed into this one gratefully, tipped my cartwheel hat forward over my face and told the boy to take us to the Avenida do Felicidade.

'I thought you said the Consulate?' Kam Foo muttered.

'Only if you had been on your own,' I told him. 'This is a brothel I'm taking you to. Much better.'

'Confucius he say, if loss of virtue appears inevitable, relax and enjoy process,' he chuckled. 'Just so's they've got coffee and clean towels.'

Avenida do Felicidade, which means 'Street of Happiness', is down on the waterfront. It is an alleyway ten feet wide and a quarter of a mile long. It contains forty-three fan-tan gambling joints, about the same number of lottery houses, twenty bars, eleven opium parlours and two factories where they cook the stuff—all at ground level. Nobody has even tried to count the brothels, because they are on the upper

41

floors of the crowded, narrow-fronted houses, some of which
go up to seven storeys. The cops, turbaned Hindus from
Goa mostly, try to head tourists away from it, and a Portuguese
soldier from the barracks on the hill behind the Plaza can
count on twenty-eight days in the cooler if caught there by
the MPs.

It never closes down altogether, but it was relatively quiet
at this dawn hour. I stopped the rickshaw well short of the
place I was looking for, left Kam Foo on deposit with the
anxious coolie, and limped off into the shadows. Paulo da
Souza's place was half-way along the Avenida, on the right.
You got to it up some stairs between a bar and a place where
they made joss-sticks. Khushipal Singh, the Sikh bouncer,
was sleeping on the bottom step. I woke him and borrowed
a Macao dollar from him and went back and got Kam Foo
out of hock, then we climbed four flights of dirty stairs and
tapped on a red lacquered door at the top.

Paulo da Souza himself opened. He had got his surname
from his grandfather, a Portuguese sea captain, so he said,
and his given one from his mamma, a Lisbon lady of great
beauty and piety, but he was a liar on both counts. Actually
he was a Goanese from Bombay. Barry had a Damocles on
him. A Damocles is just what its name implies—something
you hold over somebody to keep him in the path of virtue.
In Paulo's case it was a Hong Kong extradition order for
murder, which only needed one signature and a date to
activate it. There's nowhere to run to from Macao, except
back to Hong Kong or through the archway into China,
and he wouldn't have lasted an hour with the Comrades, so
he was completely loyal to us.

He kowtowed and said in Cantonese, 'Welcome to my
miserable abode. As the sun warms the stones of Ma Ko
Mio, so your esteemed presence lights——'

I usually played along with him in this, but I told him to
skip it now. I was too tired for bloody nonsense.

42

'Coffee, two rooms, baths, clean clothes, coffee, breakfast, coffee,' I told him. 'Strictly in that order.'

He grinned and said okay, and led us through the parlour. It was a long low room, over-furnished with heavy teakwood divans and tatty cushions, and it stank of joss-sticks, cigarette and cannabis smoke, and sweat.

'What about the roof?' he asked, but I turned it down. It would have been cool up there, and high enough to get the sea breeze, unpolluted by the stench of the alley below, but it was overlooked by the houses on the hillside behind.

The girls slept in a dormitory on the floor above when not actually working, so there were plenty of spare rooms, clean enough but redolent of those damned joss-sticks. I lowered myself on to a bed and lifted my game leg carefully with both hands. It felt and looked like a boiled suet pudding from the knee down and was burning to the touch. I heard Kam Foo tell Paulo in an undertone to get a doctor right away, but I countermanded it quickly.

'Don't be a chump,' he said. 'Who are you trying to impress?'

'Nobody—but a doctor, Chinese or Portuguese, might talk.'

'What would that matter now?'

'Plenty. This town may be wide open and fun-loving, but it's still Portuguese and cautious. They like to know who comes and goes—and how.'

'All right—so you're a sailor in a joy-house with a sore foot. What's so unusual about that?'

'Off what ship? And where are my papers? Listen, if we had a doctor here the chances are that there'd be a cop— regular or secret—round hard on his heels.'

'I think you're being over-cautious—and bloody stupid.'

'Go on thinking it. No doctor. As soon as I feel up to it I'll call Barry. With luck we should be back in Hong Kong tonight.'

But the luck ran out about that point. I had my coffee and

43

I remember being sick after it, but that's *all* I remember for some hours. He did get a doctor, a good one from the barracks, and I suppose I owe to him the fact that I've still got two legs, because gangrene was just setting in nicely when they opened it up and drained it.

Barry sent a launch across for me a week later, Kam Foo having been picked up earlier. They didn't exactly turn the garrison band out to see me off, but for all the tattered rags of security left to this lousy mission, they might just as well have done so.

Chapter Four

BARRY SAID, 'I think you're being unnecessarily hard on him.'

'You asked me for my opinion,' I told him. 'There it is.'

'But "unreliable" can mean so many things.'

'In this particular case it means just what I've said. Unreliable.'

'You wouldn't have got out if it hadn't been for him.'

'I'm fully aware of that—but the fact remains that he blew me in the process.'

'He had no option.'

'He had. He should have left me to come on in my own time when I told him.'

'You wouldn't have made it.'

'Actually I think I would. But that wasn't his pidgin anyhow. His orders were to come on and report.'

Barry sighed. 'You're an ungrateful sod,' he said.

'Maybe that's what it looks like. I'm not ungrateful, though. If the term didn't sound so corny I'd say Kam Foo was a very gallant gentleman. That's his trouble. I prefer savage rats who'll do as they're told in this business. *I'm* certainly not working with him again.'

'You won't be working at all until the dust of this one has had time to settle.' He leaned forward in his chair and topped up our drinks, sparingly, because the whisky was his and he was a mean bastard in spite of his spurious bonhomie.

'It's happened before,' I said. ' "Don't call us—we'll call you." I can't say I'm sorry.'

45

'You're not being fired, if that's what you're implying.' He looked at me straightly, frankly, openly, as he always did when he was lying, which was most of the time.

'One never is. Just indefinitely "rested". Fine. I'm delighted —and that's not sour grapes. Only for the record, Barry, this last cock-up wasn't *my* fault.'

'Nobody has said it was. But the fact remains that we've lost an expensive "Q" boat and a highly trained crew——'

'So a head must roll. All right—mine's rolling.' I flicked the clipped-together report sheets on the table between us. 'I can add nothing more to that.'

'That's not worth a damn, and you know it.' And I did know it, but I was still prepared to do battle, only he cut me short. 'That's a carefully worded bit of mendacious crap. You've been suitably modest about your own part of it, and generous about Kam Foo. You've given him every scrap of credit due to him, then you've come in here and sunk a knife between his shoulder-blades. This amounts to "There's nobody I'd prefer to have beside me in a tight corner, but at the same time he was the clot who *got* me into the tight corner." Not good enough, James. If any action of his blew this thing, you've got to have the guts to say so.'

'No action of his blew it.'

'All right, Kennelly then? You're not pulling the *de mortuis nil nisi bonum* line, are you? Did he come in too close? Hit the wrong bit of coast? Show a light accidentally?'

'Nothing like that.' I felt sick and weary. Debriefing is the worst part of any job, even the howling successes. You're cross-examined, brainwashed, led into self-contradiction, and the truth you're trying to speak is twisted by knaves to make a trap for fools—until there's no truth left in it. Just doubts—doubts not only of others, but of yourself, and the fact that you know the procedure and the reason for it is no help. And Barry was the best in the business at debriefing, after the Gaffer. God, how I was hating him.

46

'Yourself then?' he said quietly. 'Any tiny little point that you may have overlooked?'

'Quite likely. But unfortunately there's nothing I can bring to mind at the moment. If I could, I'd tell you—just to get off your hook. Why don't you ask Kam Foo?'

'I have. His report runs along much the same lines as yours. Rather more florid if anything. Wainwright the brave, the skilled, the resourceful. If I wasn't a gent I might even have suspected your cooking them up together.'

'You're not—so go ahead and suspect it,' I spat at him, which was foolish. If you want to survive in this jungle, your temper is the last thing to lose.

He smiled gently. 'It has been known. I've actually experienced it in the war. The CO and the Adjutant watched through glasses from a hilltop well to the rear, while a whole battalion of us were either scuppered or went into the bag. Then they staggered back, mutually singing each other's praises. If either of the bastards could have read a map properly, it wouldn't have happened. As it was, it was all very splendid. Nobody took a can back, and the manager collected a DSO and the bumboy an MC. You were too young for the war, weren't you?'

'By several years,' I told him. 'But I take your point. I'm sorry I can't help you more. I know what it means to you personally.'

'Why me—personally?'

'Because I know what you're trying to do. In this case there is a can to be taken back, and if you can't tie it on to me, or Kam Foo, or perhaps Kennelly, you might find it on your own tail.' It could have been wishful thinking, but I thought I saw the faintest stiffening of the gentle smile, so I pushed it. 'I think you were hoping I'd hang a clanger on Kam Foo. Maybe my criticism of him strengthened that hope. But that criticism applies to what happened *after* the job, and in no way impugns his ability, loyalty or guts. It was just that he

47

was too bloody noble about things—and his final gaffe in getting a Portuguese military doctor to me was inexcusable from a security point of view. That and——' But I realized I'd said too much, so I stopped, and covered up by helping myself to another inch of his whisky.

'Go on,' he said quietly. 'That and what else?'

'Just this. I still don't know who we were supposed to bring out. I was just told to go up the estuary with the fishing fleet, and be prepared to do a slip. You handed me my sealed orders on the junk, five minutes before we sailed. I didn't break them open until just before midnight. I read them through twice, and burned them——'

'I'm not checking you on procedure,' he said sharply. 'Come to the point.'

But this had suddenly become terribly important and I wouldn't be hurried. 'I then briefed Kennelly and Kam Foo,' I went on. 'Until then not a soul on board knew the pick-up point, the infra-red code or the passwords. Kennelly did his stuff, bang on, as always. We didn't hit the wrong bit of coast, Barry. We didn't fetch up off a Communist fort. The lights were there—dead where they should have been—and there were two men there, with their hands on their heads, all as per book. But there was also a reception committee there, and an armed scow—and the guns were ready on the cliffs above the beach.'

He tapped the report in front of him. 'You've said all that here.'

'I know. But a report is just a bare recital of events. It could all have been sheer bad luck. A patrol that happened to be passing. A scow anchored for the night, suddenly alerted by the firing on the beach. The guns there by perfectly explainable happenstance. I'm giving you my *opinion* now. More than my opinion. My absolute, cast-iron conviction. This thing was blown long before we got there, Barry. They were waiting for us.'

'That's been known too,' he said. 'What you're really implying is that it was blown from somewhere up here in the heights. That it?'

'That would be a bit too hairy even for me,' I told him. 'No, not quite that—but I am saying that your information was questionable. This sort of pick-up should only be used when you've got the local commandant by the short and curlies.'

'We've got him completely compromised. He's holding over a million Hong Kong dollars' worth of heroin on that side, and he's got a huge sum of money on deposit *this* side. We've got a tape-recording and two photos of him that would have his head on a pole within an hour of our slipping them across the border. Go on.'

'A really safe bit of coast——'

'You've seen it. I haven't. All I know is that the client himself picked it—and if he's not a vitally interested party, who is? What else?'

'You've just said it. The client himself. This method is strictly for the VIPs—people who are highly unlikely to sell us out beforehand.'

'Kowalski. Anything known against?'

That, of course, shot me down. He was our biggest. He was also *their* biggest. The classic double-treble-quadruple spy—a Shanghai Mig who had spied for the Russians in China, and then switched sides. He spied for the Japanese then—again in China—and again switched sides. Then for the Japs against us during the war. We caught him in India, tried him and sentenced him to death. We sprang him from Trimulgherry Military Prison ourselves the night before he was due to be shot, fed him a beautiful furbler and eased him back through Burma to the Japanese lines at Kalewa. The furbler caused the Japs hurriedly to move two divisions out of the Shan Hills to meet a threat of an Allied landing on the Arrakan coast. The resultant gap let the Fourteenth Army storm through and cross the Chindwin en route for Mandalay, Rangoon and the complete reconquest of Burma—so it wasn't Errol Flynn after all. The Bomb on Hiroshima saved Kowalski from a Japanese firing squad by a short whisker. He worked for Chiang Kai-shek next—then for the Americans in Formosa, checking on Chiang for them and so doubling his pay, before completing the circle and going back to Chairman Mao. But the Russians caught up with him in Vladivostok and eventually swapped him for another big leaguer we were holding—one Carter—and the Chinese hijacked him back.* Well might you ask what earthly use he was to any side at all since this was public knowledge in every Intelligence agency in the Far East. The answer lies, of course, in the fact that he was so bloody good when he *was* working for one that a lot could be winked at. That is the strength, and incidentally the life-insurance, of the real top-class professional multiple spy. Everybody knows the worst of him, but hopes for the best—and the best is often forth-coming, and it makes up for an awful lot of peccadilloes. He is also a good bargaining piece for whoever happens to be carrying him on their payroll, like a top-grade footballer who is transferred between clubs.

I realized, without Barry having to tell me, that nobody would dream of risking a big fish like Kowalski to trap a minnow of my class on a dark beach at night. Kowalski himself would never have been party to it. He had his pride—and no doubt a comfortable honorarium paid into his Swiss account each month by us. He certainly wouldn't jeopardize that for peanuts. But Barry did tell me just that, very softly and kindly.

'You don't have to rub it in,' I snapped. 'All right. It was all foolproof, and we weren't blown from the other side. But we didn't blow ourselves either, so that brings the buck back to these parts, doesn't it? Who else knew about it besides you?'

* See *The Springers*.

50

'That's just a *mite* close to the knuckle, James,' he said, still softly but not quite so kindly. 'However, we must make allowances. You've had a rough time. But get that chip off your shoulder. Nobody is getting at you—and surely to God you've been debriefed often enough to know what it's all about by now.

He poured more whisky. 'Relax. The Bank is putting your leave forward, on medical grounds.'

'What have they been told?' I asked, because I hadn't reported back there yet.

'Just what we told the Portuguese,' he said. 'You and Kam Foo arranged to go night-fishing the other side of Castle Peak. Your sampan got caught in the tide-rip and you drifted over the line into Communist waters. Your outboard packed in, so you landed, pinched some local clothes and made it in to Macao on foot. You're going to get a high-powered wigging for it and Kam Foo is on a fizzer from his CO on the same charge.'

'What about Kennelly?' I asked.

'Read it in the papers,' he answered dryly, and glanced at his watch. 'His clothes and towel will have been found on the beach at Sheko about an hour ago. Swimming fatality. He was reported missing four days ago.'

'Neat,' I said, and added bitterly. 'Saves a pension too. He's got a wife in Bournemouth and two kids at school.'

'Three,' he corrected. 'And it's not saving anybody a pension. It will come in the form of an annuity that he had been buying and keeping a secret from her. You're too prickly by half, James, and just a shade fast on the draw—with your mouth. Watch it. It could conceivably land you in a little bother.'

I tried to make a dignified exit, but it is somewhat difficult with a rubber-ferruled walking stick and a slit carpet slipper and a lot of bandages on one foot.

He halted me as I reached the door. 'One final thing,' he

said. 'The two men you were picking up? Do you think you shot them?'

'I couldn't be certain,' I told him. 'Everything happened in a split second. I opened up on the crowd who were rushing us from a flank, spraying from the hip. I might have got them—or the others might have. They might even have dropped flat and got away with it.'

'Kam Foo didn't fire at all?'

'He didn't have time. He was holding the dinghy against the current. The next moment we were yanked into deep water on the line. I'd like to stress again, though, that if he hadn't been right on the ball we'd have been caught flat-footed.'

'So we don't know whether Kowalski is alive or dead,' he mused.

'We don't even know whether it *was* Kowalski,' I shot back at him. 'You yourself have just pointed out to me that they'd hardly risk a bishop to take a pawn.'

'So you still think that it leaked from somewhere over here?'

'I didn't say that. What I did say was that there is every possibility of their having rumbled Kowalski or the commandant and set a trap—in which case the two men we saw would have been decoys.'

He grinned wryly. 'Nice if we could prove it. No cans on anybody's tails then. Enjoy your leave, James, and stop fighting everybody, including yourself. You did all right—all things considered.'

I writhed, thanked him and went.

I saw Kam Foo in his quarters that night. He had been done for 'conduct to the prejudice of good order and military discipline', which covers the whole military calendar of crime from dirty buttons to flogging the Mess silver, and had stopped a month's orderly dog for it, all highly illegal because, officially, an officer can only be punished by General Court Martial. He was relieved, but a little hurt; the more so when I told him I'd put the dirt in on him with Barry.

'Was that absolutely necessary?' he asked.

'You're bloody tooting it was,' I assured him earnestly. 'You're too nice a bloke to be in this business, Foo. Does that sound a shade paternal?'

'Actually, priggish is the word,' he said quietly. 'I'm sorry we won't be working together again——'

'So am I in some ways——'

'——because if we ever did, and you plonked your clumsy European feet on another spike, you could stay there and rot so far as I'm concerned.'

'Now look, Foo——' I began, but he cut me short again.

'Get stuffed, Wainwright,' he said with cold venom. 'I'll give you a drink in the Mess, shake hands with you and wish you a happy time on leave, but I'll never forgive you. You've made me lose face. We don't like that to happen—in Hampstead or Hong Kong.'

And then he was grinning again, and he thumped me playfully in the ribs.

But what I had seen in that moment really frightened me. There is nothing more dangerous than a good Chinese who has been done, or thinks he has been done, gratuitous dirt—and Kam Foo *was* a good Chinese and I had really put the knock on him. Whatever my motives, and to this day I still think I was acting in his best interests, to him it was treachery of the worst kind and I was a Judas Iscariot.

I wondered if I'd ever get straight with him again.

Chapter Five

I DIDN'T GET AWAY for ten days. I had a lot of handing over to do at the bank, then there was a nonsense over the tickets. They always fixed them up for us in the office, and when mine arrived I was fed up to find that instead of the plush BOAC direct flight to London I had hoped for, the best they could do for me was a thing that involved a night stop in Calcutta and the QANTAS plane on from there the next day. I beefed about it, but it didn't do me the least bit of good. It was that or wait another week for a vacant seat, and all I wanted to do at that moment was to get out. Get out anywhere. Kam Foo had complained about losing face. What about me? For all I knew this was curtains. If you were dropped by 'The Firm' it usually meant that your cover job went with it; and, strangely enough, I liked my cover job. I could have soldiered along in the bank indefinitely. England meant little to me as a place to live and work in, and London gave me the horrors. I'd been born and bred in Shanghai, and had lived out East most of my life, except for four years at school.

Of course I hadn't actually *been* fired. One never was. One was just quietly dropped, but sooner or later the final chop came. Your secret salary failed to arrive after a time, then, eventually, you would be called in by your boss in your cover job and told regretfully that owing to reorganization and retrenchment in your particular department, etc., etc., etc.—and you got a golden handshake of six months' salary, and that was it. Or so I had been told when I was first recruited. I had also been told, very clearly, that once having worked for 'The Firm' one was never thereafter completely free from surveillance—just in case one ever suffered a political change of heart and thought about gliding softly over to the Opposition. Not that that would have been easy anyhow. One wouldn't have been much good to them in the lower echelons. Your real top-flight professional double agent was born, not made.

I sat and gloomed out of the window as the Boeing rose over the harbour and swung right-handed round the Peak. What a Babylon this place was. A miniature New York, nine miles long and four hundred yards wide. High-rise office and apartment buildings perched along a narrow shelf and overshadowed by a mountain that glowered over them. Then that marvellous harbour, and Kowloon to the north, flatter and more symmetrical than Hong Kong, and the distant ring of jagged peaks that were the southern bastions of China proper. And in a matter of minutes we were over Macao, a tiny jewelled ring of red, white, blue and ochre-washed buildings on an absurdly tiny finger of land jutting out into the China Sea, with the river we had come down a dirty yellow sweep to the right of it. It all looked so small and flat from up here, and I wondered what the fuss had been about.

There were two stewardesses—pretty Philippino girls—but they were in rich men's country up front. At the tourist end we had an Australian queer to tend to us. I watched him jessying round the passengers in front of me, dispensing pillows, papers, magazines and charm, and when he came to me I pretended to be asleep. But it didn't work. I got a waft of gorgeous after-shave lotion and felt a hand that I knew would be soft and white gently shaking my shoulder. I opened one eye and snarled at him. Yes, I know—we should be sympathetic and try and understand their peculiar problems. But I can't help it. They make my flesh creep. He made kissing noises of disapproval and moved on to the next gent. The women were only getting the most cursory attention.

He came round again later, this time to frig about with those stupid collapsible tables which only seem to live up to their name when you've got a plastic tray with a drink, soup and bits in front of you. Fixing mine would have involved him in leaning over the two passengers between me and the aisle, and a hell of a lot of fiddling. I tried to do it myself to save him the trouble, but I was hamfisted about it. He was a trier, though—he insisted on helping, so I got up and excused myself to the others and pushed off to the tail of the plane.

There was a small service bar and pantry there, and the girls were making quick birdlike descents on it for trays of drinks which they hefted back through the curtain to the first class. I put it on one of them for a brandy and ginger ale, but then this other grot came back and took the order over, fluffing and blinking at her angrily. Since he couldn't get his big bum into the bar while they were there he had to wait until they had gone before serving me—and when he did, he gave me a slip of paper and lisped under his breath, 'For Cri' thake will you *pleath* take thith. I've been trying to slip you the bloody thing ever since Honkers.'

Yes, they recruit us in all shapes, sizes and sexes.

I went into the gents to read it. It was written in pencil, and there were two tiny marks on it which vouched for its authenticity. 'Get off in Calcutta. Great Eastern. Own name,' I read. I tore it up and flushed it down the pan, then I went back to my seat, sipped my drink and mulled.

It was a basic rule with us that we never wrote anything if it could be safely transmitted verbally. Barry could have got in touch with me direct at any time up till I actually got on the plane at Kai Tak. So why this? The writing wasn't his, naturally, but the identifying marks had been there all right. Just the slightest thickening of the second consonant and the fifth vowel—in this case the 't' in 'get' and the 'u' in 'Calcutta' respectively—as if the writer had accidentally pressed more heavily on his pencil there. In ink, the letters would have been faintly smudged; if typed, the key hit just that fraction harder. Oh yes, this was from The Firm all right. I had been convinced that I was being dropped, either permanently or, at best, for a long period of 'rest' before being reposted to less sensitive duties. That might still be the case, but it certainly didn't look as if—I gave it up. I knew it wouldn't be the slightest use asking the pansy who had given him the note, and when? He was obviously just a passer and dropper. We had many such on the airlines. He probably wouldn't even know who he was working for, because the heroin and gold boys used the same methods—and very often the same people. They just got a letter or a small package and a hundred-Hong-Kong-dollar bill. The bill was theirs—the letter or package they passed on. If they ever slipped up, double-crossed or talked, things could happen to them—things like being beaten up in places like Calcutta or Beirut, or having a one-ounce ingot of gold planted on them in Karachi—which could mean anything up to five years' curry and rice when found by the Customs.

So I was still in business. It was something like dodging the guillotine to be faced with a life stretch on Devil's Island. I had another three brandies, ducked the soup and bits, and went to sleep.

Dum Dum, Calcutta's international airport, was still its sweet, charming self—a mixture of a Turkish bath and the Chicago stockyards. We were herded through the transit shed to the airport bus, and I sidled up beside the steward and told him I was going to peel off as I didn't like the Majestic, where the rest of the passengers would be night-stopping, and handed him my baggage chits.

'All covered, ducks,' he cooed. 'Your stuff won't be put on the bus. Call the airline office tomorrow before take-off

57

time and tell 'em you're feeling an icksy bit icky-boo and want a stopover—it'll save me an awful lot of bitching about.' He slipped me a thin roll of notes. 'Fifty rupees—taxi and tip money, until you can change some of your own,' he explained. They thought of everything.

I retrieved my two suitcases, fought off a solid phalanx of howling coolies and bribed my way into a taxi. Travelling west we had almost stayed abreast of time, and it was still short of midday here. The steamy heat was at its worst, beating back in almost perceptible waves from the streaked, yellow-washed buildings and the acres of tin and hessian hovels that form the outer suburbs of this most desolate of Eastern cities. And yet it had a sad, ravaged beauty of its own, and even a dignity, like an aged duchess turned beggar. A mosque at the end of a festering alley, faced with marble slabs that have sloughed away in patches to disclose the fungus-covered mud bricks beneath; three slender palms arching out of the roof of the beat-up lean-to hut built round their feet; a Mogul gateway that was probably old when Clive was here, plastered with Bengali advertisements for pile cures and vitality pills; a woman, slender and lovely as a Tanagra figure, carrying a yellow plastic dustbin on her head. And children, teeming thousands of them, lying in patches of shade with the lassitude of the ever-hungry, until a car or taxi is brought to a halt by the press of bullock carts and ancient trucks, then rising and smothering it like swarms of flies— small clawing hands plucking at you. Give any one of them a copper paisa and the rest will engulf you, wrenching open doors or even wriggling through the windows. Throw a handful of coins into the dust to draw them off and you know you'll probably start a fight that could easily leave one small figure still lying there when the car moves on. That, seen through the rear window, is rather apt to stay with one.

We bumped down over the potholes on Chittaranjan

Avenue, across the top of Chowringhee, past the Auchter-lonie Monument and pulled up in front of the Great Eastern Hotel. There was the usual mêlée between the luggage coolies, the legitimate ones who kicked back half of their take to the Pathan hall porter, and the bigger band of freelances who squat and chew betel nut on the pavement all day and sleep there at night. I settled for the minimum four, who toiled and grunted under the regulation twenty-two kilos my bags totalled, plus another four who managed to get two fingers apiece on them and just grunted, and we made it into the cramped and gloomy lobby in a wedge. Yes, the old Parsee desk clerk told me, there was a room for Mr Wainwright—but no messages. I paid off the first contingent and hired another for the safari upstairs.

The Great Eastern was built in 1863, and nobody has done much to it since—a vast, echoing labyrinth of dark corridors smelling of curry and Victorian wickedness that radiate from a central airshaft which has balconies running round it and is crossed at each floor level by little concrete bridges. The bedrooms open off these balconies, and the windows in the outer walls used at one time to open on the world but now they are all 'air-conditioned' (my quotes), which means they are boarded up, with boxes at the bottom which house clanking machinery when the electricity is on, and, in theory, suck air from the outside and spew it into the room. Whether or not this cools it in the process, I wouldn't be knowing.

The cavern my column showed me into—reinforced on the passage upstairs by three Goanese bellhops and a turbaned floor-bearer—was registering at a guess about a hundred and thirty Fahrenheit. They demonstrated the modern marvel of the air-conditioner and the unspeakable luxuries of the bathroom, glossing over the piffling fact that the taps emitted hollow noises but no water, collected my quadruple over-tip and started a battle over it. I heaved them out in a body and

59

sat on the bed. What the hell now? I wondered. But I didn't have to wonder long, because the door opened then, without preliminary courtesies, and the Gaffer came in.

I hadn't seen the bastard for over three years. The interim hadn't done much for him. The same jaundiced St Bernard face—I mean the dog, not the saint himself—and the same disgusting habit of twisting one side of his blubbery mouth into a grin while sucking his yellow, nicotined teeth on the other. It's quite a feat. Try it some time. The only thing that had changed were his clothes. The shiny, cigarette-ash-dusted navy-blue serge, celluloid collar and made-up tie he invariably wore in London were replaced by a crumpled white duck suit that only a missionary of the old school or a really with-it Carnaby Street lizard would dare to be seen in nowadays, and on the back of his head was a battered Bombay bowler—the small flat topee that Eurasian ticket collectors wear in mufti.

Yes—the Gaffer. The maestro himself. I found myself wishing that I had taken more than those four duty-free brandies on the plane. I could have borne it better.

He said, 'Don't get up,' and waved a pudgy hand.

'I wasn't going to,' I told him, and added, because I was genuinely interested, 'Where the bloody hell did you get that suit?'

He squinted down his bulging front with pride and flicked it appreciatively. 'Good drop of whistle, this,' he said. 'You should have recognized the style. Made by old Hing Lo in Shanghai—before the war.'

'Which war?' I asked.

He dragged the single chair forward and sat down.

'Once is funny, twice is cheeky,' he grunted. 'Don't push things, boy.' He put a cigarette in the corner of his mouth and lighted it. It would stay there now until it was burnt down to the last sodden centimetre, the ash blown off in horrid little popping puffs at regular intervals to add to the grey guano runnel down the front of his jacket. I once put my bare feet into a sleeping-bag and found them in contact with the warty hide of a giant mendak toad. My reactions were just the same now.

'Made another cock of things, so they tell me,' he said, as conversationally as he would have said that it was going to turn out nice if it didn't rain, and as inevitably. I didn't answer, so he went on, 'Their own damn silly fault, of course. You don't risk heavy aces on lightweight jacks.'

Like a fool I fell for it and said thanks.

'I was referring to that fancy boat of theirs,' he said. 'Cost a lot of money, that did. Still, it's meant a trip back out here for me. I was ready for it. That damn London smog was getting in my tubes.' He cleared his throat reminiscently and removed the cigarette long enough to spit at the washbasin in the corner. His aim was inaccurate. There was silence for a time. He was waiting for me to say something, so he could turn it back on me, but I wasn't giving him any more openings. It seemed to annoy him, which delighted me.

'This feller Kam Foo,' he said. 'How bad is he really?'

'He isn't bad at all.'

'Then what did you put the mockers on him for?'

'I didn't.'

'What do you call "unreliable"?'

'I made it all clear to Barry.'

'Make it clear to me.'

'Personal involvement. He stayed with me when I was sick, then he got the best doctor in Macao for me. A government one.'

'Too much of a gent, in other words?'

'Exactly. A disadvantage in this business—as you'd be the first to appreciate.'

If it registered with him he didn't show it. He just went on: 'Nothing more than that?'

'That's plenty for me. Anybody I'm teaming with has got

to be ready to stick a knife in his blind grandmother if it appears necessary. That's why I'm so glad to be getting out of it.' I hoped that this last would bring either confirmation or a grudging disclaimer, but it did neither.

'What I mean is,' he said, 'this caper was obviously blown beforehand. Could he have had anything to do with it?'

'By Christ, he would have had to have been dedicated,' I told him. 'He was right there with me when the crap hit the fan.'

'Ah yes, but did he know it was going to turn out that way?'

'He didn't know anything until just before H-hour—so if he blew it he would have had to have done so from the junk. It was all in my report.'

'Never read 'em. Too long-winded. Barry said yours was useless, anyhow.' He paused the barest moment to allow that one to register, then went off at a tangent. 'Know Alipore?'

'Two. One's a town on the west coast near Bombay, the other's the Central Jail here.'

'The second. There's a feller called Bowyer coming out of there tomorrow. I want him tailed. It's a chance for you.'

'A chance of what?'

'Just a chance. Lose him and you can pick up your ticket and be on your way. Tell me where he finishes up, and you're still in business.'

'Stuff it,' I said. 'I've had enough. It's always been the same with you people. You send me out half briefed, and win, lose or draw, I finish up as the object of your elephantine wit or Barry's bitchiness. You don't trust me. You never did.'

'I don't trust anybody,' he said mildly. 'That's why I'm still in business—after thirty years of it. Isn't that a cardinal rule that I'm always trying to rub into you youngsters?'

'Sure. But when I do, for the very first time, voice certain doubts about somebody, I'm accused of knifing him in the back.'

'Best bloody place to knife *anybody*. Shows you're learning, anyhow.' He grinned suddenly, yellowly, like a hyena. 'All right, cool it. Nobody's blaming you for this last one——'

'Big of them.'

'Shut up and listen. This is important. There are fourteen hundred cons of various colours in Alipore—all of them in for something they didn't do. They'll tell you that themselves, and they ought to know. Only in Bowyer's case it's true. He was framed, and stopped seven years.'

'Who framed him?'

'Me—or rather Kowalski on my orders. He planted four four-ounce ingots on him and tipped the Customs off here.'

'What for?'

'That doesn't come into it. Actually it seemed expedient at the time, although in the light of subsequent events I should have done it the other way round and kept Kowalski on ice until we needed him again. Well, Bowyer's coming out after three years. Full remission plus the fact that the Indians always cut Europeans' stretches short. They're an embarrassment in local nicks.'

'That means he'll be deported to England as soon as he comes through the gate.'

'He won't. Officially he's Seaforth Highlander on his father's side, Madrassi on his mother's.'

'Eurasian?'

'Only on his papers. The Madrassi was a foster mother but that gives him an Indian passport. They say he's actually some colonel's daughter's by-blow. He's as English as you or me—probably more so. I always have my doubts about some of you Shanghai Migs. Only my little joke, of course——'

'And you want to know where he goes when he comes out?'

'Just that.'

'Well, that should be simple enough. I know Calcutta quite well, although it's not exactly in my parish.'

'Dead simple,' he agreed. 'All you've got to do is to stay on his track without wise-ing him up. Actually I think he'll be making for Rangoon, then over the bloody hills to China—per boot.'

I gaped at him. He lit another cigarette from the stub of the last, puffed, blew, coughed, and went on.

'Kowalski told us this, but he wasn't able to go into full details. That's why we were bringing Kowalski out—to get the whole picture.'

I said, 'You're serious about this?'

'Naw,' he answered with heavy sarcasm. 'I've just flown seven thousand miles to pull your bloody leg.'

'You really expect me to walk over the Hump?'

'Not all the way. You can run part of it.'

'But why me? That isn't my territory at all.'

'Availability mostly—plus the fact that you pee'd in your own chips when you put the squeak in against Kam Foo. He was down for it originally.' He grinned nastily. 'You'll never learn the facts of life, will you? "He who would bury Caesar should first praise him." Do you know who said that?'

'No—but look here——'

'Neither do I. I just made it up. All right—joke's over. Now listen. Bowyer will be coming out broke, less the twenty rupees they give 'em at the gate. He's entitled to a ticket to any place he wants to go. The further it is, the better they like it. He's asked for one to Karachi, but that's just a blind, we think. They'd never let him into Pakistan, and he knows it. He's got some gelt in the Swadeshi Bank here in another name. He'll probably draw it and make his way to Rangoon. He may not, of course—but wherever he goes you'll tail him—and you'll keep tailing him until he finally arrives where he's heading for, or you're called off.'

'What are you giving me, Gaffney?' I raged. 'One white man tailing another through black country? We'll stick out like two fantail pigeons in a flock of crows.'

He dropped the banter for the first time. 'You don't think I don't realize that, do you? You're not being sent bare-arsed and flat-footed. You'll have two legmen for the close work.'

'Then why send me at all?'

'Be your age. I said legmen. They won't even know who they're working for, other than you. One of them's pretty good, though. You may know him. Idwal Rees——'

'I know him. Shanghai Welshman—and suspect for a start.'

'A professional working for the cheque.' The Gaffer nodded. 'But he doesn't bite the hand that's feeding him— and he's never been known to work for *them*.'

'Who's the other?'

'A local. Rees's man and a hundred per cent reliable—to Rees.'

'All right,' I said. 'What are we after—really after? Tell me for once, Gaffney—without any of your "nods and becks and wreathèd smiles." Just trust me——'

He held up his hand and stopped me in mid-spate.

'I don't know,' he said. 'You needn't believe that if you find it a strain, but it's the truth. All we know is that there's something going on up there. It's been building up over the last three or four years. There's a nest of them—Chinese and Europeans—coming and going. It's a line—a line running through the hills—with breaks in it. It surfaces for a time on the Tibet-Kashmir border. There's a side line into Kabul. It comes up again in Upper Iraq, near Mosul, and then it's lost, until it finally comes up in Tirana—Albania.'

'The Break?' I said.

'The Break used to be in Tirana,' he agreed. 'But now it's somewhere nearer here. That's your answer. Find the Break. Find out what they're running along the line. Why they're going through the most difficult terrain in the world—the Himalayas themselves. There are easier ways to pass men and information than that. Kowalski has been feeding us bum steers for a long time. He came out here to Calcutta in the early days, promising us a lead, but he said Bowyer was on to him, and asked us to ease the pressure. That's when we framed Bowyer. But Kowalski got the hell out of it then, and we've only had whispers from him since. Then he said he was coming out with the lot—before Bowyer got back up there—but you know what happened. All right, somebody's got to go back in on Bowyer's tail.'

'But are you certain that he *is* going back in?' I asked.

'Kowalski was, anyhow. Bowyer's had no mail at all since he's been in Alipore, but we're positive that he's got a grapevine going—maybe through a bent warder. Everything is probably laid on for him. He'll just come through the gate and disappear, unless we're on the ball.' He stood up and stretched. 'I want a bath. I've been talking to Rees all morning in a dirty little dump over in Howrah. See you here about six. Better eat here in the room if you can bear it. We don't want to be seen together in the dining-room—just in case.' He paused at the door and turned. 'No shoulder chips, Wainwright,' he said. 'I've come completely clean with you. I'll tell you something more. I asked for you on this.' He took my passport then and went out looking as near embarrassment as anyone of his temperament possibly could. It was like a sergeant-major complimenting a particularly ill-favoured rookie—but I wasn't fooled by it. I was being put on this job for the reasons he gave the first time. I was available—and expendable.

'The Break.' We'd been trying to sort that out for years. The Break was that point in the espionage line where the Chinese handed over to, and took over from, Europeans, for the very obvious reason that Chinese can no more spy in Europe or America than we can in China. It's as simple as that. Time was when the Russians did it for them, but those days, thank God, have gone for ever—or so we fervently hope. The Chinese have only one Caucasian ally—Albania.

It's the hardest country in Europe in which to infiltrate agents—and I'm not excluding Russia itself—but it's so small and sparsely populated that it's relatively easy for our regular Embassy-based Intelligence people to keep tabs on Chinese arrivals and departures. They are perfectly aware of this, so the Break is no longer there. The Break is not just a spot where cryptic messages are handed over like batons in a relay race. The Break is where briefings and debriefings are done, payments made, conferences held. It's like two contiguous countries with railway systems of different gauges. Somewhere there must be a transfer point—unloading ramps —sidings—marshalling yards. It's got to be organized. And anything that is organized is vulnerable—if you can find it. There are probably more breaks than one. In distances such as these there would have to be staging-posts, but the concept that continually exercised our section was *the* Break—the Big One—where Chinese first handed over to Caucasians.

So we were putting a rabbit down a deep, dark hole to find where the snakes were.

It could be quite interesting—if one wasn't the rabbit.

Chapter Six

HE CAME BACK AT SIX with a Bengali, a floridly handsome man with the lightish skin of a Brahmin, dressed in a white shirt, dhoti and pillbox khaddar cap. Other than that he was in no way disguised, but I had to look twice at him before I realized it was Rees. As a small boy I had seen him playing cricket in Shanghai at the Concession Club. On another occasion he had come round to have a drink with my father in Hong Kong. He was a major in a British infantry regiment then, so it must have been during the Korean war. Off and on I had seen him since in the Hong Kong Club in ordinary mufti. Each time he was just exactly what he purported to be at the moment—just as he was now.

He gave an Indian *namaste* sign—both palms together in an attitude of prayer—which does duty for the caste-conscious Brahmin as a handshake, then disregarded the chair I pulled forward, and squatted by the wall. He wasn't hamming anything. That was Rees. If he was dressed as a Brahmin, he was a Brahmin—like the actor who blacks himself all over to play Othello.

The Gaffer wasted no time on unnecessary courtesies. He grunted, 'Tell him the score, Rees.'

Rees said, 'I have one man who watches from now until Bowyer comes out. When he does, the man will follow him and report to me.' Just like that. No Peter Sellers chi-chi or babu's hyperbole. Straight English a little over-precisely delivered—and the effect was perfect. He was an upper-crust Hindu to the life, a graduate of either Calcutta or Benares

University, civil servant or schoolmaster, pulling down a hundred rupees a month. There were half a million such divided between this city, Delhi and Bombay, and ove rflowing into Burma and Malaysia. Outside he would be as noticeable as a golf-ball on a white pebble beach; here he made me feel slightly uncomfortable. If he remembered me he certainly gave no sign of it.

'What time do you think he will actually be coming out?' I asked.

'The normal time is eight o'clock, but tomorrow there are two hangings, so it will be an hour early, or an hour later,' he answered. 'I am sorry that I could not ascertain which.'

'Any chance of them letting him out much earlier on that account?'

'A possibility—but not to worry. My man is already in position.'

'Only one man?'

'And one link between him and myself, of course.'

'All right—Bowyer comes out. What then?'

'My man stays with him. I am informed. I inform you.'

'Rees stays with you as long as you want him,' the Gaffer put in.

'The name at the moment is Sri Prem Nath,' Rees said. He got up and stretched. 'As this gentleman says, I stay with you as long as you require me—up to a time limit of one month from today's date. That point should be clearly understood. I take it I can get in touch with you here at any time?' I nodded and he made *namaste* again and moved to the door, opened it, went through and closed it softly behind him. When I say moved, I mean just that. He didn't walk in the accepted sense of the word—it was more a sidle, without his back ever being turned completely towards us, with the contemptuous mock-servility of the Brahmin. There was no conscious straining after effect. It was just as I said before— perfect.

The Gaffer chuckled. 'Bloody good, isn't he?' he said. 'I wish to Christ we had him on the payroll permanent.'

'Why don't you?' I asked a little sourly.

'Not the temperament for it,' he said. 'Anyhow, why should he tie himself up? He makes more freelancing for one month than you and me put together would draw in a year.'

'So who's in charge?'

'You, sonny boy. We can deal with you afterwards if things get loused up—that's if you're still around. He just draws his cheque and gives us the two-finger salute.' He grinned at me sardonically. 'What's the matter? Anything worrying you?'

'No more than usual,' I answered. 'Two things do rather come to mind, though.'

'What?'

'You told me I was getting a couple of legmen who wouldn't be knowing who they were working for—then you bring in Rees. You mean to tell me that *he* doesn't know anything?'

'If he did he wouldn't shove it at you,' the Gaffer said. 'He's engaged as a legman—foreman legman, if you like— and he wouldn't presume to step out of that role unless you asked him. He could give you some bloody good advice, though, if you ever felt you needed it. I wouldn't be too proud about it if I were you. What's the other thing?'

'Oh, nothing much, except just what the hell I'm supposed to be on, other than putting a tail on an ex-convict? I mean, all this vague talk about the line and the Break——'

'Don't come the idiot boy with me, Wainwright,' he said sharply. 'There's nothing vague about it at all. There *is* a line. It starts somewhere over the China border and comes up in Albania. There's a lot of activity on it, and it's increasing. We'd like to know what's moving up and down it. That's for starters. Anything else you find out is a bonus. We don't expect you to do the whole distance per boot, for God's sake. Just find this end of it—and what it's being used for—and we'll love you for it.'

'The Break, though——?'

'Forget the Break. The Middle East Section is working on that. If we can tell them what's moving along it from this end it will help them. They'll know what to look for. See what I mean?'

'More or less,' I sighed. 'But whether you like the word or not, it *is* vague.'

'Of course it's vague in that sense. It's vague because we haven't got anything definite to go on. If we had we wouldn't be piddling around sending valuable men in on flimsy leads——'

'Thanks,' I said drily.

'My pleasure,' he came back as quick as a flash. 'Although actually I was referring to Rees and his blokes.' He had the grace to grin, though, and to call me a crafty bastard, and strangely, I felt a little mollified. Even though it was a slip of the tongue, coming on top of the fact that he had asked for me, it was quite a morale booster. And Lord knows I needed one just then.

He opened a briefcase and handed me my passport and a wad of paper money. 'Ten one-thousand-rupee notes and five hundred in small stuff,' he explained. That was a little over seven hundred pounds at current rates. 'If you need any more you'll have to go to your own bank in Rangoon— but I'd rather you didn't if you can possibly avoid it. You're visa'd for Burma, but that will only get you in at the docks or airport. They're as tight as all hell on movement up-country, so once out of town you'll have to lie, bribe or gumshoe your way along. Rees can help there, of course. Any questions? Not that I've got any answers.'

'Who do I report to?' I asked.

'Me—and me only,' he said emphatically. 'When you come out. Don't risk trying to send anything. You won't have the means, anyhow. I stress that—*me only*.'

'Will you be here?'

71

'Hardly likely. You'll come on to London in the ordinary way. Give us your tickets and they'll be amended and waiting for you at the airline office.' He dug into the briefcase again and produced four picture-postcards—a view of the Tower, one of the Abbey and two of Eastbourne. 'Address these to four of your pals at the Hong Kong bank. Don't date them. "Wish you was here—the beer's lovely"—you know the sort of thing. I'll post them when I get back to London.'

Dinner came up then; brown Windsor soup, stringy mutton, dehydrated spuds and canned Japanese pears. It was ghastly, but the Gaffer ploughed steadily through his, and then sat back burping gently and picking his teeth with the edge of 'Eastbourne Esplanade from the Pier,' which I had earmarked for young Reggie Smollet of the Foreign Exchange Department. He watched me reproachfully as I sunk a couple of stiff whiskies to hold the mess down. Among his other shortcomings he was a teetotaller, and a bore with it. He asked me if I was carrying any hardware, and of course I wasn't. Who does on holiday? So he dug into the briefcase again and gave me a flat Browning .38 and a carton of fifty rounds, and made me sign for it in duplicate. Then he hauled himself to his feet, grunted so long and went. In the doorway he broke wind loudly and waggled his fingers at me playfully.

What a repulsive old swine he was. And how magnificent at his job.

A gentle, insistent tapping at the door wakened me. I swung off the creaking bed and went and unlocked it. The man on the other side was small, wizened and European. He had a creased and yellow face, like a worn tobacco pouch, rheumy eyes and a drooping, nicotine-stained white moustache. He wore a dingy white shirt and flapping Army surplus khaki shorts, wrinkled golf stockings and local chapli sandals. The lot was crowned by a battered topi. He had poor-white written all over him.

72

I said 'Yes?'

'You'd better let me in,' he muttered. 'Message.' I stepped aside. He came in and removed his topi, revealing straggling grey hair in a fringe round a bald patch. His eye lighted on the bottle of scotch on the table, and I saw his throat working dryly. He started a slow search through his pockets and produced a box of matches.

'Bugger it,' he grunted. 'Must've left me smokes behind.'

I gave him a cigarette and said, 'The message?' He lit the cigarette and drew deeply on it, then his eye went back to the bottle.

'All right, I'll give you a drink,' I told him, 'but let's have the message first.'

'Oh, sure. Begins, "the goods is out and is holed up, but there's something funny going on and I'd like to see you." Ends.'

'Who'd like to see me?'

'Sri Prem Nath—who else?'

'The bit about "the goods". I don't understand that.' I looked at my watch. It was three o'clock.

'Came out at midnight,' he said. 'There's two toppings there in the morning. One of 'em's a political, so there'll be a bunch of students shouting the odds outside. Releases was done early in consequence.'

It confirmed what Rees had said, but this little squirt was such an unlikely figure that I was still doubtful.

'Are you certain about all this?' I asked.

'My bloody oath I am,' he said. 'I been watching them gates since six o'clock last night. There's a nullah running along under the wall outside—it's a sewer for the bustees— full of dead goats, crap and mosquitoes. It doesn't half come up. I could do with that drink.'

I poured a shot and held the glass in my hand.

'All right, so Sri Prem Nath wants to see me. Where?' I demanded.

73

'I'll take you. I've got a gharry waiting round the back.' His hand was reaching out beseechingly.

'Where?' I repeated.

'Howrah—other side of the river. The goods is in a hotel one side of an alley—Sri Prem Nath is in another the other side, watching. You're making that bloody scotch warm in your 'ands.'

I still didn't give it to him. 'What's this something funny that's going on?'

'Oh, for Christ's sake,' he wailed. 'I was told to give you the message, and nothing else.'

'I want to know,' I insisted.

'Okay, but don't let on to him I told you. The goods was picked up by two blokes as soon as he came out of the gate, and whisked off in a car. Bloody nigh gave us the slip.'

'How did you manage to stay with him if he was in a car?'

He looked at me pityingly. 'Blimey, you don't think Mr Rees—Sri Prem Nath—would let us get caught flat-footed, do you? We had another one parked up an alley.'

I gave him the drink and started to get dressed. He swallowed it like an oyster and looked wistful. I didn't fall for it. I loaded the gun and the spare magazine and planted the money and my passport inside my shirt. I was hoping to get back here for my kit, but one doesn't leave valuables around in an Indian hotel bedroom. I said, 'Let's go.'

He seemed to share my views on the sanctity of property because he said, 'You're not leaving that bottle there, are you? The room boy will be helping his bleeding self and topping it up with cold tea.'

I got him by his skinny arm and propelled him firmly out on to the balcony and along towards the main stairway, but he pulled away from me. 'Back way,' he said sullenly. 'You never know who's hanging around out front.'

He certainly knew the place, because he led me unerringly through a maze of dimly lighted corridors and down flights of dark and smelly stairs until we reached the kitchen regions and a back door that opened into an alley. There was a *chowkidar* (watchman) outside, huddled in a cotton sheet, but he had evidently been suborned, because he pretended not to see us. The little man led me to a car which bulked darkly at the end of the alley. I had been expecting a horse carriage, but then I remembered that all wheeled vehicles were 'gharries' in the bazaar patois. He slid in behind the wheel, but stopped me when I started to get in beside him. 'Back seat,' he directed. 'Looks better. This is a taxi.'

He drove out of the alley and turned right, and right again, then left on to the approach road to the soaring Howrah Bridge which spans the Hooghli River. I knew these parts fairly well. The main railway terminal is the other side, and round it cluster slums almost as ghastly as those of the eastern suburbs.

Calcutta at night is a city of the dead. Apart from the very occasional prowling taxi nothing moves except the packs of scavenging dogs that come out to feed on the festering rubbish tips after dark. The homeless lie asleep on the pavements in huddled masses, and that heightens the ghastly necroscopic atmosphere of the place, particularly when the wind comes up-river just before dawn, bringing with it the heavy, acrid smoke of the burning ghats that line the banks beneath the bridge.

The little man drove into the dark station forecourt and parked. We got out and I followed him down a narrow street that led to the river. It was lined on both sides with heavily shuttered shops and 'hotels'. One has to put the word in quotes in this context because they usually have splendid names like 'Pearl Palace', 'Lotus Garden' and 'Shalimar', but are never more than squalid doss-houses reeking of unwashed bodies and stale cooking. The street ended at a ramshackle wharf that jutted out into the river. The little man turned aside and went through a narrow door in the last house. A steep flight of stairs led up from the tiny lobby, which was inadequately lighted by an oil-lamp. A *chowkidar* slept on the bottom step. He opened one eye and started to get up to bar our passage, but my guide muttered something in Hindi and he let us pass. We climbed three flights in the darkness, then the man tapped at a door. Rees opened it and let us in.

He said, 'Right—take post at the window, Major, and don't go to sleep,' then, as the little man passed him in the darkness he grabbed his arm and spun him round. 'You've been drinking,' he said softly.

'One bloody peg,' wailed the little man, 'that *he* give me. Blimey, you're worse than my mother-in-law—and she's a bleeding Madrassi Christian with a nose like a mongoose.'

'Get on with it,' Rees told him, then guided me sideways to a charpoy string bed that seemed to be the stifling little room's only furnishing. We sat down, and he said, 'Nothing to do but wait now, but I thought you would prefer to be here in case of a quick move.'

'Where is he?' I asked.

'Holed up in the corresponding building to this, the other side of the street,' he answered. 'They let him out at midnight. There were two men waiting for him. I know one of them—a fellow called Snaith—petty crook. As a matter of fact there was somebody else waiting also—a detective, West Bengal Police—a man by the name of Chatterjee.'

'Why would the police be waiting for him *outside*?' I asked. 'They've had him on tap for the last three years.'

'Same reason as ourselves, I suppose. They want to know where he's going. Actually it helped us considerably. Bowyer and his friends were so preoccupied with giving Chatterjee the slip that they didn't notice the Major and my other man on their tail.'

'Are the police around now?'

'They bloody ain't,' the Major chuckled from the window.

76

'Shook the bastards cold, they did. Pretty to watch. They hopped out of the car in Chowringhee and dodged into the Majestic. The dick's after them like a long-dog but he's not quick enough. They shot out of a side door in Hunyuman Street and grabbed a taxi and carried on. I bet Chatterjee's been drumming every room in the joint. There's seven hundred of 'em.'

'Don't talk so much, Major,' Rees told him. 'Just watch.'

'I *am* watching,' the Major said. 'And I'll tell you something. They ain't bloody there any more.'

'Nonsense,' said Rees. 'There are two exits to that place. The one you're watching, and the one the other side that Safaraz is covering. Nobody has come out. They're still there all right.'

'You want to bet?' the Major said. 'They was in that room bang opposite—right? One of 'em was smoking like a chimney —one cigarette after the other. That'd be our client making up for lost time. You could see the glow rising and falling. Well, nobody's smoking now. Come and look for yourself.'

'Probably sleeping,' Rees said, but he crossed to the window nevertheless.

'Sleeping? First night out of the nick?' the Major snorted scornfully. 'Come off it. You smoke, you drink, you talk, and maybe you shake a little. You don't sleep—not for three or four days you don't. You're talking to an expert.'

Surprisingly, Rees appeared to be grudgingly impressed with the little man's theorizing. I couldn't think why. I'd have trusted his opinions as much as his honesty—both about as far as I could throw a bull by the tail.

'I bet they slipped past that randy wog of yours when he was laying a bit of stuff round the back of the wharf somewhere,' the Major went on. 'The river-banks is stiff with sand-rats. Half a rupee a go.'

'Shut up,' said Rees, and moved away from the window. 'Keep watching. I'll go and do a recce.' But then there was a

77

soft tapping at the door. Rees unlocked it and there was a scuffling noise as two dark figures entered, and I could hear someone moaning faintly. Rees said, 'Drop the blind and give us a light.'

The Major lit an oil-lamp and I saw a tall Pathan standing by the door, shaking water from his soaked clothes and kicking a huddled figure on the floor. It was the figure who was moaning.

'What did I tell you?' the Major said triumphantly. 'They shook him—shook him cold.'

The Pathan was speaking to Rees in an undertone. I know a few words of Urdu, but this, even if it was Urdu, was far too fast and low-pitched for me to follow. Rees heard him through, then turned to me.

'They went out through the back way,' he said quietly. 'A boat came for them. Safaraz had no opportunity of giving us a flash on his torch as arranged. He slid into the water and held on to the back of the boat. They went about a mile downriver. Bowyer and one of the others got on a rice dhow which got under way immediately. This one came back.' He stirred the prone man with his foot. 'Get up, Snaith,' he said softly.

The man twitched and moaned louder, then uncoiled and got painfully to his knees, and I saw that he was a Eurasian, tall and lanky in the ruins of a European suit, and with a swathe of smallpox pits across his face. He staggered to the bed and sat drooping on the edge of it, his eyes darting from one to the other of us in turn, the tip of his tongue moistening his thin lips nervously.

'I'll have you for this, Mr Rees,' he said breathlessly. 'Before God I will. There's still a law in this damned place.'

'What have *I* done?' Rees asked mildly.

'This black bastard is your man. Think I don't know? Unprovoked murderous assault . . . He can get five years for that.'

78

'Go and get Chatterjee,' Rees said over his shoulder to the Major. 'You'll find him waiting in the Majestic lounge. Mr Snaith can lay his charges now.'

The Major moved to the door. Snaith looked startled, then he sneered and shrugged. 'You can't frighten me with that sort of bluff,' he said.

'Pity. I was hoping I could.' Rees nodded to Safaraz. 'I don't like this sort of thing.'

Neither did I, and I'm sure Snaith loathed it because Safaraz stepped across and lifted him to his feet by his hair, chopped him under the nose and brought his knee up painfully. Snaith's scream ended in a nasty bubbling slobber and he writhed on the floor beside the bed. Safaraz picked him up and looked questioningly at Rees. Rees shook his head. Safaraz reseated him on the bed.

'Give a man a chance, Mr Rees,' Snaith snuffled. 'We're all only trying to make a living—things are bad enough in this town without *us* leaning on each other——'

'Who's the client?' Rees asked.

'You know bloody well who he is.'

'You tell me.'

'Bowyer——'

'Who's running him out—where to and why?'

'I don't know.'

Rees nodded to Safaraz again and Snaith screamed.

'I tell you I don't—I *don't*! This Burmese bloke came and saw me——'

'What Burmese bloke?'

'I don't know his name—he never told me. He just came along to my bungalow on Monday and said someone wanted Bowyer brought from Alipore Jail when he came out and put on a dhow.'

'What dhow?'

'Rice boat—name of *Jainti*—regular run between here and Bassein. He said the job had to be done quiet and foolproof

79

with no tails, because there were some fellers waiting for Bowyer that he didn't want to see. He offered two hundred that I managed to up to four, plus another one for expenses. Mr Rees, that's the God's truth—and if you killed me I couldn't tell you any more.' He sat looking piteously up at Rees, with one eye cocked on the impassive Safaraz, gently massaging his outraged groin with one hand and cupping his streaming nose with the other.

'What did Bowyer tell you?' Rees asked.

'Not a blind word. He talked a bit to the other feller, but it was in Burmese, and I don't understand it. All he did most of the time was chain smoke—'

'So you don't know what it was all about?'

Snaith stopped mopping his nose long enough to raise his hand heavenwards. 'As true as I'm sitting here——' he began.

'All right, I'll tell you,' Rees said. 'You've just helped a gold-smuggler back into business. They're not going to love you for that along at headquarters.'

'But I didn't know! I *didn't*, I tell you,' Snaith squealed. 'They can't hang anything on me just because——'

'You watch them,' Rees said drily. 'They'll pull you in on an accessory charge and throw the book at you.'

'*Throw* it at him?' the Major croaked. 'With his bleeding record they'll ram it *up* him without Vaseline. Making a monkey out of Chatterjee's not going to help either. The curry and rice'll be running out of his goddam ears by the time he breaks surface again.'

'Mr Rees,' Snaith pleaded, 'I had no idea—no idea, I tell you— Give me a chance—give me a chance for God's sake.' He fumbled in his pocket. 'Look, the feller paid me off tonight—'

'That makes sense,' the Major said approvingly and held out his hand. 'The Police Sunshine Fund——' He tailed off as Rees looked at him.

'All right, Snaith,' Rees said. 'Nobody wants to lean on

you—not unless you ask for it. Just forget tonight—completely and absolutely. It never happened—any of it. Do you understand?'

'Sure, sure, Mr Ree '

'Good. Then beat it.'

Snaith climbed to his feet and limped to the door and Safaraz let him out. I suddenly felt sorry for him.

'So the poor bastard was roughed up for nothing,' I said.

'Not entirely.' Rees shrugged. 'To get the truth out of the Snaiths of this world you either have to have a lot of time—or a lot of very sudden action.'

'I think a hundred rupees out of expenses——' I began.

'Good idea,' the Major chipped in. 'Poke in the kisser and a kick in the cods—fifty rats apiece. Give it to me and I'll see he gets it.'

'You're in charge, Mr Wainwright,' Rees said primly, 'but I personally have the greatest objection to coddling the criminal classes. Major, run Mr Wainwright back to his hotel.'

'But what about Bowyer?' I asked.

'Calcutta to Bassein, just over seven hundred miles,' Rees answered. 'That's five days' sailing. The dhows are as regular as clockwork except during the monsoon. Flying time two hours. You can relax for a bit, Mr Wainwright, because there's not a damned thing we can do in the meantime.'

Chapter Seven

I ONCE HEARD someone describe war as five per cent action, ten per cent fear and eighty-five per cent sitting on your arse waiting for something to happen. He could just as well have been referring to this business, because I eighty-five-per-cented for the next couple of days, sweltering in that ghastly room, not caring to risk going out in case I happened to run into somebody from the Calcutta branch of the bank.

I did take one chance and slipped out to Thacker and Spink's bookshop and got a fistful of assorted reading matter, including a Burma Government handbook. Bassein, I learned, was a town of twenty-five thousand inhabitants a hundred miles to the west of Rangoon, situated on the banks of one of the many mouths of the Irrawaddy Delta—sixty-seven per cent Buddhist, fifteen per cent Hindu, ten per cent Muslim, etc., etc.; there was a rail connection with Rangoon, with an asterisk against it. The footnote said the rail service was 'unreliable'. There was also a road connection, and another asterisk. That footnote said, 'subject to seasonal weather conditions.' There was a very fine pagoda there—footnote, 'extensively damaged by gunfire (British) during World War II and not rehabilitated.' They produced an average of thirty-four million maunds of rice per annum—'subject to monsoon'. It sounded quite a place.

Rees came round on the third day and gave me an air ticket and told me I was booked on the morning flight for Rangoon the next day. He was going out the same night as he didn't think it advisable to travel together.

'I've been worrying,' I told him. 'What if our client gets off before Bassein?'

'I told you,' he said. 'Rice dhow—regular run. There are no intermediate stops.'

'Bassein's eighty miles up-river. He could be dropped in a boat.'

'I doubt it. Pretty wild country round there. But if he's *not* on the dhow when it arrives, Safaraz will lean gently on a crew member until he finds out the form. He's over there already.'

'And the other ancient villain?'

'The Major? Yes, he's there too. I got him out quickly because I heard Chatterjee was asking after him. He must have spotted him around when Bowyer gave him the slip.'

'Why do you call the old rip "Major"?'

Rees grinned—the first time I had ever seen him do so. 'Because he was a major once,' he told me. 'Quartermaster in the Bhil Coolie Corps during the war. He was an old soldier who took his pension out here, married in the bazaar and went native, then got called up again and given a temporary commission.'

'He hinted that he'd been in jail.'

'He wasn't hinting—he was telling you. He takes a perverse pride in it. He was court-martialled and busted for fiddling his men's pay, and got a couple of years. Since then he's been in and out of every jug in India that has a European wing.' He rose and looked down at me. 'Don't give him anything to drink again, ever,' he said. 'It's like giving blood to a tiger.'

'Reforming him, are you?' I tried not to make it sound like a sneer, but I don't think I was successful.

He shook his head gravely. 'He can drown in it when he's not working for me,' he said. 'At the moment he is—and I'm working for you. I try to give value for money, Mr Wainwright. There's a reservation for you at the Bristol

83

Hotel in Rangoon. I'll contact you there.' He bowed out, Brahmin-wise again, and went. I found myself disliking him very much indeed, but he certainly seemed to know his job. If I'd been on my own I'd undoubtedly have lost Bowyer before we even started. I suppose I should have been grateful, but somehow I wasn't.

I bumped into Rangoon on the Bristol Hotel bus. There were no messages for me at the desk, but at least the room was an improvement on the one in Calcutta. It wasn't air-conditioned, which meant that one could at least see out of the window, but I'd had enough of being cooped up, so I went out after lunch.

I stood outside the main entrance for a few moments, trying to make up my mind where to go, because Rangoon is about as uninteresting a town for aimless walking as any in the East. I decided on the Shwe Dagon Pagoda. At least there were open courtyards and terraces there, and the yellow-robed monks kept the swarms of beggars outside.

I held up my finger for the one taxi on the rank across the road, but then a European woman came out of the hotel behind me and signalled it also. It pulled up at the kerb, and the driver looked uncertainly at us. The woman realized then that I had the prior claim, and stepped back with an apology.

I said, 'I'm not in a hurry. You take it.'

'Oh, I wouldn't dream of it,' she answered. 'I'm only killing time.'

'That's all I'm doing,' I told her. 'Go ahead.' I opened the door for her but she still hesitated. It was fast developing into one of those stupid situations, like two Frenchmen at a swing-door bowing and saying '*après vous*', which wouldn't resolve itself until one side or the other did something positive. 'I was going up to the Shwe Dagon,' I added.

'So was I,' she said, and I could have kicked myself. The obvious thing now was for us to share the cab, which under

84

present circumstances was sheer professional lunacy. But we did. I make no excuse. There wasn't one.

'Well, in that case——' I began, and she moved over and made room for me. Then, inevitably, we made another false start: 'Is this your first visit to Ran——?' we began simultaneously, then both apologized—then I yielded the floor to her and gathered, in the five-minute run to the pagoda that (a) it *was* her first visit, (b) she was staying at the Bristol, (c) whatever else she was she was certainly not a tourist in the accepted sense of the word, and (d) she was really very pretty; bronze redhead with skin that looked as if it had some blood behind it and so saved it from the chalky pallidness that so often mars that genre. Eyes? I couldn't tell then, because she was wearing sunglasses. Age? I couldn't tell that either, with any certainty. All redheads range five years both ways from their real age, according to how you're feeling at the moment. This one could have been anything from twenty-five to thirty-five. Figure? I can remember that all right, because she had preceded me into the cab and she was wearing a simple but good green linen dress that certainly hadn't been hacked out by a bazaar *dharzai*. It fitted her like a second skin without striving after effect. Only Bond Street and one Chinese dressmaker in Bombay make them quite like that. They are the nearest approach to the cheongsam that a European woman can wear without looking as if she were going to a fancy dress ball. No, there was nothing wrong with her figure—at all. I couldn't see whether or not she was married, because she was wearing gloves, which probably sounds fussy in a temperature that was ranging round the hundred mark, but no woman with any sense goes bare-handed in the tropics.

We pulled up in front of the pagoda and the beggars swooped in a solid phalanx. She was insisting on paying her half of the fare and she had her opened purse in her hand, and a skinny claw swooped on it. I jumped out and caught the thief—an ancient villain clad in a G-string and a plaster of mud and ashes—just as he was passing it to a small boy. It was a natural reaction round those parts and I had no intention of doing anything more than recovering it, but the old devil started to shriek that I was murdering him, and the small boy jumped on my back and clung there like a monkey and I realized too late that I'd fallen for the oldest hustle in the East, and was going to have my pocket picked in the confusion, as the rest of the mob surged round clawing and tearing at me.

I did the only thing advisable under the circumstances and clamped one hand firmly over my wallet while I laid about me with the other—hard. Then the cops arrived—three muscular Shans armed with bamboo lathis—and the pagoda steps were cleared in a minute and a half flat.

I went back to her, looking sheepish, and gave her the purse. She thanked me, but her tone implied that since she only had loose change in it there had been no real necessity to be brutal to an old man and a small boy over it. I was rather glad, because it gave me an excuse to be coldly polite and formal and so break things off. There were other Europeans about and I'd committed the cardinal sin of making myself conspicuous.

I said, 'It's inadvisable to flash money in a crowd round places like this, madam. Good afternoon.' And I turned and went up the steps to the place where you take your shoes off and exchange them for grass slippers before going through the gate. She caught up with me, looking contrite.

'I'm so sorry,' she said. 'That sounded ungrateful. I'm not —but it was all so sudden, and horrible, that I was frightened. Do forgive me.'

So what could I do without appearing an absolute churl? I mumbled that it was all right and waited while she checked her shoes in with the attendant and we just naturally drifted into the pagoda together.

86

I said, 'My name's James Wainwright.' There was no point in not doing so. I was travelling on my own passport and she could have checked on me in the hotel register had she been sufficiently interested.

'Mine is Paola Alberghetti,' she told me, which surprised me. There are plenty of redheaded Italians in the Northern Provinces, but this girl looked and sounded completely English.

We went into the main temple and gazed up at the huge seated Gautama Buddha. She took her sunglasses off in order to see the detail of the carving more clearly, and I saw that her eyes were—well, what? I still can't put a name to that colour. Green? Maybe. Perhaps something between that and grey—but the sort of grey that you see on a pigeon's underwing rather than on the side of a battleship. And there were flecks of amber in them. It's no good—I can't describe them. I'll settle for them being the most beautiful eyes I've ever seen in a human head—and the most disturbing. And for the life of me I couldn't define that disturbing quality. It wasn't their sheer beauty alone. There was something else there. And then, as we came back out into the courtyard I thought I had it.

The three policemen came in, obviously looking for me. They came up and told me in pidgin English that they wanted both of us to go to the station with them.

'What for?' I asked.

'Make charge against one man—one boy,' the guy with two stripes answered. 'We have car. Come.'

'Forget it,' I said. 'They didn't steal anything.'

'Make attempt. That is offence in law.'

'Well, I'm not charging them.'

'Must do. Law,' he insisted.

'Fine,' I told them. 'You go along and get a subpoena—Duke and Duchess of Piccadilly. We'll be here when you come back—maybe.'

87

They started to argue but I grinned and dropped them a five-kyat note and they gave up the attempt regretfully. I turned to collect the girl, but she was walking away rapidly. I went after her and caught her up, and then I knew what it was. She was scared. Just plain, plumb scared.

She said, 'Have they gone?'

'Sure. Nothing to worry about,' I told her. 'It's a quiet afternoon and they're just looking for a case.'

But she was badly shaken and she wanted to get back to the hotel, so we went out and reclaimed our shoes and I managed to get a taxi. I put it down purely to the normal reaction of a girl, perhaps a bit over-sensitive and unused to the East, seeing a microcosm of life in the raw for the first time, and I tried to reassure her, but it was no use. She hardly heard what I said on that short ride back, and when we pulled up before the hotel she muttered her thanks, jumped out and went in through the lobby quickly.

I started to go across to the desk to check on who she was and where she came from, and whether there was a Signor Alberghetti around, but I let it go. I was hardly likely to meet her again, and I'd been indiscreet enough already. I went up to my room.

But I was still intrigued, and I remember reflecting as I walked down the corridor on how nice she smelt in the taxi. It was a mixture of good toilet water and a scent that was neither overpowering nor too subtle—just fresh and clean and delightful. But the idyll ended as I opened the door.

The Major was sitting there looking at an empty glass and burping reminiscently.

He said pleasantly, 'Ah, here you are. Took the liberty of ordering a little room service while I was waiting—but I could use another. Been a real bleeder down that lousy river it has.'

'What's the score?' I asked, ignoring the hint.

'Bowyer got in to Bassein at sparrow-fart this morning,'

he told me. 'Tried to get a train to Letpadam—that's about sixty miles north of here, where the Bassein and Mandalay railway joins, but there's three bridges down since last monsoon, so he had to go by teak steamer. Didn't like it, and I don't blame him. The bloody things swarm with bugs.'

'On his own?'

'No, the bloke that got on the dhow with him is still around. So's Safaraz, only the client don't know it. The black bastard's travelling in among about a hundred deck passengers—and looking just like 'em.'

'Where's Mr Rees?'

'He'll be in Letpadam by now. I spoke to him here on the phone this morning, and got my orders off him.'

'And what were they?'

'To come in and contact you when you arrived, and take you up there.'

'Train?'

'Naw. Too dodgy. They check on passports at the station. I got a gharry outside.' He pointed with his foot to a canvas hold-all. 'He fixed up some clothes for you. Yours are too fancy for up-country.'

I took them out. They weren't new, but they were clean—khaki slacks and bush shirt.

'When do we start?' I asked.

'Plenty of time. It'll take the steamer the best part of two days against the current. We can do it by road in two hours. What about that drink?'

'What about my luggage?' I countered. 'Do I leave it here?'

'All fixed. They'll lock it up for you and act dumb if the cops come round checking. Look, Mr Wainwright, I don't want to seem a bum, but I been sitting on my tail down that river for days—with malaria mosquitoes as big as shite-hawks making a bleeding pincushion out of me—and Mr Rees didn't see fit to leave me more than petrol and eating money——'

'I'll be with you in a few minutes,' I told him, and went through to the bathroom to change. I packed a few odds and ends of gear in the hold-all and rejoined him. He was still looking wistfully at the empty glass, but he sighed and gave it up in the end.

'The gharry's round the back,' he said. 'You don't want to come in the front way dressed like a ponce and go out looking like a teak-logger.'

We went down the service stairs and out into a yard. The sudden tropical twilight was drawing in, and from the nearest of Rangoon's three mosques I could hear the muezzin's wailing call to evening prayer. The 'gharry' turned out to be a battered and dated Buick.

He said, 'You'd better get in back and lie on the floor until we pass the police post at Mingladon. I'll shove a blanket over you.'

I lay there stifling for the better part of an hour as he belted the ancient car along a road which seemed to be an equal proportion of boulders and pot-holes, then I surfaced wrathfully. It was pitch dark now and we were running through dense jungle with not a light to be seen except our own.

'What the hell's the idea of keeping me smothered so long under that damned blanket?' I demanded.

'You never know who you're likely to run into out here,' he said innocently, and I knew that the old goat was getting his own back for the drink I wouldn't let him have.

'You may be Mr Rees's man, but I'm paymaster,' I told him grimly. 'Watch it, my friend.'

'Sure,' he agreed, and chuckled wheezingly. And then we blew a tyre.

We got out and rummaged through the miscellaneous junk in the boot—and naturally we didn't have a jack, which scared him much more than my threat.

'Gorblimey,' he moaned. 'The thieving bastards I hired

her from swore she had a full set of tools. Mr Rees'll kill me for this.'

'Bloody good job,' I snarled. 'How far are we from where we're going?'

'Er—ten—fifteen miles—something like that,' he said uncertainly, and I swore again, in earnest this time.

'Any villages—anywhere at all we can get help nearer than that?' I asked.

'Not a damn thing,' he answered gloomily. 'Bare as a frog's rump from here to Letpadam.'

'Then we'd better start walking,' I said, and he yelped with terror.

'Are you nuts? This bloody road's stiff with dacoits, thugs and Christ knows what. They'd cut your throat as soon as look at you—just for your boots.'

'Please yourself,' I said. 'Stay here if you want to. Where do I meet Rees?'

'You'd never find the place on your own,' he answered, seizing on this.

'So you'll have to come along, won't you?' I said nastily.

'Look, Mr Wainwright,' he implored, clawing at my arm. 'I know what I'm talking about. This road's dangerous. Our best bet is to get into the bush and lie low till daylight. What the hell does it matter, anyhow? If the client comes through, Mr Rees will tail him and leave Safaraz to contact us——'

But I wasn't risking it. 'Where do I meet him?' I insisted. 'If you don't come on you'd better——' I broke off as the headlights of a car appeared far down the road in the direction we had come.

'There you are. What did I tell you?' he demanded triumphantly. 'Cops, I'll bet you a hundred chips. Come on, into the flipping bush—quick.' He grabbed my canvas hold-all and loped off into the darkness.

I suppose he was right. If they were police I'd be in trouble, because an ordinary visa didn't permit foreigners to travel outside the towns. Reluctantly I followed him. He waded through the undergrowth for some yards until he stumbled on a dried nullah which gave us complete cover.

The lights came on, then stopped when they came up to our car, because we had skidded and it was blocking the road. A Burmese in a singlet and lungi came into the glare of his own headlights and stared at the obstacle dumbly. I couldn't see what the other vehicle was, but I knew it was neither a bus nor a police car. Had there been other Burmese there in quantity they'd have been swarming all over our car by now, chattering like monkeys.

I was about to say as much to the Major, but he anticipated me.

'On his tod. If there was another bloke with him they'd be shouting the odds,' he said. 'Lovely. You got a gun—just in case?'

'I have,' I told him. 'You go forward and talk to him. I'll cover you from the scrub—just in case.'

He didn't like it, but it must have appeared preferable to walking or sitting it out in the jungle, because he grunted sourly and moved forward.

At the edge of the road he stopped and said uncertainly, 'Look, I got a better idea——'

'Get on with it,' I told him, and shoved him forward. 'Big Brother is watching o'er you.'

The Burmese heard us and spun round, and the light fell square on his face. He was really frightened, and I cheered up accordingly, but still waited in the dark—just in case. The Major spoke rapidly in Burmese, which I don't understand, and the man looked blank and shook his head. The Major swore.

'A bloody Shan,' he said. 'Not many of 'em speak Burmese —and nobody but them and the bleeding orang-outangs speak their *bhat*.' But he seemed reassured because he stepped

92

out into the light and pointed to our flat tyre and mimed our need of a jack.

The driver looked relieved. He dived for the boot of his own car, which I could see by now was something big, battered and American like our own, and the Major followed him, then, as I was about to put my gun out of sight but still handy, I heard him say, 'Uh? Oh, sorry, miss—I didn't mean to startle you—flat tyre—just want to borrow a jack——'

A girl came out from the shadows into the light. She was wearing slacks and a shirt and a dust scarf round her hair, but there was no mistaking her.

It was Paola Alberghetti.

Chapter Eight

I HEARD HER SAY, 'Oh, thank the Lord! I thought we
were being held up or something.' And like the driver she
seemed very relieved indeed.

'You could have been at that,' the Major said, and added
reprovingly, 'Pardon my saying so, but these bleeding roads
is no place for a lady at night—white, black or tan.'

'Could you tell me where we are exactly?' she asked.

'Yeah, right where Kipling wrote his little ditty—On the
Road to Mandalay. Present moment we're about fifteen
miles south of Letpadam. If it's not a rude question, where
would you be going, miss?'

She hesitated a moment, then said, 'Well, actually to
Letpadam. There's a resthouse there, isn't there?'

'Used to be before these monkeys took the country over
and goosed it up,' he told her. 'It's a truck-driver's bug-
house now. Blimey! You wasn't thinking of putting up there,
was you?'

'Don't you think you ought to help my driver change your
wheel?' she countered pointedly.

'Oh—yes—sure,' he said and peered round to see where
I was, but I was well back in the shadows again. He obviously
guessed that I wasn't coming out and he swooped on the
opportunity like a kitehawk. 'You ain't a lady doctor by any
chance, are you?' he asked.

'Why do you ask?'

'Well, it's like this. I had me luggage pinched, and there
was a bottle of scotch in it, and now I've got me malaria
coming on, and I'm out of quinine and——'

94

'I've a little brandy——' she began, and the Major beamed.

'Just the job,' he said.

'But I suggest you get on with that first.' She pointed to where the driver was lying on his belly pushing the jack into place. And she was pointing with a small automatic that she'd been holding out of sight until then. The Major gawped at it and took the point.

'Yeah, yeah, see what you mean,' he mumbled, and went and got the spare out of our boot. The girl got back into the other car and I saw the flare of a match as she lit a cigarette.

They finished the change quickly and the Major came back, wiping his hands on the seat of his slacks. She handed him a small metal cup out of the window. He looked rather askance at the size of it, but accepted it with good grace and tossed it back in one gulp.

The girl said, 'Now, if you'd be good enough either to get going or to pull to one side, I'd be obliged. I'm in rather a hurry.'

Whether it was the brandy or the gun that did it, I wouldn't be knowing, but the Major moved back to our car with a new alacrity, started up and pulled into the verge. The other car jerked forward and shot off up the road. I came out of the undergrowth.

'Blimey! Did you see that?' the Major asked in tones of deep wonder.

'Yes—all of it,' I told him as I climbed in. 'Come on, get a move on. I'm fed up with travelling round Asia with an ancient lush.'

'That's uncalled for, Mr Wainwright,' he said with dignity. 'A lush is a man who can't carry his liquor, but keeps trying. The day you see me with more than my issue aboard, the sun will rise in the west.'

'What did you make of her?' I asked.

'Lady—new to the country—could be a missionary, but if she is she's an improvement on any I ever seen. Might be

one of these Voluntary Service Organization people—doctor
—teacher—something like that,' he mused. 'But then she
was carrying a gun—something the do-gooders never do.
Search me. Actually I seen her before.'

'Where?'

'The airport—the day I went down to Bassein. She was
coming off a Pan-Am plane.'

'Where from?' I asked quickly.

'Let's see—that would have been the New York–Paris–
Delhi flight,' he said. 'Could have been from any of those
places. *You* know her, by any chance?'

'She mentioned the resthouse,' I said, ignoring his question.
'That's not where we're going, is it?'

'Not bloody likely. That's probably where Bowyer will be
staying. We go to a store owned by a Sikh. Feller by the
name of Puram Singh.'

We had been further along the road than the Major
thought, because we reached Letpadam in less than a quarter
of an hour. It was a typical up-country Burmese town—one
that had been fought and re-fought over in 1945 and rebuilt
with battle wreckage—a brick post-office, a sandbagged
police post, with tin shanties and the ubiquitous bamboo
bashas lining a wide and dusty street, all seen darkly in the
guttering light of a string of oil-lamps on poles that had once
held electric standards.

The Major swung the car into a compound at the far end
of the street and drove round the back of a big double-
storeyed building and stopped. The place was in total darkness.

He said, 'Well, here we are. I hope they've got something
for supper that ain't dal and curried brinjal. That's what my
old woman fills me up on, seven days a week. Burned a
bleeding hole in me guts it has.'

I picked up my hold-all and followed him through the dust
on to a rickety verandah. He tapped at a door.

'Don't smoke inside,' the Major told me. 'Sikhs don't like it—but you can drink all they offer you. It was pinch-bottle scotch last time I was here. Does himself proud, does old Puram Singh. Lovely.'

The door opened but no light came through because we were up against a heavy curtain. Then the door was closed behind us by a man I couldn't see, and the curtain was pulled aside. We were in a huge room that was lighted by Petromax lamps and piled from floor to ceiling with boxes and crates on which American and British trade names predominated: cornflakes, peanut butter, patent medicines and canned fish, soap, bales of cloth and truck tyres in stacks. You name it, they had it.

There was a relatively clear space in the centre of the room and half a dozen men sat cross-legged on mats, drinking and playing carom. Three of them were Sikhs, two Pathans, and one a possible pot-pourri of the lot—an unlikely assembly in India itself but quite usual outside, where nationality often overrides caste and religion. There were, of course, no Burmese, because there you have the true oil and water. The man who had opened for us was a short and stocky eastern hillman—either a Sherpa or a Nepalese.

One of the Sikhs rose and came forward. He was an old man with a grey-shot beard and was minus his turban, with his long hair gathered in a knot on top of his head and tied with an absurd pink bow, like a small girl about to have her ears washed.

He said, 'Salaam, sahib,' shook hands, then snapped his fingers, and the Sherpa conjured a tumbler of whisky out of thin air. It was filled right to the rim, with not a half millimetre left for water. I knew I was expected to knock it back and hold it out for a refill, and I looked round despairingly at the Major, but there was no help there. He was already on his second.

The Sikh said, 'You will take drink then eat—no?' But

my wits had returned by now, and I told him that my father had only been buried a month, so strong drink was *sakt manna*—verboten—for yet another month. That's the only thing they won't argue about. Behind me I could hear the Major belching joyously and insulting one of the Pathans in gutter Urdu—and I realized it was Safaraz. The Sikh rumbled his condolences, lost interest in me and went back to his game.

The Sherpa led us round a stack of crates into another, smaller, space. There were mats and cushions here, so we sat down, and soon he brought bowls of food on a brass tray. Dal and curried brinjal, but the Major, softened by the liquor, looked at it tolerantly.

I said angrily, 'If you're not completely anaesthetized, you old rip, you'll tell me what goes on.'

He beamed at me, belched again, and said, 'My hitch ends here, Mr Wainwright. I was just told to deliver you, that's all. Can't say I'm sorry. About the only things you and my old ma-in-law ain't got in common is sex and colour.'

They brought in string beds and mosquito nets later and at my request took the Petromax out, but I couldn't get to sleep for a long time. The Major took another couple of lethal slugs and snored his head off on the other bed, but it wasn't that which was causing my insomnia. I just couldn't stop puzzling over that girl. Who was she? Had that meeting in Rangoon been fixed? Was she on my tail? It certainly looked like it. Her car was only a bare five minutes after ours. But who the hell would set a girl, a white girl, to tail a man in this country? And supposing she *was* shadowing me, why would she tip her hand to me in Rangoon? She was frightened of something—of that I was certain—yet she seemed pretty much on top of things on the road, what with the gun and the way she handled the Major. And she was going to the resthouse—and that's where Rees expected Bowyer to go—although that didn't really signify anything, because there was no hotel in this dump, and the resthouse would be the only place one could stay. I gave it up in the end and went to sleep.

They had walled us in by the time I woke. I couldn't see any daylight but my watch was showing just after six. The Major was still snoring and I decided that I'd had enough of this place, so I rolled off the bed, stretched and was about to start an assault on the wall when a case of condensed milk was moved aside and a tray with a mug of tea, bread and fruit was pushed through. I took the tray and peered through the hole. The Sherpa grinned at me cheerfully from the other side.

I said, 'Come on, get these cases out of the way.'

'Puram Singh say stay here,' he answered. 'Seven o'clock police come to collect baksheesh. After that you come out. *Thik hai?*' and he blocked up the hole again. I suppose it made sense, so I sat and ate a solitary breakfast, hoping that the Major wouldn't wake up—but he did, and he had the father and mother of all hangovers, for which I was sourly gratified. He sat on the edge of his bed moaning softly, and he snarled at me when I offered him a banana. The store evidently opened early for business because I could hear a sustained chatter from the other side of the wall, and outside there was a constant rumble of trucks arriving and departing, and all the time the heat was building up on the tin roof until the place was a furnace and the reek of oil, soap, curry powder, cayenne pepper and salt fish in that confined space was damn nearly asphyxiating us.

Rees arrived at mid-morning, crawling through a tunnel of baked beans. He was still in his Brahmin clothes and was looking quietly pleased with himself.

'So far so good,' he said. 'They arrived at Bassein on time and came on up here. Nobody met them and there were no messages for them downriver, but a woman was waiting for them at the resthouse—a European woman, according to Safaraz, who had spent half the night up on the roof looking down on them through a skylight. She had brought a couple of cases of heavy gear with her—sheepskin coats, Gilgit boots and stuff like that, so that means mountains. They've got a car ordered for tonight.'

If he was expecting congratulations he was disappointed, because I asked him what he'd managed to find out about her, and looked politely puzzled when he told me nothing, except that Safaraz had said that she was quite a looker.

'Her name's Paola Alberghetti,' I told him casually, and had the satisfaction of getting a quick reaction from him.

'How do you know that?' he asked.

'I have my methods, Watson,' I said, then realizing the childishness of it, I told him—and, of course, he turned it back on me.

'A pity you had any contact with her,' he said. 'If she recognizes you further along the road she'll know you're tailing her.'

'How the hell was I to know that she was coming up here?' I demanded. 'She was just a tourist taking in the Shwe Dagon as far as I was concerned.'

'Paola Alberghetti,' he mused, ignoring my outburst. 'Now where does *she* fit into it?'

'Do you know her?' I asked.

'*Of* her,' he said. 'I've never actually met her, but European eyebrows will shoot up in every part of India if her name is mentioned.'

'Who is she?'

'Quite a long story. She and her husband ran a business in New Delhi—smart photographers. They did all the Embassy work—pictures for the glossies in London, New York, Paris. She was very good with make-up—you know, she could blank out the bags under a lady diplomat's eyes, stick on false eyelashes and monkey their hair around. They were very much in demand. They expanded into quite a big thing—beauticians, *haute couture*—and were making a packet, but then Alberghetti turned a car over on himself one night and was killed. She stayed on running the business, but she had competition—a couple of bright gals from Paris had moved in with a clever Hungarian photographer, and Paola began to feel the pinch, so she branched out. A small, very discreet club much favoured by the younger unmarried Embassy men —and one or two not-so-young Indian politicians. She imported half a dozen hostesses and she was doing all right. She wouldn't have lasted a week if she hadn't had what amounted to almost diplomatic immunity—but I heard that the jig was up a year or so ago and her licence was revoked.'

Illogically, I felt a sinking in my stomach. A madam—a whorehouse-keeper. But she hadn't seemed that type at all.

I said, 'Are you sure we're speaking about the same woman?'

'*You* told me her name. I merely told you what I know about her.'

'But she seemed a—well—a——'

'Go on—say it—a lady? So I've heard. What does that mean? A Russian duchess ran the best-known knocking-shop in Shanghai for years.'

'But this girl is English,' I said foolishly and he looked at me in amazement. 'What I mean,' I added hastily, 'is that in spite of her Italian name——'

He laughed shortly. 'You'd probably find that she started out as Sandra Bloggs or something, if you started digging. Anyhow, that's her background. I'm sorry if I've shattered any illusions. I wonder when she took up with Bowyer?'

'What's our next move?' I asked, to change the subject.

'Up to you,' he said. 'If you'd care for a suggestion I would say that we ought to follow them in one of Puram Singh's trucks. They go right up to the northern border. We'll need to get some heavy clothes, though—like theirs.'

'Can that be arranged?'

'Leave it to me.' He rose and stirred the sleeping Major,

who grunted and snarled peevishly. 'I think it might be a good idea to get on up the road ahead of them. If they have a few hours without anybody on their tail at first it will put them off guard.'

'Always assuming that we go up the right road,' I said.

'There are only two out of here—the one you came up, and the one to the north,' he told me. 'If they do work us a flanker and double back to Rangoon the Major will get a message up to us in good time.'

They went out through the tunnel, nose to tail like two moles, and once again I was left to wait. I was really hating it all now. This bloody man Rees was running the whole show, politely and even respectfully, but still as a matter of bounden right, and I was being pushed into the position of fifth wheel to the vehicle. I really didn't need to be here at all, and I found myself wondering for about the tenth time since we started why the hell the Gaffer had sent me. If I could have got in touch with him by any means whatsoever I'd have asked to be taken off it, or thrown my hand in. But that was out of the question now, because cable and telephonic communication was a dicey business in Burma, even from the bigger towns. From a dump like this an overseas call would be impossible. No, I'd just have to go along for the ride, and hope that Bowyer would show signs of putting down the anchor somewhere before my nerves really frazzled.

The Sherpa came for me in a couple of hours and led me through the tunnel and along a passageway to a back door in the store that was also a loading bay. There was a truck backed into the bay and he signed to me to climb over the load. I did so, and found myself in a cleared space in the middle of which Rees and Safaraz were already sitting. I squatted down beside them and the Sherpa stamped on the floorboards and we drove out.

The place we were in was quite comfortable and there was plenty of room for the four of us. Clear of the town we could stand up with our heads just over the top of the surrounding load and catch our own breeze.

'What's going to happen if we're stopped by the police?' I asked Rees. 'You others might be able to talk your way out of it, but my passport doesn't run up here.'

'We won't be stopped,' he said confidently. 'Certainly not south of the Naga Hills. Puram Singh pays tribute to both sides—police and bandits.'

'And north of the Naga Hills?'

'We'll just have to take things as they come. The road ends there anyhow.'

'How far are they?'

'The hills? Just short of eight hundred miles,' he said, and I gulped painfully. 'Of course,' he went on, 'we don't know that they'll be going that far, do we? They may branch off on to the old Burma Road through Lashio.'

'Is there anywhere else they could branch off?' I asked, because this running with our quarry behind us was worrying me.

'They could turn west through Shwebo and go back over the Chindwin into India,' he answered, and then, as if he was reading my thoughts, he added, 'Don't worry. I'll drop a man at each turn-off, just in case. That's the advantage of leading the chase instead of following it.' And I had to admit he was right—but, as always, the 'I'll' irritated me.

We ran into Toungoo, a town so like Letpadam that I had an absurd certainty that I'd been here before, just as darkness was falling. Even the store was identical—and so was the corral amid the groceries they showed us into. I looked questioningly at Rees.

'Yes, one of the Puram Singh chain,' he said. 'He's got them at two-hundred-mile intervals right up to the Chinese border.'

'How does he survive?' I asked. 'I thought capitalists were unpopular in this part of the world.'

'They are, politically, but you don't burn the pub down just because you don't like the landlord. Not if there's no other pub. Without Puram Singh to fetch, carry and sell, they'd starve up in the north.'

'Can he be trusted?'

'At the moment, yes. We've been mutually useful to each other in the past, and he knows that I could blow a smuggling route of his in India.'

The Sherpa, whose name I had found out to be Lumding, came into the enclave with our bags. He muttered something to Rees. Rees gave him curt instructions in some language I couldn't understand, and turned to me. Lumding backed out through the tunnel.

'The Major rang through an hour ago,' Rees told me. 'Bowyer and his party left shortly after we did. They'll undoubtedly halt here, because this is the last place they can get petrol for over a hundred miles.'

'Do you think they'll night-stop here?' I asked.

'Quite possibly,' he answered. 'There's a resthouse down the road. I've sent Safaraz along to watch it.'

We ate after that and, dog-tired from the bumpy, dusty ride, I slept like a log until Rees wakened me at four the next morning.

'We're ready to move,' he told me. 'We've got about a hundred miles to do to the first turn-off to Shwebo.'

'The others—?'

'Got in shortly after us and refuelled. There are lights on in the resthouse so it looks as if they're going to make an early start too.'

I gulped a mug of scalding tea and chewed on a leathery chapatti without enthusiasm, then followed him out into the dark compound. It was a different truck this time—a big six-wheeled job that looked powerful but slow—and I remarked on this to Rees.

'That's the way it is,' he told me. 'The trucks stick to their own stages and change loads where necessary. Suits us. They won't get used to seeing the same one even if they do happen to pass us, or stop at the same place.'

And that's just what happened on this stage. They overtook us soon after dawn. Lumding, lying on top of the load, reported them in plenty of time for us to get down into our hollow, and we heard them come right up behind us, and there was a peremptory blast from their horn for us to get off the crown of the beat-up road and let them pass, but our driver, in the manner of the East, kept blithely to the middle, and through a crack in the load I saw his hand come out of the cab and give a rude two-finger salute. I swore angrily because I could see no point in keeping them on our tail like this, but once again Rees was ahead of me.

'He has his orders,' he told me. 'If he lets them get ahead of us before the fork-roads at Thazi we won't know whether they have turned off to Shwebo or not, will we?' And, of course, he was right, but I didn't love him for it.

But they were impatient and they eventually made a desperate attempt to pass us while we were doing a rock-steady forty-five. There was a roar and an enormous cloud of dust to one side of us, and then the tooting of their horn diminished and was lost in the rumble of our own sedate passage. Rees risked a quick look over the rim of our hollow.

'They're ditched in the soft dust,' he said. 'The bloody fool of a driver is gunning his engine like mad, and settling down further. Stopped now—getting out——' And then we were round a bend and they were out of sight. Rees stretched over the load and pounded on the roof of the driver's cab, and we pulled up. He spoke rapidly in Burmese, then translated for me.

'We're going to back up to them and our driver is going to offer to pull them out for twenty kyats,' he told me. 'That will be bang in character under the circumstances.'

The truck rolled back in reverse and we lay out of sight

and listened to the knock-down-drag-out bargaining session between our driver and theirs, with a Greek chorus supplied by the two hairy gents who rode shotgun on our truck, and the passengers in the car. It was all in Burmese, of course, but I heard one phrase in pure accentless English in the midst of the babel.

A man said, 'Chuck me that flask, darling. This blasted dust is choking me.'

I would have given a lot for a quick look over the top, but it wasn't to be thought of. The deal was eventually settled for fifteen kyats, which was supposed to include our driver's pulling over and yielding right of way to them, but he double-crossed them on that and, having recovered his tow-rope, we drove on, still in front, and we stayed that way until, forty miles on, we passed the fork-roads and the driver pulled up, ostensibly to cool his engine. They shot past us then, on the Mandalay road, and I heard Rees grunt with satisfaction.

'No turn-off until Mandalay,' he said. 'We can relax.'

'But they'll be in Mandalay long before us,' I said. 'So how will we know which road they've taken out of there?'

'Puram Singh's people will be watching for them,' he answered. 'I phoned forward from Toungoo.'

The bastard thought of everything.

Chapter Nine

AND SO IT WENT ON for three more days. We were five hours behind them at Mandalay. They had taken the Bhamo road we were told at Puram Singh's store. That was a hundred and fifty miles north, and from it they could bend back into China along the wartime Burma Road, or continue north to Myitkyina. And from there they had another choice—along the Burma Road again north-west back into Assam—or on into Chamdo—and Tibet—due north the whole way.

I looked up from the map in dismay. 'Christ! Surely not that,' I said. 'That would mean crossing the Himalayas themselves. It *must* be back into Assam.'

'He could have reached any part of Assam by train from Calcutta in under twenty-four hours,' Rees said quietly. 'So why would he waste a couple of weeks doing it the hard way through Burma?'

'We know why, don't we?' I said. 'The Indian police were breathing down his neck. He's thrown them now.'

'He threw them in Calcutta. All he needed to do that night was to change into Indian clothes and lose himself in five and a half million people. Oh yes—he could have got to Assam all right—without any frontiers to cross.'

'I know *you* can get away with Indian clothes——' I began, but he interrupted me.

'Bowyer can too,' he said. 'No—it's not Assam. I'm afraid all signs point to the Tibetan trail.'

'Or east into China,' I said, still clinging to what was marginally the easier of two ghastly alternatives. 'Don't forget they've got a woman with them.'

'That doesn't mean a thing. A lady missionary came out over the Gangtok trail—two eighteen-thousand-foot passes—in 1965.' He squinted at the map. 'There's nothing over sixteen thousand this way.'

'Yes—and the Russian lady weightlifter at the Olympic Games was found to be a longshoreman from Murmansk,' I said sourly. 'I'm a bank penpusher in private life—not a bloody mountain goat.'

But all hopes faded at Bhamo. They had stopped there only long enough to take on gas for the next stage—to Myitkyina. And this time we overtook them. They had busted a water-hose and were sitting helplessly at the side of the road, and once more we squatted in our hollow and waited while our driver, a different one this time, struck a bargain before making crude repairs with insulating tape. We went on ahead of them and arrived in Myitkyina at sundown, and I slept that night in a bed, glumly conscious of the fact that this was likely to be the last for a longer time than I cared to contemplate.

They had gone when I woke next morning. Four of them, Rees told me; Bowyer and one of the men who had come up with them from Rangoon, another who had been waiting for them here—like Lumding, a Sherpa—and, of course, the woman.

'They've got a pony for the woman and a mule for the baggage, but that will only be for the first fifty miles. After that it will all be on foot,' he told me. 'I've done the same thing—a pony for you and a pack mule.'

I blew up then. It had been simmering for a long time, but this was the final straw. 'Stop mothering me, will you!' I stormed. 'I didn't ask for you. You were wished on me. You've been helpful, but you haven't done a thing I couldn't have done on my own if I'd had to. I'm not taking any more of your thinly veiled superiority, Rees.'

But he didn't even blink. 'Say the word any time you like,'

he answered, 'and I'd be happy to go back. Actually one pony and one mule is a matter of pure common sense. You've recently hurt your foot, and any strain we can save on it in the early stages will be a bonus later on.'

'Ponies all round then,' I said, but he shook his head.

'I'll want Safaraz and Lumding on foot ahead of us the whole way,' he told me. 'If they come round a blind bend and stumbled on their camp, they'd just be two hillmen on their lawful occasions, whereas if the whole lot of us overtook them on ponies it would give the show away. The woman knows you, doesn't she?'

And of course the bastard was right, as always.

We gave them a six-hour start before hitting the trail. It lay along the banks of the Irrawaddy, which here was narrow, rock-strewn and deep. The teak and sal trees soared up to a hundred feet plus on either side, and the narrow path constantly crossed the stream, sometimes by ford, which meant a waistdeep wade through water that struck at the pit of one's belly like the thrust of an ice dagger, at others over log bridges that for the most part had all but rotted away.

And that bloody pony wasn't anybody's bonus, because it shied at everything that moved in the jungle, and a lot of things that didn't, and it liked cold water even less than I did. When I was riding it I was stuck with leading the mule; when I wasn't, I had to wrestle with both, and the damn things, in the manner of their kind, always wanted to pick their own paths, graze, or stop dead and contemplate infinity. And Rees just strode ahead, never once turning to see how I was getting on, and certainly never offering to help. He went out of sight finally and I struggled along for about an hour on my own, cursing and tugging at the leading reins, until in the end I just dropped them and followed Rees's example, leaving the ornery brutes to find their own way—which is exactly what I should have done in the first place, because thereafter they followed me like twin lambs.

I enjoyed the walk after this. We were steadily rising the whole time and although I sweated while I walked, I could feel the air getting fresher, and there was a slight chill in it when I sat and rested. There were flowers up here—not the frangipani and *gul mohur* of the lower jungles, but primroses, violets and, in places, clumps of mimosa.

For the first time I was enjoying the trip for itself alone. The heavy boots Rees had got for me were wearing in and fitting like gloves, and my foot wasn't hurting any more, and I felt I could go on like this for ever. I found myself hoping wryly that Bowyer wasn't reacting in the same way. If he would only go to ground somewhere before the going got too rugged, and give me some vague idea of what the hell his objective was, I could turn round and make my way back without dodging rabbitlike from hole to hole, make my report to the Gaffer and then, presumably, bow out from this crazy business.

I was still feeling good when I came up with Rees at sundown. He was sitting smoking at the side of the path, and in the trees I could see that Safaraz had made a small smokeless fire of dry wood. It gleamed a bright welcome, with promises of whisky, hot food, and blankets and sleeping-bags on pine needles. We unloaded the mule and fed and watered both animals.

Rees said, 'They're two miles further along—just where the teak ends and the pines begin. Lumding is up where he can see them.'

'Just so as they stay put until morning,' I said. 'We can all do with a night in the sack. Are you keeping a constant watch on them?'

'Four-hour hitches.'

'You can count me in on that.'

'Thanks. That'll be after me then—midnight till four. You just come up the trail until I halt you.'

'How much have we done today?' I asked.

'About fifteen miles. I reckon they'll do another night stop before they reach Kadan.'

'What's Kadan exactly?'

'It's a Kachin village—where the main pass up to Chamdo starts. You've got a gun, haven't you?'

I nodded and patted the bulge under my bush shirt.

'What are you like with a rifle?' he asked.

'Reasonable. Why?'

'I've got a couple of Rigby expresses in the pack. I'll carry one and I'd be obliged if you'd take the other.'

'Are you expecting trouble?'

He shrugged. 'Could be. The Nagas are fighting the Indians away to the west—and the Kachins round here have got a constant thing on with the Burmese—banditry more than political strife—and both sides enjoy sniping. One well-placed shot can often nip trouble in the bud.'

My earlier euphoria passed off quickly. 'That can cut both ways,' I said gloomily. But then Safaraz came over with scotch in two mugs, and from the fire I could smell canned stew being heated and I realized that I was really hungry for the first time in weeks.

We ate and then rolled into our sleeping-bags and it seemed only ten minutes later that Lumding was gently shaking me. The fire was out now and the air struck really chill and I was glad of the sheepskin *poshteen* he held out to me, the poshteen being a long coat of Afghan sheepskin with the fleece side in.

I walked up the trail only half awake. There was no moon and the sleep was still in my eyes so I stumbled along in a cavern of blackness, cursing the whole silly business. Why did they need to be watched through the night anyhow. We could have sent someone forward at daybreak and then followed in our own time. Rees was just doing it the hard way to impress me. He didn't need to. He got paid—win, lose or draw—which were better terms than I was on.

A hand came out of the darkness and fastened gently on

my arm, and that didn't improve my temper, because I jumped and yelped and felt an absolute bloody fool.

He said, 'All quiet. They've been bedded down since sunset.'

'What the hell else did you expect?' I asked, and then put into words what I'd been thinking. 'We could all have had a decent night's rest without this nonsense. One of us could have come forward at daybreak——'

'The trail forks a little way past where they are camping,' he said quietly. 'If they'd started in the dark we might have been somewhat confused.'

'If they started in the dark you couldn't bloody well see them anyhow,' I said cleverly.

'No, but I'd have heard them and followed on until they reached the fork, then we'd have known which one they'd taken, wouldn't we?' His voice was just like that of a particularly kind and patient schoolmaster I'd suffered under as a kid. I'd hated his guts also.

'Screw off,' I told him shortly.

'By all means,' he answered without a trace of resentment, and then added apropos of nothing, 'Do you remember Ringdo?'

Surprised, I repeated, 'Ringdo? I only ever knew one—and he was a dog.'

'Exactly,' he interrupted. 'A golden retriever your father used to take duck-shooting outside Shanghai.'

'But what the hell—?' I began, but once again he cut across me.

'Best bird-dog I ever saw,' he went on as if I hadn't spoken. 'At least he was after your father had retrained him and given him his confidence back. The idiot he bought him from had mishandled him sadly. He expected too much from him as a young dog—and used to kick him in the ribs when he made a mistake or failed to understand a whistle, with the consequence that the poor brute didn't know if he was on his head or his heels half the time, and used to snarl and snap at people who tried to make friends with him.'

I got his point immediately, and the enormity of it took my breath away, but before I could cut loose with something really blistering he had turned away and the darkness had swallowed him. The cheeky bastard! Who the hell did he think he was? A damned two-bit private eye ('Confidential Investigations—Divorce a Speciality'), a snooper at motel windows. But I realized the absurdity of this while I was still raking the splenetic gutters of my mind for ammunition. No—whatever else he was, he certainly wasn't a two-bitter. I'd have been up the creek long before this had it not been for him—and, fair play to him, he hadn't in any way crowed over me.

Maybe there was a modicum of truth in what he said. I *was* too quick to take offence—to imagine that my superiors were riding me into the ground just for the hell of it—to be suspicious of my colleagues and to treat the depressed minority of those unfortunate to be lower than I on the totem pole with something less than courtesy. But then, like Ringdo, hadn't I been mishandled by various controllers ever since I finished my training? Hadn't I been whipping-boy for the lot? The Gaffer, old Walters, Barry. This policy of theirs of telling the field man as little as he absolutely had to know to carry out a specific mission didn't exactly make for self-confidence. It worked only so long as things ran along expected lines—and how often was that? If they took a sudden twist and you had to make a spot decision, and it turned out to be the wrong one, your head was on the block. If it was the right one it wasn't even remarked upon.

Oh yes, there was a reason for it all. The less you knew, the less you could spill if you landed in the bag the other side —or defected. Logical, no doubt, but hardly calculated to boost one's morale.

I don't know how long this session of alternating autoanalysis and self-justification went on, but I certainly came out of it feeling somewhat better. Rees's words had had a cathartic effect and I stopped being sorry for myself. Results were all that mattered in this business, and to get anything that was worth a damn out of this vague assignment was going to be difficult enough without fighting with the one man who could help me.

I watched them through the glasses as dawn broke. They were too far away for me to make out details, although the girl's hair was unmistakable as she sat on a rock and combed it. They had camped in an open glade without any attempt to hide, which indicated that they were still unaware of being followed.

They had a quick meal, loaded the animals and set out up the trail. I could plainly see where it forked some distance ahead of their position. They took the one to the right and moved steadily up to the crest of the next ridge, and over it out of sight.

I came out of cover and went back to our camp. They were already packed up except for the coffee-pot and a skillet in which Rees was cooking some bacon—for me, as it turned out. I mumbled my thanks, feeling awkward.

'Safaraz pretends he can't touch pig because of his religion,' Rees explained, 'and Lumding's nose always drips in the morning.'

I thought of apologizing for the previous night, but then decided to let sleeping dogs lie and just told him about the others. He nodded and sent Safaraz and Lumding up the trail, then, when I had finished my breakfast, we set out, leading both the animals, and since the trail wasn't wide enough to walk abreast no conversation was necessary.

We plugged steadily onward until mid-afternoon and then came up with our scouts. They were lying on their bellies at the top of a rise, and at first I thought they were asleep. Rees, who was in front, dropped flat and crawled up beside them to avoid appearing over the skyline, and I saw then that they were looking down into a long bare valley. It was a couple of miles wide, and the other side the real Himalayas rose in steps until their distant crests were lost in cloud, which was perhaps just as well, because the lower slopes looked bad enough—bleak, desolate and deeply fissured with crevasses that even as early in the winter as this were already holding the snow. I shivered.

Safaraz was pointing. Following his finger I saw a village strung along the rocky bank of the river that marked the floor of the valley—a dozen or more houses roughly built of stone that merged into the background, so that unless one knew where to look or had the unbelievably keen eyes of a Pathan it would have remained unnoticed until one had got considerably nearer to it than we were here. And then I saw movement—four tiny figures and the two animals moving along the trail towards it. I was about to draw attention to them, but then I realized that, as usual, they were away ahead of me and Rees was already studying them through the glasses.

'That woman must be very fit,' he said. 'We haven't been idling, but they've made a good half-hour on us.'

'Is this Kadan?' I asked.

He nodded. 'And it could be awkward. We can't move down the trail because we'll be in view.'

'So we wait until dark.'

'No good.'

He held up his hand. 'Listen.'

I heard nothing for some moments, then it came to me: the shrill and sustained yapping of dogs.

'These hill dogs can get a stranger's scent a good mile away, even up-wind,' he said. 'If we approach by night all hell will break loose.'

'So we wait until morning?' I couldn't see any problem, or any alternative.

115

He nodded. 'They'll night-stop there and drop the animals, I should imagine.'

'So we camp here?'

'I wouldn't advise it. The valley will be under a heavy pall of mist in the morning, and we wouldn't know when they'd moved on. If they make a late start we could quite easily walk into their backs. If it's all right with you, we'll make a wide detour and hit the trail again well on the other side of the village. We'll be in position then to follow on when they pass us.'

'But what about *our* animals? Don't we have to drop them there too?'

'We'll turn them loose in the valley. The locals will regard them as a gift from heaven.'

My heart sank. Now that we'd stopped, the prospect of going on again immediately didn't appeal to me in the slightest, but I saw the wisdom of his proposal, and this time he had at least advanced it tactfully.

We struck off from the trail right-handed, keeping below the skyline, and picked our way across the slope for a couple of miles before crossing the crest out of sight of the village, and descending into the valley.

It was dark when we got to the bottom. We unloaded the animals and dumped their harness into a crevasse, then turned them loose in the pasturage that ran along each side of the stream.

Rees issued our heavy clothing then—poshteens, sweaters and woollen shirts, karakul caps and mitts—he'd thought of everything, even to snow glasses. Then he shared the loads between us, meticulously, judging the weight of each article as he stowed it in one or other of the four rucksacks; Tibetan tsampa and brick tea, compressed rations that had probably been stolen from American Air Force survival packs many years before, an alcohol stove, ice-axes, a rope, and finally our sleeping-bags. I reckoned that each of us was carrying upwards of forty-five pounds, but so well-balanced and distributed was the load that it didn't seem too burdensome —at least, not at first.

Then he handed me a rifle. It was an unfamiliar pattern to me and I fumbled awkwardly with it in the darkness. He took it back and loaded it for me, then expertly guided my hand on to the breech-bolt, safety-catch and rear-sight. And this time I felt no resentment. Maybe the threat of those mountains looming unseen above us in the darkness was forcing some plain common sense into me. It was going to be hairy enough without any 'prima donna-ing' on my part.

We set out along the river bank until the barking of dogs told us we were near the village, then Safaraz, who was leading, swung away obliquely to the right, and we started to climb, gently at first and on fairly even ground, but soon the slope increased and we found ourselves among outcroppings of rock that alternated with patches of scree that slipped and shifted underfoot.

It had been cold during the halt, but within that first half hour of climbing I was soaked in sweat under my poshteen and my breath was coming in short, panting gasps. But Safaraz never paused. He just led straight on and up with Rees hard on his heels and then me, nearly busting a gut in my efforts not to let the gap between us widen, and finally Lumding bringing up the rear, easily and effortlessly and even singing softly to himself. Then, when I thought I'd have to turn chicken and drop out for a breather. Safaraz halted and waited for Rees to come up with him.

I sat down flat on the ground I was standing on and lay back against my rucksack drawing in great gouts of that thin mountain air that didn't seem to ease my tortured lungs. Rees came back to me.

'We're on the trail now,' he told me.

'Good,' I mumbled. 'So we stay here till morning do we?'

117

'No, we'll have to move off it and get under cover higher up,' he said, and I suppressed a groan and climbed to my feet again.

My eyes were becoming accustomed to the dark now and I could see that the narrow path we had struck ran sharply downhill to our left, presumably to the village, while to the right it wound upwards towards a patch of snow that I could see gleaming dully under the stars.

Rees set off uphill and I followed miserably. My forty-five pound pack that had seemed so comfortable a short time ago was now weighing a ton, and the straps were cutting into my shoulders.

Rees set off uphill and I followed miserably. My forty-five-age—a jumble of loose boulders in a hollow to one side of the trail. He led us into the middle of them and I was hoping that he was going to make a proper camp, but he didn't. He just sloughed his pack and told the rest of us to snatch some sleep while he watched the trail. I remember slumping down again, and then nothing more until I felt a hand shaking me gently.

'Safaraz can hear somebody coming up the trail,' Rees said softly, 'and I'm afraid you were snoring.'

We were in the sickly grey light of pre-dawn and there was a heavy wet mist enveloping everything that was more than an arm's-length away. I was cold, damp, sore and stiff and I started to react as peevishly as most people do when they've been accused of snoring, but Safaraz reached out and gripped my arm warningly.

I couldn't hear anything, and I doubt if Rees could at that stage, but a Pathan's ears are as sharp as his eyes, and after a crawling five minutes during which I had to wrestle with an incipient sneeze, I heard the faint crunching of scree under boots. They were moving slowly through the mist and as the footsteps grew louder I felt certain that they were making directly for our spot, and I looked questioningly at

Rees, expecting him to signal to us to move further in among the rocks, but he shook his head.

Then they were level with us and a man's voice muttered something I didn't catch, and a woman laughed, softly but clearly and unmistakably, and the footsteps receded as they went on up the trail.

One can tell a lot from a laugh—more than from an ordinary speaking voice. That woman was enjoying life far more than I was. Bordello madam or not, I suddenly felt sorry to be gumshoeing along on her trail like this. Whatever her morals, she certainly had guts.

Chapter Ten

WE GAVE THEM four hours' start, then sent Lumding on ahead to keep contact. There was some slight dispute about this because Safaraz with his prickly Pathan pride considered himself no small potatoes as a scout, with no doubt every justification, but Rees thought Lumding the more advisable choice in case he ran into any of the locals coming downhill. Safaraz spoke only Urdu in addition to his native Pashto, and that was no good up here. He sulked as the Sherpa set off ahead of us, and I heard him muttering and was surprised that Rees let him get away with it. But he did—until mid-morning, when Lumding showed up on the skyline high above us and gave the prearranged hand signal that told us that he had the others in sight. Then Safaraz spat and said something about dirty eastern hillmen who didn't know better than to stand upright on a crest, even a rearward sloping one, in enemy country. It was unfortunate that a trick of the wind carried the spittle the wrong way. I saw Rees look expressionlessly at his gloved hand, then, still expressionlessly, he removed the glove and stepped across to the big Pathan and belted him with it across the face. Twice. Right and left.

It wasn't a particularly hard blow, but it was no love-tap either. Safaraz's hand went flying to his knife, but it was purely a reflex action. He didn't draw it from its sheath. He merely reached forward and took the glove, wiped it carefully on his own poshteen and returned it to Rees, who received it with a courteous bow as if the other had retrieved it from the ground.

I wouldn't have believed it if I hadn't seen it. I'd been brought up in the belief that a Pathan couldn't even wallop his own son, over the age of twelve, and get away with it. I certainly wouldn't have risked it. I'd rather handle a tiger by the tail. There was no more muttering after that.

We toiled on up the track for most of that day until, when I thought I couldn't go another step, we came upon Lumding high on the third ridge, looking down into the next valley, where, thank God, the others had made camp. What the hell was that woman made of I wondered?—or Bowyer for that matter? Three years in a Calcutta prison couldn't be adjudged the best training for this sort of thing, but it didn't seem to be slowing him up any.

The sun went down behind the hills, and with it the temperature. There was a cold northerly breeze that seemed to cut through our poshteens like a knife, and I sat hunched miserably with my back to it, until shame drove me to help them build a small windbreak with loose rocks. Then we brewed up over the alcohol stove—Tibetan tea and a stew of tsampa and canned beef which tasted foul but was hot and sustaining.

I wondered what Rees was going to do now. It was important that we knew when they were starting in the morning so we could keep distance: too close on their heels and we ran the risk of discovery; let them get too far ahead and there was always the chance of losing them up one of the tracks that bifurcated from the main one further up the valley. I realized now, of course, that the fact that we had them in sight in the evening didn't mean that we would in the morning, when mist tended to lie in the ravines and crevasses until the sun was high overhead.

There was only one thing for it; one of us had to go forward and hide up within earshot of them as we had done previously. The thought appalled me. Here, huddled together in the lee of the windbreak, was security and comparative comfort. A night alone out in the blue was another matter altogether, because even I could see that reliefs were out of the question in a terrain like this. Once up there the sentry was a fixture. I wondered who the unlucky one would be. I knew he wouldn't send Lumding because, scouting as he had been all day, the Sherpa had probably covered twice our direct distance already. That made it Safaraz then. Good—that would salve his wounded pride. I snuggled down into my sleeping-bag.

But then, just as the first waves of sleep were sweeping up over me like a healing balm, I saw Rees rise and roll his bag and blanket, and like a fool I asked him where he was going.

'Forward, naturally,' he said shortly.

'Why not Safaraz?'

'Part of his punishment. More effective than the swipe across the jaw I gave him.'

'Seems a hell of a way to enforce discipline, if you ask me,' I mumbled.

'I'm not asking you,' he answered. It was the first time he had been directly rude to me and it brought back my rancorous dislike for him with a rush.

'There's no need to make a bloody martyr of yourself,' I said, and started reluctantly to crawl out of the sack. 'You've been carrying most of Lumding's kit all day.'

And to my horror the bastard took me up on it. 'Much obliged,' he said, and pointed into the fast-gathering gloom. 'Actually I was thinking of making for that spur out there. It overlooks them and will probably be within hearing of their camp when the wind drops. You please yourself, of course, but if you go round to the left you'll be screened from them all the way up.'

Of course he was dead right as usual. If there had been any alternative way I'd have chosen it, but there wasn't. I rolled my bag and blanket, picked up my rifle and set out.

'Thanks,' he called softly after me. 'As a matter of fact I am feeling rather pooped.' I doubted it, but somehow it went a long way towards putting things right again.

It was a nightmare of a climb to the top of the first ridge, and worse going down the other side, but at least from there I could see the spur I was making for dimly outlined against the dying afterglow in the eastern sky. I made it just as darkness fell completely and suddenly as it always does in the hills.

I found a niche which gave a faint illusion of shelter from that murderous wind and curled into it like a dyspeptic snail. I could only guess at the position of their camp at first but after a time a pinpoint of light glowed for an instant in roughly the area I had fixed, as if someone were lighting a cigarette. I wished I could do the same, but my fingers, sheepskin mitts notwithstanding, were too numbed to open the fastenings of my poshteen.

And then it began to snow—softly and silently and at first unseen until I noticed the windward side of the surrounding rocks becoming perceptibly lighter than the rest of the all but absolute darkness.

The snow steadily built up over me, and since it was powder-dry it insulated me from the outer cold, so much so that I began to worry about stories I had heard of people going to sleep in the damned stuff and never waking up. With a supreme effort of will I dug myself out of it once and stood up in the icy blast, stamping my feet and swinging my arms, but that only seemed to make me colder so I crawled back into my cocoon and settled for comfortable euthanasia if necessary.

I slept in fitful, restless snatches, stirring myself from time to time to clear a tunnel from my head to the lee side of the drift. I was warm enough, even comfortable, and after a struggle I was able to get at my cigarettes and lighter and some compressed oatmeal and chocolate bars I'd shoved in my pocket before leaving camp. Smoking and chewing relieved the tension and I dropped off into a deep sleep after that.

It was the noise that awakened me. Low and sustained at first, like distant thunder, but growing in volume and taking on a higher, howling note. It seemed to be all round me and was closing in on me as if I were in the epicentre of a cyclone, and there was a rumbling underneath me. I fought myself out of the snow tunnel in blind panic. It was still pitch dark and the snow was being blown sideways in a solid white sheet that had particles of ice in it as sharp as razor blades. But it wasn't the wind that was making the noise. This was something different: something solid that had a pounding quality in it, something that screamed and howled and grated, unlike anything I had ever heard before. I thought immediately of earthquakes. I had been in a minor one in Shanghai as a kid, and I knew that we were right in the 'quake belt here. But somehow that didn't match up either. Earthquakes happened, then stopped, in a matter of seconds. This kept up. It kept up for what seemed some hellish hours and was probably its equivalent in minutes, although God knows that was enough. Then it stopped, not suddenly like the turning off of a tap, but in a fairly swift rundown—and with it the wind dropped and the snow cleared, and the silence that followed was almost as terrifying as the noise that had preceded it.

I peered down into the valley where their camp was, and back down the slope to our own, but it was still too dark to see anything, although the sky was now lightening over the eastern peaks. I sat down on a rock that had been swept clear of snow by the wind and tried to puzzle out what the hell had caused this rumpus, discarding outlandish theories almost as quickly as I formulated them. It would have to wait until morning. Rees, as always, would have an explanation, damn him. Something perfectly normal, no doubt, that he had experienced before—with politely masked surprise that I hadn't also. I almost made up my mind not to mention it—and if he did to swear blind that I had slept through it and hadn't heard a thing.

I saw them moving in the pre-dawn light. Someone lit a stove, then dimly through my binoculars I saw first Bowyer, then the girl crawl out of snow-covered sleeping-bags, shake and fold blankets and generally set about the business of breaking camp. They had a coffee-pot on the go, and plates of something that steamed, and I felt the saliva drooling down my by now quite noticeable beard and freezing there. I hoped to God that they would move soon, then my hitch would be up and I could go back for my own breakfast—and there'd be no more volunteering for this lousy duty—not for four clear nights, anyhow.

They pulled out just as the sun came up, and made off up the track—first their Sherpa, then the girl, then Bowyer, with the remaining man bringing up the rear. I timed it at exactly five past seven. They were all dressed as we were, in poshteens, Gilgit boots and parkas, and they seemed to be carrying similar packs—that of the girl being somewhat smaller than the others.

I turned then and went back down the track towards our own camp. I came round the first bend, a huge jutting bastion from the main massif, and stopped dead. From here I should have been able to see the windbreak we had built—but I couldn't. I could see nothing but a smooth slope of snow— a frozen white river of it—half a mile or so across, and stretching down the valley out of sight.

And then I understood. The horror of it hit me like a punch in the midriff. An avalanche.

One could see plainly what had happened. The snow on the peaks which soared up on either side of the pass we had been climbing had funnelled into it at the top, gathering bulk and momentum as it came roaring down, stripping the slopes bare and bringing rocks and scree with it, then more snow—the softer stuff which had fallen in the night—to cover the scars it had made. And our camp had been bang in the middle of its path. They wouldn't have had a chance.

I could feel the nerves and muscles in my stomach knotting and twisting, and I think I was sick, then after a time I shook myself out of my paralysis and went forward towards the spot where I judged the camp had been, but I knew it was hopeless even before I started. This was the sort of thing they used electro-detectors and trained dogs for when it happened in the Alps—and with infrequent success at that—but I did try.

I stripped off my poshteen and started to burrow above the spot like a demented terrier, but after an hour of it, spent and exhausted, I was still nowhere near solid rock. Snow—just snow all the way, with here and there an admixture of scree that tore the nails from my frozen fingers as I dug. And, looking at the steep rock face beside me, I reckoned there must have been another thirty to fifty feet of it beneath me before I could hope to strike bottom, and now the stuff was hard-packed and solid by the sheer weight above it. Hopeless.

I crawled out of the hole and sat for a time fully considering my own problem. There was only one. That of getting back alive. That was relatively simple. One long day's march down the valley the way we had come—to Kadan—hire a pony there and go on to Bhamo, and throw myself on to the resources of Puram Singh to get me out of Burma and back to Calcutta. It would be the end, of course. It was only a second chance they had given me, at best. Or was it a third or fourth? What the hell did it matter, anyway? I'd screwed it up again, that was the uncomplicated view of things the Gaffer would take anyway. I could hear him: 'Bit of snow falls on you and you quit and come home—leaving your blokes in the crap. Have a good holiday, Wainwright. Don't call us—we'll call you.'

The sweat I had worked up digging was now freezing on me, so I got up, put on my poshteen, slung my rifle over my shoulder and started out. And made five yards. The soft upper snow just swallowed me.

I struggled out on to the hard upper slope and looked for an alternative route. It should have been easy enough. The track we had come up through the main pass was under fifty feet or so of snow—but surely I could find some sort of toehold along the edges.

I took time over it on my second attempt, and thought I had found it. It was a ledge no more than six inches wide that ran along the side wall. I made fifty yards this time, clinging like a fly, but then it petered out into glass-smooth rock and I had to come back. The whole hundred yards had taken me over an hour. So this side was clearly out, even as things stood now. If it came on to snow again I'd had it, probably for weeks.

I tried the other side of the valley then—going back up the snow-free slopes and crossing at the head of it. But that proved to be the side from which the avalanche had started, and it was even more hopeless. In short my retreat down the pass was cut off and my only course was to go forward.

I was on high ground now and through my glasses I could see four dots moving slowly up the slopes of the pass above—briefly for a moment as they crossed a patch of snow, then they were lost against the darker rock background. That route seemed clear enough. To the point where they were now they had taken three and a half hours by my reckoning. Chamdo was another two days' march ahead, according to Rees. I sat down and turned my pockets out.

I had a bar and a half of this compressed ration stuff—about eight or ten ounces altogether. The faded printing on the wrapper claimed that it was 'fortified', whatever that meant, and was chock-full of vitamins, extra calories and God knows what. I hoped the guy who had written the blurb circa

1945 wasn't kidding. Besides this I had fifteen cigarettes, a lighter, a knife, a watch, pistol, rifle and a total of a hundred rounds between the two, a pair of sunglasses, a ball-point pen and a tiny notebook. Next to my skin I was carrying a wad of paper money and my passport, neither of which were likely to be of the damnedest bit of use to me up here and would probably land me into a lot of extra grief if I stumbled into a border patrol between here and Chamdo. I debated for quite a time on whether or not to ditch it, and I couldn't bring myself to do it. With a bit of luck I might conceivably meet a Tibetan trade party or something on the way down, which would relieve me of the necessity of going all the way into Chamdo which was just as likely as not to be garrisoned by Chinese. In the former case I could use the money and passport, in the latter it wouldn't matter a damn what I was carrying; as a European I'd be whipped inside and the heat would be on. But what the hell else could I do? It was a choice between going on and taking a chance or staying here and starving.

A third alternative did occur to me. That of catching up the party in front and throwing myself on their mercy, but I discarded that. An ex-con, particularly one who knew he'd been framed, could hardly be expected to be brimming over with charity, particularly since he had fish of his own to fry up there in the hills, and brothel madams with hearts of gold don't exist outside a certain type of literature, or so I've been given to understand. No, there was nothing for it but the long haul to Chamdo and hope for the best.

I turned and looked down into the pass we'd come up. I'm not a sentimentalist but I did feel a slight tightening in my throat. Rees hadn't been a bad sort of bloke. Sure, he worked for the cheque at the end of it—but if it came to that, who didn't? And he never swopped sides as some of the big operators did; and he'd been patient and courteous with me in face of some bloody bad manners on my part. And the two others.

Safaraz? I didn't know what his material recompense was, but I knew what he gave Rees in return for it. Complete and unquestioning loyalty. And the other man—the good-natured, grinning little Sherpa? He had no part in this except as a modestly paid factotum. Swept away—for what? I couldn't answer that myself, except that someone had sent me up here on a vague mission to follow somebody who had already received the dirty end of the stick from us. Oh yes, I could no doubt shuffle the responsibility on to the next man up the ladder, and he, if he were sufficiently interested, could pass the buck up higher—and higher—until it lost itself in the rarefied atmosphere of something they called 'political expediency.' But the Gaffer wouldn't be sufficiently interested to pass it up higher. All he would say if I ever did manage to get back would be, 'Rees bought it, did he? Hard luck. Useful feller him, in his time.' And that would be his epitaph. The other two wouldn't rate a mention. Only one thing was certain. I'd get the blame for it. A lopsided grin and the inevitable sucking of his teeth: 'Made a balls of things again, eh, Wainwright?'

I was wallowing in self-pity by this time and I had the sense —just enough—to realize that it wasn't doing me the damnedest bit of good. I had to move on, fast, if I wanted to survive at all, even in a Chinese School of Meditation, Realization and Self-Correction, which is what they call their political prison camps. *Some* survived. Kowalski had.

I pushed on down into the next valley. There was no sign of the avalanche this side and, sheltered on all sides from that horrible wind, it was warmer here—so much so that I worked myself into a muck-sweat crossing the stream at the bottom and starting the climb up the other side. I passed their camp site at the end of the first hour and commenced to time myself carefully from this point on.

They were now something over four hours ahead of me, but I reckoned I was travelling faster than they—though how long I could keep up the pace when the lack of food started to make itself felt was anybody's guess. I was already missing my breakfast horribly, and my hand kept straying to that damned 'fortified' Toffo bar, but I steeled myself against temptation and settled for half a cigarette and a long drink of water at each hourly halt. There was plenty of water fortunately—wherever the sun fell directly on the snow fringe which lined this upper pass. During the night it would no doubt freeze solid again. It was probably this alternation which weakened the structure of the snow cap above and caused these horrible avalanches. I determined to camp high tonight, right out of the pass, even if it meant settling for the wind on the exposed mountainside.

The track was well defined here. In fact in some places it was man-made—cut into the cliff face to an average width of three or four feet, with the sheer wall going up one side and a belly-turning drop to the valley floor the other, and where it did emerge into open country on the intermediate plateaux it was marked by stupas—piles of stones, usually topped with a stunted pole and ragged white prayer flags. Devout Buddhists, which means about ninety-nine per cent of all Tibetans, would never dream of passing one of these without tossing another stone on to it, so Rees had told me. Each stone apparently meant the equivalent of a thousand recitations of the Buddhist prayer of '*Om mane padme hum*'—'Hail to the Jewel in the Lotus.' A million million such prayers meant Nirvana. It seemed to me a hell of a good idea, whatever the theology or mathematics of it were.

I finally came out of the pass at mid-afternoon—suddenly and dramatically. It was like walking down a long dark corridor and stepping out on to a balcony in brilliant sunlight. Before me was yet another valley, wider and longer than any I had seen so far, and far in the distance the sun was glinting on a wide river. I trained my glasses on it. It looked a bare ten miles or so away, but I was becoming aware of how deceptive great heights and crystal-clear air can be. It was possibly a good twenty-five miles off. I scanned up and down the valley. It was as lunar and desolate as the hills through which I had come, but here and there I was able to pick out a green patch of cultivation and at least one tiny village, while on an eminence half-way across it I could see a huge fort-like building from which smoke was arising from a cluster of chimney-pots. That, I decided, could only be a Lamaist monastery or a Chinese barracks. I'd have swapped all my worldly goods at that moment for a map of the area—even the Toffo bars which were burning a hole in my pocket. Rees had the whole series—a quarter-inch to the mile, beautifully printed on silk finer than cigarette papers. I tried to recall the last one we had studied together. This, if I was right, could only be the valley of the Salween, a river which rose far to the north in central Tibet and ran the entire length of Burma, emptying itself finally into the Gulf of Mataban at Moulmein. Further across the valley, if I was right again, was yet another river, the Mekong, running parallel to it for a time before bending to the east and traversing Siam and Vietnam until finding the South China Sea south of Saigon. I strained my eyes through the glasses to find this second river, but if it was there it was too far away for me to see it.

This was exciting. I sat down on a rock and allowed myself a whole cigarette, and then got really reckless and wolfed the half bar. I needn't make for Chamdo at all. With a modicum of luck and a lot of guile, providing the Chinese weren't too much in evidence, I might be able to beg, buy or even trade some help in one of the villages down there. Food, and a couple of men with those inflated bullock-skin rafts they use, and then a long float down the Salween until I was safely back into Burma. How far? My memory wasn't good enough for that. By the land route we had taken I was now about fifty miles inside Tibet, but the river—again if my memory served me right—bent to the east just south of here and entered China proper before swinging west again and re-entering Burma. Call it two—three—hundred miles. What did it matter on a swift-flowing river? Always providing that there weren't too many booms, checks and traps along it, manned by unfriendly characters. I seemed to be developing a thing about floating down Chinese rivers.

I got up and continued on my way. It was downhill now and fairly smooth and I made good time. I wondered how far ahead the others were—then I started to worry. Back there in the blocked pass I had had no option. I would have been justified in quitting because I had no means of survival in the mountains. The fact that I had come forward instead of going back was beside the point. I had no option there, either. Had I been able to go back then I should have done so without hesitation—and I'd have been justified in my decision. Even the Gaffer, whatever he may have said to the contrary, would have had to concede that. But now it was different. The man I had been ordered to follow was still ahead of me—and going forward. I could no longer make an excuse of having no supplies. It was up to such wit and low cunning as I possessed to obtain more. There was civilization of a sort ahead of me—and South Tibetans spoke, in addition to their own language, a sort of Chinese patois which I could cope with, and, since they hated the Chinese, I might even be able to enlist help if I could convince them of my bona fides.

No, I decided regretfully, the Salween as a means of escape was out—until I knew where this son-of-a-bitch was going and what he was doing.

I was still making good time when I saw them in front of me.

Chapter Eleven

FOR A MOMENT I thought they'd seen me too. I was walking right in the middle of the track, and they had halted and made camp by the side of it, not two hundred yards in front of me. I froze for a full minute before I was able to convince myself that I had got away with it, then I slipped into the cover of some loose rocks at the foot of the cliff. They had evidently been here for some time because their blankets and sleeping-bags were spread out to air in the evening sunlight, and the girl had evidently been doing some laundry in a small stream that crossed the track further down the hill because there were some white garments pegged out to dry by the side of it. I squirmed in my sweaty underwear at the thought of it. Me, I'd rather be lousy and warm.

There were just the two of them—Bowyer and the girl. He appeared to be dozing, his back against a sloping rock, facing me. I got my glasses on him. It was the first opportunity I had of studying him closely. I wondered how he could ever have passed as a Eurasian. His face was deeply sun-and-wind-tanned but his hair and close-clipped moustache were blond, and his features were wholly European. His eyes were closed, but I guessed that they would be blue or grey. It was a wholly unremarkable face, the sort that one could see a hundred times in one day in messes and clubs throughout the East. The sort of face, in fact, that caused the Chinese to say that we all looked alike to them.

The girl was sitting on a rock a few yards away from him drying her hair with a towel. She got up as I looked and crossed towards an opened rucksack, passing him on the way. She paused, bent over him and kissed him on the end of his nose. He reached up lazily and pulled her down to him, and I felt like a Peeping Tom, but I still kept the glasses on them. She unclinched after a time and started to do things round their alcohol stove. I was glad that I couldn't smell what she was cooking as I sat there nibbling on my Toffo bar. Who the hell was she, I wondered for the thousandth time? There was a freedom and a freshness about her that somehow just did not jibe with a bordello background. Had Rees got the whole thing wrong? But when had the bloody man ever been wrong, blast him? Anyhow, what did it matter? Whoever she was, she was now kittens-in-a-basket with an ex-con. But was that altogether fair? The bloke had been framed—by us. Still, mine not to reason why. All I had to do was to follow them, not analyse them.

I foresaw another freezing night in the open because they certainly looked as if they were bedded down until morning. I wondered where the other two were, but not for long, because I saw them in the distance before Bowyer and the girl did. They were coming from the direction of the village which I'd seen from higher up, riding two ponies, leading another two and driving a yak before them. They started to call as they crossed the stream, and Bowyer got up, cautiously at first, but then, when he was sure who they were, he stepped from behind the cover of a rock and waved to them. I saw the pattern of things then. This is how they would manage on the road to wherever the hell they were going—Bowyer and the girl lying low while the Sherpa and the Indian, both common enough in Western Tibet, went into villages for supplies. That no doubt had been Rees's plan also. Head down and parkas up they could get away with it indefinitely —unless they were pulled in by border guards, many of whom were quislings for the Chinese. But that risk would decrease the further they got into the interior. All right for them, but not so good for me as a loner. Tibetan villagers, petty officials apart, hated the guts of their Chinese overlords, which made them potential allies once they had accepted one —but against that they were as inquisitive as monkeys, and they gossiped too readily. A single European on foot trying to buy his way along with Indian money would be a talking-point in any bazaar. I thought of trying to pass myself off as a Russian, but I discarded the idea even as it came to me. Granted, as the rift between the Russians and Chinese widened, so it proportionately narrowed between the Tibetans and the Russians—but it was only a matter of degree. In the last analysis there's only one person a Tibetan trusts—another Tibetan, and then only if they were born and raised within a day's march of each other.

No, I concluded at last, it would be best to play this as simply as possible. I was an American soldier—a prisoner taken by the Vietcong and passed over to the Chinese for brainwashing purposes. I'd escaped from a hell-camp and was attempting the long haul round to the north and into Kashmir and then Pakistan because I'd heard that the nearer passes were heavily guarded and, in some cases, closed by avalanches. How much of that I could get over in my bastard Chinese remained to be seen. At least it was feasible. Some Yanks had, in fact, escaped out of the bag and had performed near-miracles on foot before recapture, death or, in at least three happy cases, eventual freedom. How would I account for my serviceable clothes, boots, sleeping-bag, etc.? I'd been helped by charitable and patriotic Tibetans—and I hoped that the same help would continue to be forthcoming. Nothing like a good example to dangle before the uncertain.

I decided to shift my position. Here I was screened from them, but I was too close to the track for safety should any-body come up or down it, but then, as I was casting round for an alternative I saw with some dismay that there was no need. They were moving. Their two men linked their packs and other gear together and slung them over the back of the yak, then they all got mounted on their ponies and set off. This was hell. Night-tracking is tricky business even when all things were even. Now they had the legs of me—twenty of them to my two—and they were fed and rested. I would have to step it out to keep within reasonable distance, with the constant risk of over-running them in the dark. I swore viciously and peevishly.

But after a mile or so in that fast-fading light I found I had little to worry about other than my near-exhaustion. Five animals make more noise on the track than an equivalent number of people on foot—and the yak even had a bell on it, and the same beast, even if it lightened their load, decidedly slowed them up. I could hear the Sherpa howling curses at it and belabouring it with a stick, but if it felt it at all through that foot-thick coat of shaggy hair it certainly didn't hurry it in any way. I found, in fact, that I could sit down for quite long intervals, and even risk a cigarette at times, and still hear them—and when I was walking the problem was to keep my pace down.

In any case they didn't go far—just to the village, which was about four miles away. They made it just as night finally fell. They were evidently expected because the whole populace, I suppose about fifty men, women and kids all told, were out in the space between the huddle of mud and stone huts to greet them.

I got in close, not worrying about the dogs which were creating bedlam round the visitors, and heard Bowyer telling the Sherpa in Hindi to tell the villagers for God's sake to keep it quiet, as he didn't want the Chinese along for a look-see. The Sherpa did so, and then translated back that there was nothing to worry about—there wasn't a Chinese within fifty miles. Bowyer grunted non-committally and said they'd turn in—and he hoped the hut allotted to him and the memsahib was reasonably free from fleas. The Sherpa laughed and said

136

this was Tibet and what was wrong with fleas anyhow? They were only our smaller, and much younger, brothers. Bowyer said something rude and told him to be ready to start at an hour after sun-up, and went off.

So that was something. At least I had them fixed until morning. All I had to worry about was something to eat and a reasonably warm place to sleep, fleas or not. I looked as longingly at that beat-up village as if it had been the Hilton.

One by one the villagers drifted off, slamming their heavy doors behind them and blotting out the glow of fires inside, leaving me out in the cold, shivering like Little Orphan Annie. I toyed with the idea of risking it and knocking up the denizens of one of the nearer huts, pretending I was one of the party—but I knew that would be madness. I sighed gustily and moved back up the track—and heard a bell ring away to my right, and then the low hollow moan of the *kyoche*, the ten-foot-long trumpet that calls to prayer in Buddhist monasteries.

I remembered then the high-walled building I had seen across the valley from higher up. Down here it was hidden from view. If the villagers were to be believed it wasn't a Chinese barracks. Monks were traditionally hospitable. One gained merit in feeding the hungry. Jesus! In me they had a passport straight to heaven. I set off towards the sound and, topping a rise, I saw the dim lights of the place about half a mile away.

If I had not been so desperately hungry, dog-tired and cold, I would never have plucked up the courage to brazen it out that first time. My knowledge of the monasteries was at best academic. I'd heard the monks were steadfastly anti-Chinese, but against that I knew that they had endured absolute hell under the invaders who were determined to break the power they had held for centuries over the lay population. Not all the monks were pure Tibetan, even as far west as this. Many were Chinese Buddhists and it would have been an easy matter for spies to be infiltrated under the all-enveloping guise of the yellow robe and shaven head. I had read in Intelligence summaries that certain monasteries had, in fact, been accused of harbouring 'undesirable reactionary elements' and that their shrift had been short—usually beheading for the Lama and an arbitrarily selected ten per cent of his flock, forced labour for life for the remainder, and complete destruction by fire of the monastery itself. If someone sent for the cops when I showed up, one could hardly have blamed him, looking at it strictly impartially. But I wasn't looking at anything impartially right at that moment. All I wanted to do was to eat, and to hell with the consequences.

The big double teakwood doors of the place were open and I could see into a courtyard where monks were gathered before moving up some wide steps into a temple. They were chanting in a low, humming monotone—a weird and unearthly sound, punctuated with blasts on the kyoche and backed by a continuous ringing of small silver bells inside the temple itself. There was an air of complete, withdrawn absorption about them as, eyes downcast and hands clasped before them, they moved across the courtyard and up the steps—and that reassured me somewhat. Then I noticed a group of people squatting in a semi-circle outside the gate, beyond the patch of flickering light cast by the torches that flared from sconces each side of the temple door. There were about fifty of them and I suppose the generic term bum would have covered the poor devils, because I could see, as my eyes got accustomed to the change of light, that they were gaunt, ragged and filthy, and indescribably hairy—unusual for Tibetans who, while not bigots about washing, generally manage to keep their faces shaven and their hair to a short all-round fringe. The monks, of course, shave all over.

As the last of the monks disappeared up the temple steps, the crowd outside rose and shuffled forward to the gate and

I saw with amazement that they were linked together in pairs by the ankles with bloody great murderous iron bars with leg-cuffs at each end. Then I remembered reading somewhere about the Tibetan penal system. They have no prisons. Criminals under sentence are shackled together like this and turned loose for terms ranging from a year to life. How they survive is their own affair, just so long as they are not caught stealing. They can earn a pittance roadmaking or drain-cleaning, and the disposal of corpses is theirs by tradition, because no orthodox Buddhist will willingly touch a dead body. But usually they have to rely on the charity of the monasteries.

This was what was happening now. Through a small postern-gate I could see an old monk handing out huge chunks of bread—a whole flat native loaf about a foot in diameter and some four inches thick—to each pair, and ladling something that steamed from a big iron pot into their wooden tea bowls, which most of them carried slung on a string round their necks.

I wondered how I could get into the queue as a loner, then I noticed that there were in fact a few solos already—some still retaining their own half of the leg-cuff, some without. Cons whose partners had been released or had died and legitimate law-abiding hobos respectively I assumed them to be. I tailed on to the chow-line hoping to be taken for one of the latter. I was hampered by the lack of a tea bowl but that didn't matter, because some of the others were without also, and in those cases the old monk lent them one, which, having drained the contents, they licked clean and handed back. Leprosy, syphilis and yaws are endemic in these parts, I remembered, but you try being hygienic after a three-day hike through the Himalayas on a Toffo bar and a bit. I hauled my parka up over my head and face and shuffled past, showing my empty hand to the monk as the other bowl-less ones were doing, took it brimming from the old man and drained it in one. I even licked it, as protocol demanded. It was tea and tsampa, as hot as hell, and at that moment I wouldn't have swapped it for Beluga caviar. I took my loaf, a whole one since I wasn't partnered, and got out of the dim light quickly. But I needn't have worried. The others were far too preoccupied with the basic business of survival to bother about anybody else in the line. I don't suppose I was even noticed, in spite of my better clothes. All they were concerned with, having got their food, was to get to the *kang*.

I had seen this thing earlier, and thought it to be the oven where they baked the bread. It possibly was, but it was serving a dual purpose. It was a long clay platform about three feet clear of the ground and beneath it was a smouldering fire of wood and yak dung, under a projecting roof that ran between two buttresses in the outside wall. These people, having fed, were now clambering up on top of it and stretching out like codfish on a smoke-rack. Being the last in the line I only got a strip about eighteen inches wide, and even that was made untenable by the hacking cough of my immediate neighbour, so I settled for the floor alongside it. It was out of the freezing wind and was blissfully warm. I munched steadily through half my loaf. Dry bread can be hell to eat on its own, but this was solid, soggy and greasy and needed no extraneous lubrication—and by God it was filling. After ten minutes I felt as if I had been ballasted with a small bag of cement. I sighed contentedly and drifted out on a deep, dreamless stream.

The bugs woke me before dawn. Anyhow, let's call them bugs. I was virgin territory to them and they were really having a ball. I sat up, scratching in all directions, and looked wistfully at the postern-gate, wondering whether breakfast was included in the bill, but I decided not to push things too hard. These kindly people had done me very well. I picked up my bedding roll from the patch of shadow I had dropped it in the night before. I hadn't cared to use it as none of the others were so encumbered, and I'd have been conspicuous.

The rifle I had left with it worried me. Carrying it openly in these relatively populous parts would be asking for trouble. I considered dumping it, but couldn't bring myself to do it. It could, in the last resort, be a valuable trading asset at some time in the future. It was a 'take-down' model, breaking into two pieces, so I compromised in the end by wrapping them inside the bedding roll.

I walked down to the road. There was only one way for them to come from the village, so I started to walk in the other direction in order to get well ahead of them. An hour after sunlight, Bowyer had said. I reckoned that was still an hour off, so that gave me a leeway of two. The track was level here and I kept up a steady clip that I judged had put me a good six miles ahead of them by the time they started. The morning was cold, but gloriously clear and crisp. I moved off the track and drank from a stream, ate half my remaining bread and smoked a cigarette. I was beginning to feel fit—really fit. My muscles were toning up and I was no longer panting now that my lungs were attuning themselves to this high air.

I climbed on to a crag and scanned down the track with my glasses. They were not in sight so I got out of the wind and stripped down to the buff and had a bug hunt. I didn't find any, they were evidently home-lovers, but I could see where they had been browsing. I screwed up my courage and had a quick dip in a near-by pool, shook my clothes and crawled shiveringly back into them. Then I saw the others in the distance. They came on slowly and passed underneath my position. The Sherpa was still having trouble with the yak. In the manner of its kind it was taking its time, balking, wandering, stopping still and even occasionally lying down. I wondered why they were bothering with it, until I saw that it was now quite heavily laden. They had taken a lot

141

more stores aboard somewhere, and it worried me. This looked like a long trek ahead of them—fully kitted up and provisioned. What the hell was *I* going to do?

I looked up the track after they had passed. North and east. That still meant Chamdo—by my reckoning another two days' march ahead. Where then? The centre and the north were strongly Chinese held. Even if I succeeded in keeping them in view, hand-to-mouthing it as I was, how was I to get out again. Where was it all going to end? What was the object of it, anyhow? Just to see where he was going and what he was doing at the end of it. What a crazy, inconclusive brief.

I think I finally made up my mind at that point. Chamdo it was, and no further. If they went on, the best of luck to them. Chamdo was a town of sorts. I remembered from various Intelligence reports that there were several Indian traders there. They were always ready to do business. I'd make a deal with one of them to get me out. I was carrying enough for a down payment. The Firm could cough up the rest on safe delivery—of me. They wouldn't like it—not if I wasn't bringing a golden egg out with me—but what the hell? I didn't like *them*, either. And I wouldn't be working for them after this. No, just let's get out, and cut losses. Wainwright was fed up right past his tonsils.

I gave them a couple of hours and then followed on. The level going had finished now, and I was climbing again. I had a bad shock about midday. I came round a bend in the track and ran right into a group of men and animals coming towards me. But they were Tibetans, travelling down to the plains with enormous rolls of the felt they make from yak hair, and goatskins full of the rancid butter on which life itself depends up here. They were friendly enough, and poked their tongues out at me, which is their way of greeting. A couple of them spoke a bit of twisted Urdu and another the peculiar Chinese Esperanto they use up here in the very high places, and between the both I managed to convey to them that I belonged to the party in front, but had been lagging because I had been drinking *sharab* in a village the night before and had a hangover. That sort of things always appeals to Tibetans, Gurkhas or Sherpas. Living the murderously hard life they do, they do not begrudge a fellow mortal indulging in a bit of dissipation when the rare opportunity arises. They wanted to know if there'd been any women at the party, and I invented a couple quickly. Houris straight from paradise—and very fat—which is how they like them. They sighed enviously. They told me that 'my' party was a couple of hours ahead, and I said the hell with it, I'd make camp and catch up with them tomorrow. They themselves were pushing on down for the first village on the plains and they invited me to turn back with them and show them the houris I'd been bedded down with. I declined regretfully and said that if I did that I'd never catch the others up. I made a deal with them then for as much as a man would need to camp out for one night on his own—a rusty tin kettle, a beautifully carved tea bowl, a two-pound hunk of block tea, a small bag of tsampa, a dollop of butter and an unsavoury lump of dried yak dung for fuel. I gave them a ten-rupee note and they considered I'd done them handsomely, and continued on their way with much poking out of tongues and lascivious advice about what to do with the maidens of Chamdo when I got there. I was now better equipped than I had been since the avalanche—but my resolve to peel off at Chamdo still held. That far and no further.

I knew Bowyer's pattern by now. They invariably set out an hour after sunrise, and marched until an hour before sunset—which at this time of the year worked out at about ten hours, allowing for an hour's halt at midday—so that this time I was prepared for it and didn't overrun them as I nearly had the day before. They had made camp in a small valley and were already brewing up and cooking. I didn't need to feel envious this time. I found myself a sheltered spot off the track and made a dull but immensely hot little fire with the yak dung and some of the butter, as the Tibetans had shown me. I brewed up a mess of tsampa tea, and then a second one. I was still hating the stuff but I have yet to find anything more sustaining. Imagine it. A thick porridge made of tea which is as often as not compressed into block form with goats' blood, coarse-ground parched barley and lumps of semi-rancid yak butter that floats in it in biliously yellow patches.

I was lying back against a rock that still retained a little of the sun's heat, half-way between sensual satisfaction and downright nausea, when I heard the shot.

I rolled over and peered over the rim of my hollow down into the valley. The sun had almost gone now but there was still enough light left for me to see fairly clearly. There were three people standing in the tiny camp and one lying sprawled some few yards away, and even as I looked I heard the second shot and saw the standing figures galvanize into action. One—I could see that it was Bowyer—shoved the girl down flat and threw himself over her. The other one jumped, spun and fell.

I hauled out my glasses and searched the surrounding slopes. They're not terribly good at this sort of thing, the eastern hillmen—not nearly as good as the Pathans—and I picked up two of them almost immediately. They were on the opposite side of the valley, moving from one patch of cover to another, closing in on the camp. Bowyer must have seen one of them at the same time, because I saw him roll over, kick the girl further under cover and then come up behind his rock and take a pot shot with a rifle. I don't think it went anywhere near either of them. Then there was another shot—this time right underneath me—and I was able to place another two of the raiders, plus a fifth, lower down the slope than the original two. This one seemed to be in charge, because, shielded from the camp, he was making signals with his hand to the remaining four. I scanned the hillside carefully. That appeared to be the lot. This was why Rees had brought rifles. He'd told me about them. Kampas —bandits; some actually Tibetan troops demobilized and scattered after the Chinese take-over, others mongrels from the border marches. They operated in groups of never more than half a dozen, preying on small unarmed parties trekking through the hills. They never risked an open confrontation. They usually stalked their quarry until just this very time —sundown, as they were making camp—then they'd pick off a couple from relatively long range, and rush in on the demoralized remainder and cut their throats for whatever small return they yielded. They seemed somewhat nonplussed in this case because Bowyer got off another couple of quick shots, nearer the mark this time. I saw and heard one of the two immediately below me jump and yelp, but if he was hit it was only slightly, because he cut loose with a fusillade of badly aimed shots in the general direction of the camp, and his pal kicked him savagely to make him stop.

I don't know what made me so illogically angry about all this. After all, it was the way of life in these Hills, as natural as the law of the jungle—or London, or Central Park after dark. The thug and the mugger doing what comes naturally. But it *did* make me angry. Possibly it was the atavistic rage of the hunter being robbed of his prey—the stalking tiger being despoiled by jackals, if you like.

Anyhow, whatever it was, I didn't stop to think. I grabbed my rifle out of the bedding-roll, assembled it quickly, cursing my maladroitness, rammed in a clip and drew a bead on one of the nearer ones to me.

Chapter Twelve

THERE IS A generally held conviction that shooting people in the back is nasty. I could never see the logic of it myself. Shooting anybody *anywhere* is nasty in my opinion, but once one is committed to it I believe it should be done as expeditiously and with as little risk to oneself as possible. The two immediately in front of me went out without knowing where it had come from, because all of them, on both sides, were now blazing away like the Fourth of July, and the echoes were coming from every direction. One stayed where he was, but the other gave a convulsive leap and slithered down towards the leader like a half-empty sack. It clearly disconcerted the leader. He goggled at the dead man then yelled to the other, and getting no answer decided to bail out from what was clearly an uncomfortable position. He started to move to a flank, but then a couple of close ones from Bowyer made him change his mind and he nipped smartly uphill towards my spot. He, at least, did know where it came from, because he came bounding over the crest literally on to the muzzle of my rifle. The impact of the round stopped him in his tracks, and for a second he stood outlined darkly against the sky, then he went back down the slope end over end.

I don't know when the two the other side decided to call it a day. I just realized that the shooting had stopped and that Bowyer was standing up peering round the slopes and that the girl had crawled across to one of their two casualties who was writhing and trying to sit up. I could just make out that it was the Indian. From the way their Sherpa was sprawled

I gathered that he was dead. Bowyer dived for the girl and the wounded man and pulled them under cover, and by then it was too dark to see any more.

I moved away a couple of hundred yards just in case the remaining two had spotted my position and were resolute types, although somehow I had little fear of that, but it seemed the sensible thing to do. I wondered if Bowyer would be doing the same thing and found myself hoping that he'd have the savvy to get up high somewhere under cover. Then I stopped and wondered why the hell I was worrying about them—wondered, in fact, why I had shoved my nose into this at all. I had enough on my plate already without playing guardian angel to people whose interests were, by the very nature of things, diametrically opposed to my own. I thought wryly that if I had let things take their course without interference I would have been off the hook. I could have gone on to Chamdo and set about the only thing that mattered—getting out myself—safe from any subsequent charge from the Gaffer of quitting.

But I suppose that deep down inside of all of us we know that there are some things one just can't do, and that the threadbare cliché of having to live with oneself afterwards does have some validity.

I gave up pondering after a time and rolled up in my sleeping-bag, and I didn't wake until dawn.

I couldn't see their camp from my new position, so I moved back round the hill until I had it in view again. It was deserted, so I assumed that Bowyer had done the wise thing and got out while the going was good, but it put me in an awkward fix now. Would he be able to see me when I moved down the track? I lay for over an hour scanning the opposite slopes, then decided to risk it. I went down the track to their site. They had evidently moved in the darkness, and in a hurry, because they'd left a blanket behind them under a rock—but then, when I got closer I saw that it was covering the dead

Sherpa. He had been pulled under cover and an attempt had been made to straighten his stiffened limbs into some semblance of dignity and even, incongruously for a Buddhist, to cross his hands on his chest. I wondered who had been responsible for this last small courtesy and guessed that it would have been the girl.

I crossed the small valley and started up the track the other side, wondering what unseen eyes, if any, were watching me, but there was nothing else for it. The cliff sides rose sheerly all round, and it was the track or nothing. I stopped several times on that long climb to the top of the next big rise, and searched the path both ahead of me and behind through my glasses, but other than some fairly fresh horse and yak droppings I saw nothing which showed that anybody had used it before for some time. I wondered where they had picketed their animals the night before, because I had not seen them during the ruckus—and then I had no time to wonder about anything else except keep a whole hide on me, because they were at the top of the hill.

I almost fell over the Indian, who should no doubt have been watching the track behind them. He was sitting on a rock with his arm in a rough sling, cradling it with the other and moaning about it in a low crooning dirge. He was an ill-used man and he was letting the world know it. I tried to slip into reverse quick, but it was too late. He looked up and saw me and let out a shrill yell of sheer terror—and then the girl came from out of a shallow cave with her arms full of camping gear and we looked full into each other's faces. Past her, some yards away, I could see Bowyer having some difficulty in loading the yak. He looked across at us as he heard the yell, and I saw him dive for a rifle, but the yak and one of the ponies chose just that minute to make a break for it, and it was only that which saved me. They dashed towards us just as Bowyer fired his first shot in my direction, then the remaining ponies took fright and joined in the general

148

mill. The Indian dived for cover, but the girl stood her ground, staring at me. Bowyer was yelling to her to drop flat, but she appeared not to hear him. I grabbed her arms and swung her to one side and took off up the track. I'd have done better to have turned and made back the way I had come, but I had no time for esoteric deliberation then because Bowyer, with the girl no longer cluttering his field of fire, was pumping them at me as fast as he could work the bolt—which, thank God, was evidently too fast, because I got round the next bend, and the next, still unpunctured. One carefully aimed shot would have done it.

I kept going down the track fast, right to the bottom, where I had to cross a stream. I was in the open for a bit then and evidently in their view, because I heard a shot faintly from high above and behind me, and the *wheep-thump* of a bullet hitting the rocks some yards to my left. I kept going, still fast, and didn't pull up until I reckoned I was a good couple of miles in front of them, then I got off the track and climbed high up a cliff to one side of it.

They didn't pass me for well over an hour, going slowly and having plenty of trouble with the yak, but I could see through the glasses that Bowyer was very much on the alert, his eyes scanning the track ahead and each side of him, rifle in hand, with the air of a man who would shoot first and ask questions afterwards. I thought it was a pretty poor return for what I'd done for him, but I could hardly blame him for his reaction. I probably looked at first sight very much like the types who had jumped them the night before. I wondered if the girl had recognized me. She had looked right into my face from a distance literally of inches. At the moment I had thought so, but on reflection I put the odds slightly in my favour. She had seen me on one occasion only, dressed in European clothes, clean-shaven and respectably short round back and sides. I hadn't seen myself in a mirror for many days now, but I guessed I looked vastly different. I had a flourishing

149

beard, a hairdo like a hippy, my face must have been sun and wind-seared almost black, and I had no doubt I must have stunk like an Aleppo goat-stable. No, at worst, I hoped, I'd given her no more than that infuriating feeling one gets at times of 'where the hell have I seen that bum before?'

I gave them plenty of time on this last occasion. More than plenty. I wasn't risking making a nonsense of it again—not with somebody as trigger-happy as Bowyer. I came down after about an hour and looked for water, then I found a really sheltered and, I hoped, tactically safe spot where, with some dry lichen which I scraped off the rocks, the remains of my invaluable yak turd and an admixture of butter, I made a fire and on it a gigantic witch's brew of tsampa tea, and smoked my last three cigarettes. And when I did start out again, late in the afternoon, I found myself out of the mountains in the first hour.

There was a road of sorts here, and people were using it, and there was cultivation in tiny terraced fields built up inside stone walls, and to one side was the river, but whether it was the Mekong or the Salween I just couldn't tell at the time. I knew Chamdo was on one or the other of them. A map was the first thing I wanted—and a quilted Tibetan coat. Afghan poshteens belonged far further west than this—not that they were totally out of place, in fact I saw one or two other wayfarers with them—but they marked one immediately as an Outlander.

Because of my late start I intended to walk far into the night and then to camp off the road somewhere before entering Chamdo the next morning—but I had overestimated the distance and I came within sight of it well before dark. In the distance it looked quite a metropolis, because it was sited round the sides of a natural amphitheatre in the hills. Normally Tibetans build their houses where it is handiest to gather their basic material, mud, from the rivers, but there appeared to be a sort of planning here. There were streets—

narrow, admittedly—but with some semblance of symmetry, and although no building appeared to be more than two storeys high, they were mostly of stone or starkly ugly concrete, which at least gave the place an atmosphere of solidity and permanence. It also gave one a peculiar traumatic feeling —like coming out of the Sahara and hitting Paris without any intervening gradations. I wondered if they ran to hotels or even doss-houses where one could at least get a little privacy and a meal that wasn't tsampa. I believe I was even soaring wilder and thinking in terms of hot water, soap and whatever they used for towels in Tibet. I know I was certainly walking faster than I normally did towards the end of the day.

But I pulled up short when a squatting figure at the side of the road uncoiled and fell into step beside me and said, 'Wainwright sahib? Very good—this way, please, sahib.'

I've often wondered what Livingstone really said when Stanley greeted him a thousand miles from nowhere. Of course he had the advantage of a sound theological training to fall back on. I only had the army and the gutter-sweepings of three otherwise imperfectly learnt Eastern languages. I used them all, then stopped to be sick—literally. I remember reflecting miserably that this was the very first time I'd ever been actually nicked by the Opposition, and wondering whether what they would undoubtedly do to me was as bad as was said, and written. I also remember wondering whether it was worth having a try to reach the .38 under my left arm —and on whom I would use it first—him or myself. I knew that the session, or rather series of sessions, ahead of me would be something *really* bloody, because I had nothing to tell them —furbler or truth. All I could say was that I was following a man named Bowyer who had recently been released from Alipore Jail, Calcutta. Why? Just to see where he was going? Who sent me? A man called the Gaffer. His real name? I didn't know. Crash! Then they'd probably tell me that it was George Henry Gaffney, but that I was a liar and that I had another controller—and what was my real mission? And so it would go on. Questions—beatings—more questions—until you were spinning in a vacuum of doubt and agony and you would swear your own and your mother's life away if only they'd let up, just for a minute.

I suppose it takes everybody that way the first time they're caught. It is something that lurks at the back of your brain right from that part of your training where they start telling you the real truth about the *modus operandi*—of both sides—because They haven't an entire monopoly in bastards who are good under the interrogation lights.

All this ran through my disordered mind in the matter of a minute, while I was puking—and it took another full two minutes before I realized that this secret policeman wasn't acting in pattern at all. First of all, he was on his own. For a straight out pinch like this he'd have had at least another two, and they'd have been behind me, with guns on a spot about four inches above the bottom of my spine, where a bullet would cripple but not kill or reduce the capacity to feel. Secondly, he let me feel in my pocket for a filthy handkerchief. And thirdly he was making sympathetic noises.

'Oh, shit, sahib! Very bad luck, sahib! Lose it bloody dinner, sahib. High mountains very bad for belly. Never mind—this way, sahib. Scotch whisky very good.'

I had time to look at him now. He was a small wizened Indian, dressed in a poshteen not unlike my own. His straggly grey beard and the beaded skullcap I could see under his parka told me he was a Muslim. He put his hand gently on my arm and said, 'Come, sahib. Night-time soon and bloody dopkas come out on streets and knock it the shit out of everybody for nothing only make it laugh.'

Then *I* started to laugh—too loudly, and I kept it up too long. I suppose it was the sheer reaction. His grip on my arm tightened a little, and he looked worried. He said, 'Come, sahib, this no good. Plenty men all look.'

Obediently I fell into step beside him and he led me along the main street where, wonder of wonders, electric street lights were coming on. He pointed up to them with pride.

'Very good,' he said, beaming like a dragoman. 'Russkies go put up—but silly Tibetan bastards make it cock-up more and more every day. Soon all finish unless Russkies come back.'

He steered me down a side street where there were no lights, pulled me into an archway and tapped an iron-studded teakwood door. They were a long time opening and I was able to look back towards the main street. There were a lot of people about, but nobody seemed to be talking much, and they were all hurrying, like ants before a rainstorm. They were Tibetans mostly, with here and there an Indian, a Sherpa and, I saw with some misgiving, occasionally Chinese, in uniform greatcoats and the Chairman Mao cloth caps their police wear—heavily armed with burp guns and pistols —and always in threes.

The little man saw me looking. 'Chinaman police,' he told me. 'All right if nobody give trouble. Dopkas the buggers. Plenty crack it head with lathi. Plenty kick up the ass for nothing.' Then a trap was lifted in the door and there was some whispering, and the door opened and we went inside.

Looking back I have no doubt whatsoever that I must have been in a state of complete shock. I just took this weird little man at his face value—a friend in need—absolutely without question. Sanity returned as I stepped inside the door. What the hell was I doing this for—going like a lamb meekly to the slaughter? Who was this guy—and how did he know my name—and obviously my expected time of arrival here?

Then it dawned on me. The girl! Of course she had recognized me—and they'd had time to set this up. What an abysmal bloody fool I'd been—walking straight into it. Well, it was too late to try and beat a retreat now. The door shut behind me and we were in complete darkness and I could

153

feel the little man's hand on my arm guiding me forward, and sensed the presence of somebody else in front of us. The little man was speaking gently, soothingly, as if he could feel my nervousness. He would have had to be pretty obtuse if he couldn't, because I was shaking by this time, with a mixture of sheer terror and rage at my own stupidity.

'All right, sahib,' he was saying as we shuffled forward through the darkness. 'Soon pretty nice. Have it scotch, have it bath, have it good dinner, have it clean clothes—*jaldi, jaldi* —same like officers' mess, by God.'

We came to a flight of stairs and he guided me up them as carefully as if I'd been his invalid aunt. I was just formulating a belated idea of getting my gun from under my arm and transferring it to my side pocket when we came up against a door. He opened it and switched on a light.

I don't know just exactly what I was expecting to see. Possibly Bowyer, and even perhaps the girl—and certainly someone with a gun. But they weren't there. There was nobody there. It was just a room furnished with dusty and tatty Victorian furniture—a couch upholstered in faded red plush, a chiffonier with wax flowers under glass domes, rickety 'occasional' tables with beadwork-framed photos on them, a couple of grandfather chairs, and, hanging from the ceiling, a mass of dusty glass chandeliers in the middle of which one low-powered electric bulb was fighting a losing battle. If there was a window it was hidden behind some of the wall hangings, which were for the most part of the 'Good Luck from Taj Mahal' genre. I just stood and gaped.

The little man chuckled and said proudly, 'Pretty bloody nice, eh? All my home from Pakistan carry up here on bloody yaks. Cost plenty money—pay myself, not that damn bugger Puram Singh—too bloody tight-assed.'

I seized on that one familiar name in a shaking and uncertain Mad Hatter's tea-party. 'Puram Singh? What's he got to do with it?'

'My boss,' he answered. 'Open up this branch for him ten years ago. Make it plenty money—for Puram Singh, not me. Pay me two hundred rupees a month and one half of one per cent on profits—but he fiddle the books on me like hell. Bloody Sikhs all the same—but what to do? Big Mussulman contractors all finish when British Army leave India, and I get no other job.'

And then it came to me in a blinding flood of light. This mixture of babu's English and monotonous soldier's profanity. The army contractors of the old Imperial India. A race apart. All Mohammedans, and formerly very wealthy indeed. Under Government contracts they fed, canteened, tailored and barbered the entire British Army. They furnished and staffed the officers' and sergeants' messes. They lent, at only slightly higher interest, and infinitely more readily than the banks, money to impecunious officers on the strength of no more than a flimsy paper chit. I had had no experience of them in India —that was all before my time—but when we pulled out several of them latched on to the regiments they were accredited to at the time, and I had met them during my national service in such places as Aden and Cyprus. There were even some of them in Singapore and Hong Kong, in murderous cut-throat competition with their Chinese opposite numbers. I looked at the little man with a new respect, and even, in my relief, a certain affection, as he took my bedding roll and helped me out of my poshteen. Then he remembered the social graces.

'Mohammed Ishaq, sahib,' he introduced himself. 'I contractor manager in Lahore, Jullundur, Ferozepur—lots of regiments—Wiltshires, Royal Scots, Worcester—oh, plenty. Before me my father. My grandfather buy two polo ponies for Winston Churchill sahib when he second lieutenant in Bangalore. Pay him two years later and send him very nice letter. Still got in box.'

He settled me in the easy chair in front of a big clay stove, placed a bottle of Johnnie Walker and a tumbler beside me, and then dragged off my Gilgit boots, never stopping talking once. I was lapsing into a feeling of complete unreality, but the stiff slug I swallowed pulled me together a little.

'Yes, yes, yes,' I interrupted. 'Fine—I've got all that—but what I want to know is how the hell you know me? How were you expecting me? Who told you?'

'I get my orders, sahib,' he answered evasively.

'Yes, but who from?'

But then the door opened and another, younger man entered. He gave me a friendly grin and a perfunctory half salaam.

'My son,' said Mohammed Ishaq. 'Don't talk English like me—only little bit.'

The young man said: '*Gusl tiar hai*—the bath is ready,' picked up my poshteen and bedding roll and started to go out again. I remembered the rifle and jumped up to stop him. I undid the straps and took the two pieces out. They did not appear in the slightest surprised. Mohammed Ishaq examined it, clucking approvingly. 'Rigby,' he said. 'Very good—cost plenty money. *Gusl* this way, sahib.'

I gave it up for the moment and followed them out into a primitive bathroom the other side of the passage. There was another clay stove here also, and a tin bath three-quarters full of steaming water. There were also some clean clothes and big coloured Swadeshi towels warming on a stool by the stove. Mohammed Ishaq checked that I had everything I wanted, clucked again, and went.

I soaked and steamed until the water, scalding at first, started to strike chill, scrubbing myself with a handful of loofah fibres and a huge cake of soap that was scented like a whore's anteroom. The clothes were comfortable Punjab style shirwani and pyjamas, with a soft but heavy Kashmir caftan to go over them. I got dressed, stowed my gun away underneath my arm, and left my own stuff where it was.

They brought the meal in as I arrived back in the other

room. It came on two huge brass trays, and I can remember it item by item to this day. There was a chicken tandoori, hot and spicy, then a beef curry which was hot enough to raise the hairs on the back of your neck, which is the way I like it. Being classic Pakistan cooking, there was no rice, but in its place, huge chapattis, leathery but at the same time crisp—a paradox that can only be achieved by a Punjabi cook who knows his business—golden and swimming in ghee. And there were about seven kinds of pickle—lime, mango, brinjal, each hotter than the one before. And then, finally, to let you down lightly and to take the tears out of your eyes, a *firni*—which is a sort of yoghurt, but much better. And, characteristically, there was tea to wash it down—good honest to God stuff, not the goat's blood ullage I had been making porridge with on the way up—which is the only beverage which goes with real curry, whatever erstwhile Empire-builders may tell you to the contrary.

I was still bursting with unanswered questions, but somehow they didn't seem quite so pressing now. They could wait until morning. All I wanted was sleep.

Mohammed Ishaq led me to another room—again delightfully warm—and I rolled on to a bed and crawled beneath a pile of soft Pachmina rugs that smelt delightfully of nim leaves.

And that, for the next ten hours, was that.

157

Chapter Thirteen

I WOKE like a diver surfacing, slowly, with many pauses between the dark depths and full consciousness. I looked at my watch. It was eight o'clock. There was no daylight in the room, only a weak electric bulb carefully screened so that the light would not fall on my face, and for a moment I wondered whether I had slept the clock round; then I remembered the blacked-out windows in the other room. I lifted the corner of a hanging. It was garishly machine-embroidered with the badge of the 16th/5th Lancers, and inscribed 'Meerut 1936'.

The small window looked on to an alley. Craning my neck, I could see a narrow slice of the main street, which in daylight did not look so impressive. It was quite wide, but was muddy and filthy, and there was a fine sleety rain falling. I looked speculatively at the warm rugs I had just crawled out of, then realized that that was plain damned nonsense. The first thing I wanted was information, then breakfast, in that order.

I crossed to the door and tried to open it. It was locked. It brought me to full suspicious wakefulness—but then, as if to offset this, I saw not only my rifle but the two boxes of ammunition that went with it, carefully laid out on the bedside table. I examined the bolt and breech mechanism just to make sure nobody had been ingenious and removed the firing-pin—but no, it was all there. I felt under my pillow. My .38 and ammo was where I had placed it the night before —together with my unviolated money-belt. Funny; if you're locking somebody up you would surely take the precaution

158

of removing his hardware first. I examined the door. It was the usual heavy, ironbound teakwood thing they built in these parts, where doors are meant to do more than keep draughts out, and I was just making up my mind to start pounding on it when it opened, and the son put his head in. He grinned guilelessly and asked me if I was ready for *chota hazri*, which is what Indians call breakfast. I nodded, then pointed to the door and went through the motions of locking it, and looked at him inquiringly.

'*Tibetani-log, sahib*,' he explained. '*Kamwallas*—workmen— all time stick it nose wrong place—damn buggers.' His English was every bit as good as his old man's, and his explanation eminently reasonable. He went off and came back shortly with a brass basin of hot water, towels, scissors, razor, soap—everything, in fact, a fastidious gent would be deemed to need for his morning toilet, even to a new tooth-brush. But most important of all, there was a good big mirror with it. I dived on this and studied myself—and nearly dropped it.

I had been prepared for a change—but hardly this. I was darker than Mohammed Ishaq, wind-burnt and blackened, and my beard had to be seen to be believed. It was fierce and luxuriant—something between that of one of the hairier San Francisco poets and a Greek Orthodox monk—and yesterday at this time it was just as dirty, with bits of tsampa and rancid butter in it, and my parka had been up, which meant that very little of my face had been showing, anyhow.

No, I decided, the girl couldn't have recognized me—not at that particular moment, anyhow. Then who? Who the hell knew I was up here, other than myself—and of course these people? The Puram Singh organization? They knew we were tailing Bowyer, certainly—but we ourselves didn't know which of half a dozen possible routes he was going to take until after we had left Myitkyina. Could the old Sikh, for reasons of his own, have had a tail on *our* party? He'd have had to have been pretty close if that were the case—above the avalanche as I was—or he could never have followed me over the last part of the route. Then who? Who? Who?

I was just about ready to beat my head against the wall when the son came back with my breakfast. It was a good one, with freshly baked native bread, boiled eggs, honey and again civilized tea.

I tried to get him into conversation while I ate—but I was just beating the wind. He went all dumb and pretended to understand neither my English nor my fractured Urdu—and certainly not my Chinese. All I could get out of him was: '*Mera bap bhagia. Thora waqt ke bad wapas aega. Us se pucho.*— My father has gone out. Soon he will come back. Ask him.' And with that I had to be content.

The old man returned about midday, came into my room and carefully stationed his son outside the door. When you do business with an Oriental—any sort of business with any sort of Oriental—you've got to be prepared for a lot of preliminary skirmishing before you come to the nub of the thing. It can be very disconcerting if they break pattern and get straight down to tintacks of their own volition. But that's what Mohammed Ishaq did.

He said, 'One sahib—one memsahib—one Indian man, bloody Bengali Hindu *hath se zachmi*—got wounded arm. Get in yesterday before you. Go to house of Chinese Number Two —that Number Two for all province, but burra sahib for this town—what we call District Commissioner back in India. You understand?'

'Yes, but——' I began, but he cut me short.

'You listen, sahib, please. Pukkha important. They there now——'

'You mean they've been arrested?'

'No—just go straight there.'

'How do you know this?'

He looked exasperated. 'Sit on bloody ass—me, first son,

first son's small boy—three bloody days, waiting—first for them, then for you—outside town. What you think?'

'But for God's sake!' I yelled. 'Why? Who told you to? How the hell did you know we were coming?'

'Sahib—I do what I get told. That dangerous enough. I'm old man now—don't like this *tamasha*. How? Why? Don't know. Don't want to know.' He sighed and sat back, his eyes closed. And you're not on your own in that, either, I thought sourly.

I tried the fellow-feeling gambit. It sometimes works with us of the lower echelons.

'You're goddam right,' I told him. 'Who wants to know? Not knowing, can't tell, eh? But we're in the same business, Mohammed Ishaq——'

'You work for Puram Singh too?' he asked, and I saw that he was deliberately misunderstanding me.

'You know damned well what I mean,' I answered. 'And you can see my position. I trust you. I've got to trust you. But at the same time I've got to know who you're working under. Tell me that—just that—and I won't ask any more questions.'

'I don't work under anybody,' he said. 'Only Puram Singh. Buy some felt for him—some hides—yak butter—little bit of jade sometimes—send down to Burma. He send up some tea for making into blocks—canned stuff—kerosene—scotch and tobacco to keep Chinamen happy.'

'Squeeze-pidgin?'

'That's right.'

'But how do I come into it? How do you know about me?'

'I get told to give you message.'

'Told by whom?'

'Just told, that's all. You don't want it—that's all right. Just say so, and I'm finished. You go on—go back—do what you like. You want some help, I give it to you.'

'Fine,' I said. 'I want to get the hell out of it—back into Burma. Can you fix that?'

'Can do—but not till next Spring. Passes closed now. That one you come up, the last.'

'What about the river? The Salween? Can't I get down that?'

'No good. What you call *mulk sakt manna hai*?'

'Forbidden Zone?'

'That's right. Plenty Chinese down that way. That's why we don't have many up this side. Build it bloody big road alongside river—built it airfield—four, five airfields. Anybody get caught down that way—head off—click-snap—*jaldi-jaldi*.'

'You mean it's heavily guarded?'

'Sahib, a mouse don't get through that way. Patrols—barbed wire in rivers—trip wires on banks—mines *bun-bunf!* all the time.'

'Then what do you advise? I can't sit on my ass here for four or five months.'

'Only one way: west to Shigatse on Brahmaputra, through Lhasa, then turn south into Nepal. One trade route stays open through winter.'

'How far is that?'

'Maybe seven, eight hundred miles—little bit more.'

I shuddered.

'Can you get me a map?' I asked.

'Can do—but more better I send man with you to show the way. Gurkha man. No trouble then about getting into Nepal. He know lamaseries and safe villages to stop at.'

This sounded a bit better. But seven or eight hundred miles plus the inevitable 'little bit more'—call it a thousand to be on the safe side—over some of the worst terrain in the world, in murderous weather? And for what? To tell them something that they knew already—that Bowyer had reached Chamdo and was holed up with a Chinese official. And this had cost the lives of three men—and as likely as not would

merely put that under the row of figures you had already, and added them up. The sum of them gave you the letter you required. You then strung the resultant numbers into one line and, for transmission, broke them down into groups of five. The random line, being purely arbitrary, sometimes resulted in some letters having the same total number—but here you used your common sense. L and S, for instance, coming out at, say, 15 could possibly result in a word being either 'subject' or 'lubject'—the correct alternative being obvious. Unbreakable? Well, the pundits say no code is, but here, at least, no key was ever committed to paper, so unless the Gaffer or myself ever coughed the random line to a third party it was as near so as one could ever get.

I worked for an hour, subtracting the random line from the groups and then transposing the letters, and got at the end of it:

Vital uinfus tdr goods xx kc minrisku xx assistfus soonest xx best.

Which, in our own rather childish shorthand, meant, I gathered:

Vital you inform us of time of departure and route of goods. Keep contact with minimum risk to yourself. Assistance will come from us at soonest opportunity. And the best of British luck to you, sucker.

I could picture the unsavoury old bastard sitting and sweating over it. He hated codes as much as I did. We used this one exclusively on the air. That meant a short-wave radio up here somewhere—but why was Mohammed Ishaq so coy about it?

As I burned the message and my decoding sheets, I decided to try him once more.

He was sitting at the top of the stairs at the end of the

passage, and he came creeping along as if he expected to be kicked when I beckoned to him.

'All clear,' I told him, and he looked mightily relieved. 'But I want a message sent back over the radio.' And then he stopped looking relieved.

'Sahib, use bloody sense for God's sake,' he implored. 'All right, you clever man, know all about radio—but operator can receive all he damn wants—no risk. Sending, that different, by God yes. Four bloody DF stations looking for him for over one year. Can send one word—two words, then got to move position bloody quick. You want to start argument with damn buggers in Burma, India, you do it some other way—pigeon, wave two flags, any damn way you want, but you don't use my radio. I only got two sons—and only one that isn't bloody fool.' He stopped for want of breath.

I understood then, of course, and I didn't blame him one little bit, particularly if his son was the operator.

'All right,' I soothed him. 'Don't blow a gasket. But you've got to trust me a bit more. If you'd told me the form earlier I wouldn't have put the pressure on.'

'Telling nothing till you got to,' he growled. 'Didn't they tell you that when you were a makee-learn? By God, they tell *me*. Okay—what you want now?'

'Are you watching the others still?' I asked.

'The sahib and memsahib? Yes. Still sit tight. Chinese doctor been up. I think he fix the Bengali's arm.'

'How many roads are there out of this place?'

'Three only. The one you come up from south-west. One going downriver, south-east to North Vietnam. One going west to Lhasa.'

'What about the north? No road up there?'

'What for? Nothing up there—not even yak shit.'

'I see. All right then—keep a tight watch on the others. When they move I've got to know immediately—day or night. Got that?'

166

He nodded.

'And I'll want to know the road they take. And then you'll *have* to transmit. Do you understand?'

'What?' he asked, looking scared again.

'Just the road and the time they leave.'

'That's all right—just two, three words. It's bloody arguments I don't want.'

'Fine. Now listen—I'll be following them. Can you fix me up with everything I need?'

'Sure. What you got all right, except that I give you a Tibetan coat.'

'Supplies?'

'*Khana*—food? Don't want too much weight. Just two-three days' tea and tsampa. This man I send with you show you good place to stay every night.'

'He'll still come with me, even though I'm not going out?'

'Sure, if you want him. Good man.'

'Trustworthy?'

'I'm still here, with head on top of neck. If he not trustworthy I go finish long time ago.'

'All right then, so I just stay on here till they move.'

He bowed courteously. 'Sahib's pleasure my honour.'

He brought me in the maps I had asked for later in the day—four adjacent sheets at twenty miles to the inch. They were, I imagine, the results of American photographic reconnaissance missions during World War II, when they used this route over the Hump from India to China, in the days when the latter were our gallant Allies, and we flooded them with supplies which they needed in their guerrilla war against the Japs, but which they mostly sold to the then emergent Mao Tse-tung.

The maps were technically excellent in their original form, photographed at mid-morning I guessed, when the sun was low enough to show the towering contours in bold relief, but high enough not to put the valleys in deep shadow. They had

167

been gridded over crudely but effectively, probably by Indian Army surveyors, and the few place names they had entered were spelt phonetically.

The whole terrain looked murderous, even on paper. I thought the two ranges I had crossed on my way in were high enough, but they were very low indeed compared with some of the stuff further to the north, and down to the south-west, where they had ringed Everest—which they spelt 'Ever-Rest'—in a white circle.

And yet Mohammed Ishaq had told me that there was a pass down here that was open all winter, when the lower ones were closed. I asked him about it later, and received scant comfort.

'Too bloody high and cold for snow. Little bit come down —wind go blow it all away,' he explained. And that was the only way out unless I stayed up here the better part of a year. It sounded lovely.

I met the Gurkha that evening. Mohammed Ishaq came in and told me he was outside, and then went to the door and threw it open. He came in stamping his feet like the Bull of Bashan, crashed to a halt in front of me, threw up a meticulously correct salute, and bellowed, 'Three-one-double-nine-six-eight-two, Naik Tulsa Gurung! S-A-H-I-B!' at the full capacity of his mountain-trained lungs.

I stared at him in dismay. He was dressed in normal Tibetan quilted coat and pants, but he had on a pair of unmistakable British Army boots that were polished until they shone like a nickel on a Nubian's navel. He was about five foot six in height, and damned nearly as broad, with the flat Mongolian features and wickedly twinkling eyes of the true Gurkha, and a grin which split his face from ear to ear, showing a set of perfect teeth. And if that wasn't enough, he was wearing a Regimental belt with a crown on it, which supported his sheathed *kukri*—the viciously sharp foot-long curved knife they all carry. Anything more un-Tibetan I had never seen.

Mohammed Ishaq must have guessed my misgivings because he said cheerfully, 'That's all right, sahib. Plenty Gurkhas in this place. All been in British Army—all crazy buggers like this. Chinamen leave them alone.'

And I didn't altogether blame the Chinamen.

'But those boots—that Army belt——' I said doubtfully.

'Only wear it for best when in city,' Mohammed Ishaq explained.

I put out my hand to the newcomer. 'Well, at least you speak English,' I said.

'Three-one-double-nine-six-eight-two, Naik Tulsa Gurung!' he bellowed again, but Mohammed Ishaq managed to stop him before that final blast of 'Sahib!'

'That all English he know, sahib,' he explained to me apologetically. 'But he very good man.'

And on that I instinctively felt complete agreement. There are some people, unfortunately few, who carry an aura of excellence with them.

This little bloke, to quote that cliché to end all clichés, was someone you would like to have behind you in a tight corner.

I gently straightened the fingers of my right hand, which felt as though I'd had it in a carpenter's vice, and remembered something old Danby, a fellow in Hong Kong who had served nearly thirty years with the Gurkhas, had once told me, and I nodded to the rifle on the bedside table and said, '*Acchha! Rifle lejao, safkaro aur wapas lao shamko*—Take that rifle away, clean it and bring it back tonight.'

'The only Easterner who doesn't give two sods in hell for flowery compliments,' the old man had said. 'Give "Johnny Gurk" a soldier's job and show trust in him, and he's your man.'

It seemed to work. Three-one-double-nine, etc., Naik Tulsa Gurung beamed, pounced on the rifle and ammunition, which, if he'd been found with them outside could have been his and my death warrant, stamped his feet, turned about smartly and stalked ramrod-stiff from the room.

Mohammed Ishaq, a damned sight more learned in the peculiar, and at times almost childish ways of the British and Indian armies than I could ever hope to be, nodded approvingly and said: 'Good man—*bloody* good man.'

Chapter Fourteen

I REMAINED COOPED UP in that room for another two days, gnawing my nails, sleeping badly and hating this whole proposition more every moment. Mohammed Ishaq received a big consignment of yak hides the second morning, filling the downstairs warehouse and overflowing up into the passage outside. Their stink was almost tangible and by late afternoon I decided I couldn't stand it any longer and said I was going for a walk round town. He shook his head firmly and told me that there were too many dopkas around to take unnecessary risks.

'What the hell are these dopkas you keep talking about?' I asked.

'Monk policemen,' he said. 'Before the Chinese came they run the town for the lamas. Still do, and take a little bit of squeeze-pidgin from Chinese at same time. Bad buggers.'

'How can you tell them?' I asked. 'I mean do they wear any sort of uniform?'

'Same like monks—red-yellow robes—but they all very big, carry big sticks and rub black stuff on faces.'

'What do they do that for?'

'Frighten hell out of poor peoples.'

It sounded very childish to me, and I'd had enough of this confinement, so I stuck to my determination to get out for a lungful of fresh air. He didn't like it, but there was nothing he could do about it, other than to send his son out to follow me.

I turned into the main street from the alley and almost

turned back again immediately because the mud was ankle-deep and there was nothing remotely resembling a sidewalk. But the air was wonderful after three days in that room, so I ploughed on.

The street was crowded; Tibetans mostly, but with an admixture of Indians, Sherpas, Nepalese and naturally quite a lot of Chinese. I was beginning to be able to tell them apart—not so much because of any difference of dress, which was pretty universal, but by some sixth sense one seems to develop after a time spent in any Eastern crowd. There was only this one thoroughfare, wide like a Western movie set, with alleys running off it each side. The centre part had been paved, raising it a foot or so above the surrounding sea of mud, and here the market was set up. There was nothing exotic about it: yak butter, brick tea in stacks, and heaps of coarse barley on the Tibetan stalls, while those of the Indians displayed cheap canned goods, hurricane-lamps, tin and brass pots and garishly dyed blankets. But markets, and the diverse types they attract, have always fascinated me, so I walked through, feeling safe and secure in my anonymity. The son closed up behind me and I could hear him twittering nervously, but pretended not to.

I wasn't doing this for sheer mule-headedness. Moving naturally through a crowd was a nervous cathartic after the weeks of skulking I'd been through. Hiding, dodging and snooping puts its mark on a man after a time. Yes, this sort of thing was all to the good. The language problem didn't worry me in the slightest because the place was an absolute Tower of Babel and lots of the trading was going on in pointee-talkee. In the event of anybody addressing me direct in any language whatsoever, I decided I'd just look blank, shrug and walk on, as many others, pestered by hawkers and beggars, seemed to be doing. In fact I did just that several times, and felt my confidence growing.

But unfortunately it didn't work with the dopkas.

I ran smack into them as I pushed through a narrow passage between two stalls—two of them, and there was no mistaking them from Mohammed Ishaq's description. They were enormous men, Tibetan in features but towering by a full head over most others around them. They wore the dull reddish robes all other monks wore, but with a difference; bitter though the wind was, these two had their right shoulders bared, which, I remembered, Rees had told me was the sign of the warrior. Their heads were completely shaved and their faces looked as if they had dipped both hands into soot and 'washed' in it, carefully avoiding their eyes, which glared from two correspondingly lighter cavities like old-time Southern minstrels, but there the similarity ended.

Anything more coldly ferocious than these two cookies I have never seen. They carried thick iron-shod staffs in their right hands, and begging bowls in their left. I suppose begging would be the technical term. These two were just shoving the bowls into people's faces, and waiting. And they didn't have to wait long in any case, as I saw in that first minute. Those so solicited dived for pocket or pouch and weighed in without question—to both. Each gift was inspected by the dopkas, and if deemed sufficient it was acknowledged with a grunt. If not, they just carried on waiting until the giver thought again and raised the ante. Nowhere did I see any-body arguing. The original protection racket, working like a dream.

I heard the son give a gasp of dismay, and turning I saw him getting the hell out of it. He was evidently the one who was not a bloody fool. I was about to do likewise because I had no coins of any description on me, and I knew instinctively that giving them Indian paper money would arouse their very unwelcome interest in me.

But it was too late. One of them, seeing the son taking it on the lam, shouted angrily and pushed past me, but the son made good his escape by dodging smartly between two stalls and diving into the crowd the other side. The second dopka deeming no doubt a bird in hand being worth two in the bush, shot out a hand as big as a soup-plate and grabbed a handful of my poshteen. I wriggled like an eel but it was no good. His pal came back then and I was trapped between them.

I looked pitiful and whined in Urdu that I was a poor man and a stranger, and broker than a mosque mouse, but if they understood me it was so much water on an alligator's back. The guy who was holding me was now fingering the finely tanned sheepskin of my poshteen with interest, and the other was shaking his bowl under my nose and whistling softly between his teeth.

I looked around helplessly. The crowd had just melted and the three of us were alone in a narrow passageway between two rows of stalls. There wasn't a thing I could do about it. If I'd taken a poke at one of them, the other would have brought me down with that damned great staff of his before I'd gone a couple of yards. In vain I tapped my pockets, showed my empty hands and shook my head. The one who was holding me nodded to the other, then spun me round and they each grabbed an arm and almost lifted me clear of the ground.

There was no mistaking it—it was a typical cop's manoeuvre. I was being given the bum's rush into whatever the Chamdo equivalent of the local police-station might be. And there, I thought desperately, I'd be searched—and I was wearing a gun and carrying a sizeable amount of money in a bodybelt. The former was a capital offence in itself, the latter would mean that I'd be put through the hoop as to where I'd got it, and who I was anyhow, and it would build up from there. I thought for one mad minute of going for my gun, but I knew that would be worse than useless; I'd never have got it out in time from under those layers of clothing, and even if I had, and had used it, I still wouldn't have had a cat in hell's

174

chance of getting away through the crowd that the shots
would inevitably bring round again.

Christ, I thought bitterly, a couple of miserable little
Tibetan copper coins in my pocket and this needn't have
happened——

And then something came with the speed of a cannon-ball
from behind us—something that took the dopka on my right
in the small of the back and sent him crashing into a stall
that collapsed with him and nearly buried him in bulbous
goat bladders of yak butter, and as the other one spun round,
something landed on his shaven skull with the sound of a
baseball bat hitting a coconut, and he went down without a
sound. The first guy backed out of the debris, glaring round
in bewilderment, his mouth just forming for a yell, but before
he could let it go, the bat landed across his skull also. I felt
my arm grasped and a chuckling voice said in my ear, '*Bhajao,
sahib—bahud jaldai*—Let us run, sahib—very quickly.' It was
the numerical Tulsa—and I swear the little devil was actually
enjoying it.

He half led, half pushed me back up the narrow passageway. Behind us I could hear the owner of the collapsed stall
shrieking to high heaven, and a rising note that told of a
crowd gathering, but this side there was nobody, and after
a few yards we slipped between a couple of stalls and got
back into the main fairway of the market. My every instinct
was to keep going back in the direction from which I had
come originally, but Tulsa would have none of it. 'Go different
way from other men, everybody look,' he muttered in his
broken Urdu. 'Same way, nobody look.'

I saw what he meant. The crowd, in the dumb way of
crowds the world over, was converging on the wreckage of
the stall, undeterred by the fact that a couple of other pairs
of dopkas had arrived on the scene and were laying about
the front ranks two-handed with their staffs, apparently just
on general principles. The proprietor of the stall, an inoffensive-

looking Tibetan, then discovered the two stricken dopkas behind the wreckage, and started to shriek his complete non-involvement with the whole affair. It was curious to note the hush that fell on the crowd immediately. Up to now it had been something amusing—but pasting dopkas was apparently serious. They gazed at each other, awe fighting with the deepest satisfaction, then started to melt away rapidly. And we melted with them—Tulsa's restraining hand holding me back against my instincts to walk too fast. Behind us the dopkas were grabbing people at random and making them squat down in the mud.

We got back to the alley and Tulsa rapped at the door—two-three, two-pause and two again—and this time there was no delay in opening it. Mohammed Ishaq must have been standing just inside—and he was jittering with fear. In the shadows behind him I could see the son, hopping from one foot to the other. The door slammed and they rushed me upstairs to the room, Mohammed Ishaq chattering: 'Bloody fool, sahib! What I say? What I tell you? Go out—trouble!' And I had no answer for that—but Tulsa, grinning like a gargoyle, said, '*Chupraho, baba!*' which was a very rude way of telling him to shut up, and made a farting noise which was even ruder.

The old man insisted on my handing over my poshteen and Gilgit boots, which he slung at the son and told him to cut up and burn, and refused point blank to give me replacements in case I decided on another promenade. He needn't have worried. I'd stuck my neck out enough for one day. I settled for two stiff slugs of scotch and a large meal and rolled into bed. One thing was clear to me, though. In Tulsa I had a jewel of price. I shuddered to think what would have been happening to me at just that moment if he hadn't decided to act as guardian angel over me on that walk.

I slept badly that night. I couldn't stop speculating on the whole business. Did whoever was controlling Mohammed

Ishaq from outside know that I was on my own, or was the assumption that I still had Rees with me? I made up my mind to force Mohammed Ishaq into sending out just two words in my own 'random' tomorrow—'Rees dead.' That might bring a reaction, and I'd be called off—officially. And then it suddenly struck me that this might be the end of the line anyhow—that Bowyer was going no further. In which case how long would they keep me up here sitting on my ass until somebody made up his mind? Sourly I reflected that that could be one hell of a long time. Nobody was likely to be screaming for Wainwright's exclusive services back there. What the hell was Bowyer doing up here, holed up with a Chinese satrap anyhow? Had he been recruited into their Intelligence? If so, how? The bloody man had been in jail for three years. Anyhow, you never brought a local recruit back to the homeland—he'd have too much to give away if ever he switched sides. *One* man recruited him, and thereafter controlled him. And finally, why the devil had he brought the girl with him? I could well imagine a man wanting some relaxation after three years inside, but not on this sort of trip.

I gave it up after a time through sheer mental weariness, and dropped off into a dream-bedevilled sleep in which I was being chased through lakes of yak butter by black-faced dopkas, so that when Mohammed Ishaq gently shook my arm I sat up with a yell.

'They go, sahib,' he told me.

'When?'

'One hour ago.'

'Which way?'

He hesitated, then sighed sympathetically: 'Bad way—south-east. Sahib, memsahib, Indian man and three Chinese soldier.'

'Where there's lots of patrols, plenty barbed wire, and head come off click-snap if caught,' I quoted back bitterly.

'That's right, sahib.'

'How are they travelling? Foot or riding?'

'Foot, sahib. Pony, yak no can go that way—road too small.' He gestured with his hands to indicate narrowness.

The bastards. I'd been hoping all along that when they did move it would be to the north-west, towards Lhasa, then up to the Kashmir passes. Things were easier up there. That, surely, would be where the Break was by any logical reckoning—towards the Middle East and Europe, not down here in this absolute wilderness.

Then Tulsa came in with a pile of clothes, grinning at me and swearing at Mohammed Ishaq, because they stank and were not fit for a sahib. Mohammed Ishaq answered tartly that if they didn't stink they'd be noticeable—anyhow, if it came to that, Tulsa stank also. All good hillmen did. Only Hindus and queers were violets.

Between them they got me into this gear. It was thin but immensely strong yak felt, soaked in the actual making with linseed oil which made it flexible and completely waterproof, and outside that was another layer, this time of quilted cotton —coat, pants and thigh-length boots—and underneath it all a shirt of finely-woven wool. I felt like the man who advertised Michelin tyres when I had it all on, but it was surprisingly light and didn't seem to hamper movement, while the warmth of one's body started to build up inside immediately. I ceased regretting my poshteen and Gilgits. Topped with a hairier version of an old-time flier's helmet which covered the head, neck and shoulders and came down hoodlike over the face when required, I was equipped with what the well-dressed Tibetan was wearing when he was damned fool enough to venture out on the high passes.

Mohammed Ishaq clucked his approval. I saw that Tulsa was dressed in the same way, and only then did I venture the question that was really bugging me. 'Is *he* coming?' I whispered to Mohammed Ishaq.

178

'Of course, sahib,' the old man answered, slightly shocked. 'He your man.'

I knew heart-stopping relief. I'd been fearing that his hitch would have been for the Nepal route only. Purely as a face-saver I said to Mohammed Ishaq, 'You can tell him that he doesn't have to come if he's got any doubts about it. Get caught down there—click-snap.'

'He don't mind that,' Mohammed Ishaq assured me.

'Tell him,' I insisted. He did, in what I suppose was rapid Gurkhali, and got a wide grin and another rude noise from Tulsa.

'All Gurkha bloody fools,' Mohammed Ishaq said, shrugging. 'He *like* this. He say he more better at click-snap than Chinese. Bloody good job he hit dopkas with piece wood and not damn kukri. All damn hell get loose if those buggers' heads come off.'

'What's his pay, anyhow?' I asked. 'We haven't settled that.'

'That all get fixed,' he assured me. 'Maybe if you got some money at end of trip, give it little bit baksheesh.'

Even for someone to assume that there *would* be an end to the trip, other than a sticky one, cheered me a little.

Mohammed Ishaq said, 'Better start, sahib. They about two hour ahead now.'

'Have you let them know *back there* yet?'

He shook his head. 'Not yet,' he said. 'No transmission for twelve hours. Set gone up in hills with number two son.'

'Why?' I asked, my heart sinking again. This shot my last pathetic hope of being called off.

'Because I bloody say so,' he snapped. 'Too much talkee-talk go on last couple of days. *My* head, sons' heads, stay where they are.' He swung a pack over my shoulder by a strap. 'Okay, sahib. Just do what Tulsa say. You'll be all right.'

I shook hands with him and with the son, who had been

179

looking hangdog in the background, and he led us down stairs and switched off the lights, eased back the bolts of the front door, and we slipped out.

The street lights were now economically dowsed, and the alley was as black as the inside of an undertaker's hat, but Tulsa set off like a cat in the dark, our soft boots making no noise on the frozen mud. It was bitterly cold, but such was the miracle of those clothes that only the tip of my nose was registering it. The rest of me was in a gentle glow after ten minutes or so.

We went up the main street, past the deserted market-place, keeping to the shadows of the buildings. Not a soul was stirring, and I didn't blame them. We were out of the town in under ten minutes and on to a deep rutted road, then Tulsa swung right over some small terraced fields and we started to climb, over loess slopes at first, then scree— and then we were on the rocks, and soon I was sweating like a June bride. Never once did Tulsa pause or hesitate. He just went on and up until we reached the top of the first ridge, although there was no sign of a track of any sort. I looked back into the valley. When we came through the streets there had been no sign of a light, but from up here one could see pinpoints, and they looked warm and safe and it wouldn't have taken much for me to have pocketed the tattered remnants of my pride and turned back.

Tulsa said in his tortured Urdu, of which I understood an average of one word in three, 'Good. This way save some time. Stay here till morning.'

I wondered what the hell for, but morning wasn't far off, and when the sun rose I saw that we were looking down on to a track in the valley the other side of our ridge—a track which led back to the north, then swung round and joined the road out of town. That, apparently, was the normal route, an easy one for pack animals. Our way, we'd crossed between the two arms of an inverted U and saved a possible six or seven miles. And then, in confirmation of this, we saw them. Six dots moving along the track. I dug my glasses out from under my coat and trained them on them. The dots became figures, but they were still too far away for me to identify them with certainty. I looked inquiringly at Tulsa and handed him the glasses. He took them for politeness' sake and made a show of using them, but he didn't need them. He knew. He nodded and grinned.

They were in view for about twenty minutes before a spur of the hill cut off our line of sight. I looked at Tulsa again and asked when he thought it would be safe to follow. He said, '*Ek sigret, ek piala char, sahib*—After one cigarette and a cup of tea,' and dug into his pack and produced a tiny solid alcohol lamp and a brass jar, then skipped like a goat downhill and got some water from where the early sun was melting the snow-edge. We drank our tea and lay back smoking. There were a thousand questions I would have liked to ask him, and I know he would have done his cheerful best to answer them, but I decided on that first day to keep them to a minimum, and when I had something really important to ask him, to formulate it properly. That way we both saved breath, and by God, the way *he* travelled, you needed to up in this thin mountain air.

He got up after a time, but instead of heading downhill into the valley, he moved to a flank—right-handed along the blind side of the ridge. It was hard going, because the ridge was saw-toothed, which meant that we were either climbing or sliding the whole way. He stopped from time to time, and I knew it was purely out of consideration for me, because he wasn't even breathing hard. And we kept it up, all that whole morning, until, when the sun was high above us, he signalled me to lie flat and to crawl with him up to the ridge and look over.

And there they were—smack below us, a mile away on the valley floor.

I looked at him and shook my head in admiration, and he grinned delightedly. The pattern of it was plain now. They had been following the track which wound with the valley. We had come by bee-line. Our going had been harder, no doubt, but they had travelled possibly twice our distance.

They were near enough to make out details now quite plainly. This was evidently a longish midday halt because they were making tea and eating—two groups, Bowyer, the girl and the Indian in one, and some yards away the three Chinese troops huddled round a communal bowl, eating with chopsticks.

Tulsa snorted and said something about Chinese being no bloody good because they hadn't got at least one look-out posted. I hoped he wasn't setting a standard for *us*.

They stayed there for about an hour, then started off again. I studied them through my glasses. I thought the girl was looking more tired than she had been formerly. Tulsa said with certainty, 'They go ten mile more. One village—one lama house.' By which he meant monastery. And he was right, although we ourselves only covered about five or six miles—but that was quite enough for me, because the going was murderous.

The village was in a wide valley set in a bend of a river which came bursting through a narrow cleft in the hills the other side, widened, then continued in a broad and shallow sweep until it disappeared into another cleft to the south. I assumed that this was the Salween, and would have liked to get my maps out and make an attempt to plot our day's march to verify it, but the light was fading and it was getting too cold for fine work on that exposed hill face. I looked at Tulsa questioningly. Where were we going to spend the night, I wondered?

He seemed to read my unspoken question, because he grinned and pointed down to the village. I didn't argue, but I was nervous. The village was only a cluster of a dozen small huts, and we didn't know whether the others had arrived yet. But he didn't seem to have any doubts, so I left it to him, and just followed him down the hillside, keeping right on his heels as he took advantage of every bit of cover—here a pile of loose rocks, there a watercourse—until we arrived at the bottom, some four hundred yards from the nearest hut.

He left me in a hollow then and melted into the shadows, and I waited a dragging half-hour, getting colder every minute, until he returned. He squeezed my arm and clucked reassuringly, and led me out of the hollow, skirting the outlying huts until we arrived at one in the centre of the cluster. It was pitch dark now, but never once did he put a foot wrong. There was nobody about as far as I could hear—people in those hills get under cover at nightfall—but the inevitable dogs were out in force, barking and howling as we passed, and once two or three of the bloody things came out at us and snapped at our heels. But it didn't faze Tulsa for one moment. He stood rock-still, searching with his cat's eyes, then planted a well-aimed kick into the ribs of the nearest of them, which sent them all back yelping.

I was out to it on my feet by this time, and I only dimly remember following him through a low doorway into a smoke-laden atmosphere that stank to high heaven of goats and unwashed humanity. But it was gloriously warm, and someone shoved a dish of hot yak milk into my hands, laced with something that tasted like sulphuric acid and which nearly lifted the top of my head off.

Tulsa spoke then for the first time. 'Others here, sahib,' he said. 'One hour before us. And they know we follow.'

Chapter Fifteen

SO THIS WAS IT, I thought dully. If they knew we were on their tail what would be the use of following further? It would only be a matter of time before they either ambushed us or, if they were really on the ball, circled round and came up behind us. This is where I peeled off and took sensible measures about getting out. I think my first feeling was one of intense relief—but I had, at least, to make a show of verifying it first.

'How do you know?' I asked him. He gestured towards the donor of the laced milk. 'My brother,' he said.

The other man grinned with a flash of white teeth. He was a Gurkha, but there the likeness between the two ended. This one was short and immensely fat, and considerably older than Tulsa—but the term *bhai* can mean anything from common parentage to membership of the same tribe.

'Bhup Nath,' he introduced himself. 'Havildar in Second Tenth Rifles, sahib. Take it pension long time. Speak little bit English—plenty Tibetan and Chinese.'

'How do you know that they know about us?' I asked him as we shook hands.

'I *munshi* for this place,' he explained, which meant that he was the official interpreter. 'Chinese captain here don't talk English or Urdu—this other sahib don't talk Chinese or Tibetan. I get sent for when they come in.'

'And he said he knew we were following him? You're sure of that?' I insisted.

He shook his head. 'He don't say it that way, sahib. He

say that other side of Chamdo he *know* somebody follow him—maybe two men. He think Europeans. Then he say one European have fight with dopkas in Chamdo. He thinks maybe these men still follow. He have big fight with number one Chinese in Chamdo—ask for more soldiers to make ambush for these men. Number one Chinese say no can do—give it three soldier only. This sahib say these soldiers no good. He tell them to stay one place to ambush these men, damn soldiers go to sleep. He ask captain here for more soldiers.'

So it still wasn't certain. It just meant that Bowyer was getting jumpy, and was making some shrewd guesses. Perhaps I'd been careless at some stage on the track to Chamdo and he had picked me up with his glasses—or, contrary to my comfortable belief that I'd got away with it when I ran into them, he or the girl *had* recognized me for a European. As, apparently, had the dopkas. I felt my conceit sinking to a new low—and then a thought struck me.

'He thinks two men follow him?' I said. Bhup Nath nodded. Why two? I wondered. He hadn't seen us up to the time the others had been scuppered by the avalanche. Not the way Rees was running things; I'd have staked my last dollar on that. And I was equally certain that he hadn't seen us today. All right then, let's assume that I, as usual, had been the goat who had tipped my hand to him—that could only have been while I was travelling solo. So why should he have mentioned *two* men to the Chinese commander?

'Two men—both Europeans?' I repeated.

'He *think* two men. He *think* European.'

Oh God, I thought desperately. Not a tip-off—not again? 'Did he say who he thought they were?' I asked.

'Capitalist-Imperialist running dogs.' Bhup Nath grinned apologetically.

'Did he give any names? Did he say what they looked like?'

'No names—but he say that one man dark like Indian, but run like European. Got it black beard. Wear poshteen.'

That was me all right. Smart of the bastard—or just instinctive. Asiatics and Europeans do run, and walk, and stand, differently. One can simulate the other when one's whole attention is on the matter—but when one is expecting a bullet up the ass, one just runs as comes naturally.

'These dopkas?' I went on. 'They knew I—this man—was a European too?'

Tulsa, who understood more pidgin that he would ever admit, butted in here. 'When they look at sahib's poshteen one say "meat eater—smell like dam' Ferenghi foreign devil".'

That was understandable. We smell differently also. If the dopkas had reported this, and described my appearance—and it had come to Bowyer's ears—he could have put two and two together. But *two* men—both Europeans. Where had that come from?

I started to question Bhup Nath again, but he closed up.

'Eat first, sahib,' he said firmly. 'Head go *idhar-udhar*—this way, that way, after long walk over khuds. Bimeby we talk again.' And wearily I agreed, and took in my surroundings for the first time.

It was a single-roomed hut, about sixteen feet square, with a *kang* running round three sides of it. In the centre was an open stone fireplace, with a minute hole in the roof above it doing an inadequate job of letting the smoke out. A small, shrivelled Gurkha woman crouched over a big iron pot stirring food, while a younger one sat on the kang feeding a baby. In what room was left, four goats and three dogs slumbered while three little devils of boys kicked a roughly-made football of yakskin around. It landed in the stew once, and the old lady fished it out with a ladle, completely unperturbed, and tossed it over her shoulder back to the players.

Bhup Nath stoked up the secondary fire under the kang,

while Tulsa made my bed down for me, augmented by a bright Pachmina rug and a padded quilt. I fended off another bowl of warm milk and firewater, and settled for a huge helping of the stew, bowed my thanks and crawled, half-dead, into the sack.

But I couldn't sleep for a long time. A combination of nervousness and shrewd guessing on Bowyer's part? Could be. If not, wasn't it a reasonable assumption that we'd been fingered? If so, by whom? Who knew for certain that we were following? The Gaffer? I wondered if he were still in Calcutta or was remote-controlling from London. Anyhow, he could be ruled out. Or could he? I disliked the old rip so much that I'd willingly have believed anything of him—but that was ridiculous! Who else? Rees himself doubling? Collecting a fat fee from both sides? Ridiculous again—but what about Kowalski, and a round dozen smaller fry I could mention? Didn't they double? Yes, but never at the same time—too risky. When they went over it was openly— as openly as anything ever was in this dingy business. Besides, I had the Gaffer's word for Rees—for what that was worth. But mightn't Rees have had the wool clamped down over the Gaffer's eyes? Possible, but not probable. I realized of course, that I didn't want to think this of Rees, and tried to be coldly objective about it, but it was no good. No, not Rees. That drunken old bastard of a Major? Could be again— but how would he have got word to them? Any time along the road through Burma. But that sort of deal would have called for a lot of chaffering and bargaining first—and he hadn't had the opportunity for that. What about the time-lapse between Bowyer getting off the rice boat and the Major meeting me in Rangoon? Again, possible but improbable. Somehow I couldn't see that old wreck mustering the guts to double-cross Rees, particularly when he had Safaraz watching him. It never occurred to me for one moment to number Safaraz among the suspects.

187

Who then? In the name of God *who*? There was nobody else—not down here at my level. So back we came to the beginning. A leak at the top. The thing that Barry had almost invited me to put into words—but I had been scared to. The Big Sell-out. Unthinkable. But was it? Wasn't a very big wheel of ours living in Moscow at this moment—writing his memoirs for a London weekly newspaper *and* drawing the pay for it? Hadn't another one—not quite such a big wheel, but infinitely further up in the firmament than I— sold nearly forty of our agents to the firing-squads and labour camps? And they weren't Kowalskis either. Englishmen—the right schools—the right accents—Oxford. What made *me* so bloody invulnerable? Couldn't there be another —and another—and another in this circus of ours? Somebody I didn't even know, but who had us poor bastards as coloured flags on a map somewhere: 'Who's this? 385/G? Oh yes— fellow by the name of Wainwright, James. Not dangerous— rather a bumbler. Following Bowyer at present on the lower passes in south-east Tibet. Don't think he's got much to talk about, but every little helps. Let him get right in, then arrest, interrogate and remove.' Who the hell could one trust— above or below? There was only one answer—the Gaffer's: 'Nobody—only your bloody self—and then not always.'

And on this hilarious note Nature had its way, and I went off to sleep.

They woke me from a deep sleep after what seemed only minutes. Tulsa was shovelling food into himself as if he were preparing for a seven-year famine. Bhup Nath handed me a huge bowl of it—boiled lentils swimming greasily in yak butter and I tried to follow Tulsa's example, but the heart had gone out of me, and with it my appetite, and I started to retch after a few spoonfuls. They both clucked sympathetically, and Bhup Nath suggested more goat's milk and firewater, which, amazingly, did seem to do something towards lifting me from the deep gloom that was upon me.

Bhup Nath said, 'Last night they give orders, sahib, that they leave at daylight. They ask captain for more soldiers. He say no, so they still got same three.'

'So what do we do now?' I asked. 'Get ahead of them again?'

'More better that way,' he nodded. 'Tulsa show you good way across khuds.'

'How tough?' I asked warily.

'Not tough, sahib. Nearly as good as yesterday—and only little bit further.' Which sounded wonderful.

I said goodbye to the old chap and tried to leave a hundred-rupee note 'as a present for the children,' but he declined it courteously and without making me feel an ignorant lout.

Why did they do this sort of thing, these people, I wondered? Loyalty to the British Raj that was? That finished over twenty years ago, and these old soldiers had little to show for their service to us save a minuscule pension which, in the case of Bhup Nath, he would have to walk the best part of a thousand miles to Katmandu to collect each year. Personal affection for the men who had been their officers in the past? That ruled me out. I was a babe in arms when this old warrior finished his service. Financial reward? That was minuscule too. I had paid some of these part-timers on occasion. He'd be lucky if he collected fifty rupees for the assistance he had rendered me—and yet he had refused a hundred from me because he would have felt he was charging me for his hospitality. And the hideous risk he was running! He'd only have to be suspected of aiding a European to be subjected to unmentionable torture before final beheading —for himself and his entire family. No, it was something beyond me.

And then, inevitably, my thoughts switched back to something I'd asked myself only a few short hours before. 'Who could one trust—above or below?' He might, at this moment, be hurrying to the Chinese command post. But that was stupid. If he'd wanted to do that he had had ample opportunity to do it during the night. I felt belittled by the very doubt, and I cleared my throat and spat as I followed Tulsa back up the hill.

It wanted another hour to dawn. The wind had risen during the night and it was freezingly cold, and I had none of the pleasant glow I had felt when leaving Chamdo. Of course we had climbed another 6,000 feet since then, and I realized now that I was suffering from the desperate depression that this rarefied air brings until one becomes fully acclimatized to it. The locals recognize it and have a name for it; the 'Hill Devil's Breath,' they call it. A full belly and a plenitude of the hooch they distil from barley is the only sure specific against it, they say.

The early part of that day's walk was a repetition of the previous one, along another razor-backed ridge, with Tulsa leaping like a chamois from crag to crag, coming back with his huge grin from time to time, to help me over the more difficult bits. I tried to stop him, because this way he was travelling twice my distance, but it was just barking at the wind.

Three times he halted and climbed cautiously to the crest above us, at points from which he knew the track in the valley below would be visible—but only once did we see them—six dots, as before, far below us. But today there were no halts for tea and cigarettes. Tulsa was really pressing on—and at midday I saw why.

The whole terrain changed here, and we were descending, and at the same time the valley floor was rising to meet us on a common, snow-covered plain beyond which, ten to twenty miles away, rose the main massif of the whole range. I have never seen anything so starkly frightening in my life. It rose, sheerly like a wall, for as far as the eye could see both right and left, snow-covered, with jagged rock teeth

190

protruding through in places where avalanches had swept down. The crests were invisible, hidden by swirling white clouds that billowed like smoke against the grey sky.

'Wind make it snow go whurr! whurr! whurr! on top,' said Tulsa conversationally. 'Very bad.'

'Where does our road go?' I asked him, dreading to hear the answer.

'Round to south, sahib,' he told me. 'Not over top. One pass.'

'Thank God for that,' I said, and meant it.

'*Bahud khabadari*, there, sahib—very careful,' he went on. 'River come out other side—go into hill—come out again. That where Chinese men are, sahib—*lakh, se lakh, se lakh*.' A *lakh* is a hundred thousand and is the usual term for a hell of a lot, in much the same way as we say 'millions'. What the hell for? I wondered dully. Troop concentrations over on the Indian and Pakistan borders, or down to the south to back the Vietcong, I could understand. But why up here in this desolate hell? A high-altitude training area? They could train and threaten India at the same time over to the west, within sight of Everest, and they had built military roads over there. Why pick on this place, in the heartland of Tibet itself, merely to train? I gave it up. If we got there maybe some explanation would offer itself, and in the more speculative case of getting out again, I might even have something fairly useful to take back. No Intelligence reports that I remembered having seen gave any hint of massive build-ups in this region.

I studied the plain in front of us. It was an unbroken carpet of powdery snow, as flat as a billiard table, and I could see no sign of a track across it. If there were *stupas* and *chortens* to mark it, then they were buried, which meant that the plain itself would be impassable without skis or snow shoes. I said as much to Tulsa.

'One way can go, sahib,' he assured me, and pointed.

'From there, where valley come out—round to left—then straight across. One time river—now all ice. Snow not thick.' In other words it was a glacier, although I could see no difference in the surface snow.

'What do we do?' I asked. 'Go ahead of them?'

He shook his head as I expected he would, because the question, on reflection, was absurd. 'They see footprints,' he said. 'We make camp here and wait till they go, then follow in same footprints after dark.'

That made sense, though how the hell even he was going to follow footprints in the snow in pitch darkness was beyond me.

He chose a spot among the last of the rocks from where we could see the spot where the valley track came out finally on to the plain, and while he prepared tea and tsampa I got out the maps and had a shot at orienting ourselves. I had no compass, but I got a rough line from the sun, and then dead-reckoned our route along the ridges from Chamdo.

The result was unpromising. The area facing us was blank, unsurveyed and unmarked, except for a line of estimated spot heights on the range across the plain. They ran up to 7,000 metres—nearly 22,000 feet. The pass we were making for was not marked. Five hundred miles to the north was the vast plain of the Koko Nor; east, the range we were looking at; south, off the edge of the snow plain, a huge bend in the headwaters of the Yangtse-kiang, here running parallel with the Salween and Mekong. Behind us, to the west, was the massif we had skirted round since leaving Burma. This in front of us, then, was the Hump itself—the hurdle that American fliers shuttling supplies from Calcutta to Chungking in World War II had to take twice in forty-eight hours, in unpressurized DCs—and where the losses by natural hazards averaged two planes a day. There were no political boundaries marked on the map, but if my reckoning was correct we were now standing at a point where the frontiers of Tibet touched the two provinces of China proper—Szechwan and Yunnan.

And as far as I knew, no Western power had had a man in this far for at least twenty years—or if they had, nobody had come out to talk about it.

We saw them at mid-afternoon. They emerged from the valley and stood looking at the barrier ahead of them, just as I had. They were about half a mile away and I could plainly see Bowyer, with his arm around the girl's shoulders, pointing out the route to her. Through the glasses she appeared as if she were now, for the first time, tiring, and her shoulders drooped under the small pack she was carrying. I would have given a lot to have heard what they were saying.

They rested for an hour and then pushed on, two Chinese soldiers leading and breaking trail. The snow appeared only knee-deep along the route they were following, and I wondered if my own estimate had been pessimistic, but once I saw the girl get slightly off-line and immediately she was floundering up to her shoulders until pulled back by Bowyer and the Indian.

They were still in sight when the sun went down—six minute dots that you had to watch for some time before you realized that they were moving. I was really worried now. Plainly they could not possibly hope to reach the unseen pass without at least one more camp. That would mean somewhere on the open plain in a scooped-out hollow. Trailing them in the dark we could easily stumble over them, particularly if Bowyer posted hidden sentries to watch their route behind.

I tried to estimate their distance in front of us as night fell, but it was almost impossible under those conditions. Our camp was above them, which gave us an advantage of sight which I knew would tend to make the gap appear smaller. Timing them I did not think that they were making more than two to two and a half miles in the hour. They were exactly two hours ahead of us as we set out, so to be on the safe side I reckoned it at four miles. Close the gap to less than that and we'd be asking for trouble.

Following their trail in the evening gloom was quite easy, and even after darkness had fallen completely it was not difficult, because although there was no moon, the night was clear and my eyes had by this time adapted themselves. To Tulsa's eyes I believe midnight or high noon was a matter of complete indifference. But this worried me even more, because the trail, trodden flat by six pairs of feet, was comparatively easy going for us, and we were making that much better time.

But we got through that night without trouble, Tulsa slowing the pace considerably and halting me at frequent intervals while he went forward to scout. Then, as dawn was breaking, he led off the track about a dozen yards, the snow coming up to our waists, then to our armpits. Having settled me in a hollow, he went back to the track and returned, smoothing the snow behind him. He grinned and told me to sleep. 'Sun come up proper, we see them,' he said with authority. But my self-respect came to the surface at this point and I insisted on taking first watch. He agreed, but only after building a low snow parapet on the lip of our hollow and scooping a peephole in it through which I could watch up-track.

They surfaced an hour after sun-up, and frightened the devil out of me. How he had judged it to this nicety I have no idea, but there they were—not three hundred yards in front of us. Like us, they had moved off-track a little and burrowed in, and I saw first their heads, then their shoulders, then the rest of them as they floundered in single file back on to higher ground.

Bowyer stood for some minutes carefully studying the route behind them through his glasses, and I felt the hair on the back of my neck prickle as they seemed to rest on our spot for a long moment before sweeping on. But he appeared to be satisfied because I saw him turn and make a thumbs-up sign to the girl before taking a long, searching look up the track ahead of them.

Tulsa was still sleeping and I was scared he would wake and say something or make some movement, so I slid slowly backwards into the hollow, and clamped my hand over his mouth and told him the score in a hoarse whisper—and the little devil didn't even look surprised. He had known where they were all right.

We were stuck here now, because the track was rising once more towards the massif in front and they would have had sight advantage over us as we had over them when the position was reversed the previous day. So there we stayed all day, drowsing in the sun, which, completely out of the piercing wind as we were in the hollow, was surprisingly warm at midday in spite of the snow around us.

We fed twice, then, as the shadows deepened an hour after the sun had gone down behind us, we crawled out back on to the track, Tulsa once more moving in reverse and smoothing the snow behind us, which I thought a bit unnecessary but which I certainly didn't argue about.

So we headed onward towards the pass.

Chapter Sixteen

EVERYTHING WAS CHANGING. First I was conscious of the fact that the wind had dropped, and then that there was no soft snow underfoot—two things that I would have hailed with joy earlier on—but this brought no relief, because the temperature had dropped also. The air now had that dead, killing quality of a refrigerating chamber. The cold was a tangible thing that seemed to work itself into every chink of one's clothing, seeking out crevices and destroying the layers of relative warmth that had been built up during the earlier part of the march. There was no feeling at all in my hands and feet, not even pain—just a nothingness which passed from the physical side of me to the mental, until I found that I could no longer think. All I was conscious of, and that only dimly, was the dark blur of Tulsa ahead of me, and the effort of keeping up with him, and the certainty that if I lost that blur I would just stop—and if I stopped I would die. This was the cold of outer space. This was what the science magazines said one would find on the dark side of the moon.

And then I bumped gently into Tulsa—gently because I was beyond all sensation and was just floating stupidly in this frozen vacuum.

He said, 'Very bad, sahib.' Which did nothing to reassure me.

'How much further?' I croaked.

'Don't know, sahib,' he answered uncertainly. 'Don't come this far before.'

It needed an almost physical effort for me to assimilate

this. 'You told me—about—Chinese troops—river—that goes in and out—a pass round to—the south,' I panted accusingly.

'That what they say,' he told me. 'I not come before.'

I think that if I'd had any reserves left whatsoever I'd have hit him, but thank God I hadn't, so I just whimpered in self-pity. All this for *nothing*. This tower of strength I'd been completely relying on was a broken reed, who had been telling me, in the age-old way of the East, just what he thought I wanted to hear. And now he'd led me right up the creek—literally.

I snuffled, 'All right—let's go back. This way leads nowhere.'

'Others come this way,' he said.

'Don't talk like a bloody fool,' I told him. 'If we can't do it, they couldn't. There's a woman with them, don't forget.'

'They come this way,' he said positively.

'How the hell could you know?' I snarled. 'Don't tell me you can see their tracks in the dark. I don't believe you could before. You were just lucky, that's all. They've turned off somewhere this time, and you've missed them.'

'No snow for tracks,' he said, and I heard him tapping with his foot. 'All ice underneath. But they come this way.'

'I don't believe you,' I said flatly. 'Come on, back we go. You'll get your pay just the same. But don't you try and lead me up the garden path again—you hear?' At least this halt was letting me get my breath back, and with it a burning resentment, against him for making a cock of things, but mostly against myself for allowing it to go this far without question. Making a cock of things was a speciality of mine, but at least in the past I'd kept command, and something which passed for self-respect. On this wretched trip I'd been leaving it to others all the way through—first Rees, now this little bloke who I was rending for it. I took a pull at myself.

'You've done very well, Tulsa,' I said. 'Not your fault. They turn aside somewhere. Come on, we'll go back. Maybe in the morning we'll pick up their trail again.' I had no intention of looking for it, but it sounded better this way.

'Sorry, sahib,' he said miserably, and I felt an utter bastard. I tried to be the bluff and hearty leader and to clap him on the shoulder, but, characteristically, my feet slipped on the ice and I sat on my ass, and it was he who had to help me up again. But that was our break—if you could call it such—because if we had already been turned in the opposite direction we wouldn't have seen the pinpoint of light which showed for an instant high up the pass in front of us. I cursed it, because this time I had really been through.

'They come this way, sahib,' he said happily, all doubts now resolved, and I groaned. I was never to get off the hook—not until I was gaffed, landed and clubbed like a salmon. He started slowly up the slope again and I followed, blindly and dumbly. But that brief halt had done something to restore me. The cold was just as intense and my limbs were as devoid of feeling, but, without the effort of climbing, my lungs had at least been able to struggle for and hold a little of the scanty oxygen in that thin air, and with that my sight improved somewhat.

The walls of the pass were closing in on both sides. They seemed to be smooth and unbroken, like the ice underfoot, and I realized that what we were, in fact, traversing was a channel in the glacier itself—a long twisting gutter in this river of age-old ice which filled the pass. I strained my eyes upward through the darkness for another glimpse of the light, and I saw it twice, and it seemed to waver and dart from side to side as if someone were using an electric torch to see the way—but it was impossible, for me at least, to judge how far ahead of us it was. I hurried forward a few steps and nudged Tulsa in the back and asked him.

'Maybe one mile—little bit more,' he said with an assurance which I hoped was justified. 'That mean they two hours in front.'

'Hadn't we better halt here then?' I asked uncertainly.

'Stop here, die here,' he answered, and *he* wasn't uncertain.

The going was getting worse the whole time. Glacier ice is not like the stuff one skates on; its surface is rough and hummocky, and if the slope is not too steep one can walk on it like concrete, but in patches where the sun can fall on it by day it tends to become polished and it calls for ice-axes, which we hadn't got. Time and time again I fell flat on my face and slid back until it seemed that I was making three paces to the rear for every one forward, but at least Tulsa wasn't doing much better, and the extra effort it called for did something to shake me out of the terrible lethargy of lower down where the going had been easier. And finally we got an ice-axe. Tulsa fell over it in a particularly nasty patch, and I guessed that one of the others had dropped it and hadn't the energy left to slide back after it. He had my entire sympathy.

The ice-axe made things marginally easier, but the clinking it made in that still air worried me. I mentioned it to Tulsa but he said not to worry. 'They out of pass now—on top,' he said with certainty. 'Wind up there go whurr—whurr—whurr. You listen.' And again he was right. When one stopped and the pounding of one's overtaxed heart had time to subside a little, one could hear the snarl and whine of it above us.

We came out of it with the dawn, into the very hell of a blizzard that seemed to blow from every direction at once—into, in fact, the white whirling clouds masking the peaks we had seen from the other side of the valley the evening before.

There was no semblance of a track here. There was nothing but a fury of flying ice particles that cut like razor-blades. I buried my face, ostrich-like, into my parka and wrapped my arms round my head, blinded and deafened, and then I felt a fumbling at my waist. Feeling down, I found that Tulsa had twisted the head of the ice-axe into my belt, and

199

was tugging. I followed blindly, unable to see him even at the distance of that three-foot handle. We were going down hill, and that was all I knew. Sometimes the wind seemed to be against us, pinning us to the rocks against the force of gravity; then it would change and beat downwards until I felt I was about to be picked up and whirled like a leaf into the valley I sensed but couldn't see below us. But always that axe held steady as Tulsa anchored himself and belayed me.

I lost all count of time. I lost all count of everything except the pull of the axe on my belt and a gibbering half prayer I kept repeating that it, and Tulsa, would hold until we got out of this whirling, shrieking hell. And then we were off the rocks, but not out of the wind, for just the moment I had to have to get some air into my lungs. The stuff that was battering us was certainly not air. One could breathe it in, but there was no body or guts to it, and one's lungs were clamouring for something to bite on.

We were in a small transverse gutter just below the bare rocks, a place where some aerodynamic fluke gave one, literally, breathing space—just time for two or three great sobbing gulps, before the wind changed again. And I had, blessedly, no sensation of falling here, so I decided—finally and irrevocably—that this was it for Wainwright. Here I stayed until the wind let up for long enough for me to scuttle back to the ice-cap and down the chute again.

But I had reckoned without that ice-axe. It was pulling at my waist again. I tried to shriek at him that this was the end of the line—we were going back—but I might just as profitably have tried shouting against Niagara. He couldn't even see me, let alone hear me. He just pulled. I tried pulling him back, but it was equally useless. I wasn't belayed on to anything and he had the advantage of the downward position, and he yanked me out of that gutter like a determined Salvationist with a Saturday-night drunk.

We were in snow again now—soft, shifting and whirling in huge eddies, and again there was no sense of direction, except downwards with the pull of that bloody axe. I lost my footing and started to slide, and the snow was sliding with me, and I remember that one clear thought, like the one they say a drowning man experiences, that this was the start of an avalanche, and so *really* the end, not being experienced enough to know that surface movement alone is not the cause of major slides.

I finished in another gutter, a deeper one this time, sloping obliquely downward into a shallow-sided crevasse—and, miraculously, the wind had ceased here at least, although I could still hear it howling above me. The axe was still twisted into my belt, but Tulsa wasn't at the other end of it. Fortunately I saw him before the full realization of it hit me, or I think that would have been the worst moment of the whole thing so far, transcending even the loss of Rees and the others. He burrowed his way out of the snow like a parti-coloured mole, shook himself and grinned, then pointed downward.

'Not bloody likely,' I said with feeling. 'We stay here a while until I really get my breath back.'

But he would have none of it. 'Up there very cold, sahib,' he said earnestly, 'but we still sweat a little bit. Stay here too long, sweat go freeze, then bad trouble.' And since he had been right all along there was no excuse for doubting him now, so with the greatest reluctance I staggered to my feet and joined him. He clucked his approval, like a nursemaid dealing with a spoiled child at last appearing to see reason, and like nursemaid promised rewards in the near future.

'Stop little way down, sahib,' he said. 'Make it breakfast, take it proper rest.'

I tugged out my glasses with frozen fingers and swept the valley below us, but there was nothing to be seen from here because the walls of the crevasse restricted all but a long slope to the east, but what could be seen looked unpromising enough—just snow and rocks, although, far away through the snowblink I thought I could make out the line of a river.

We went on down the slope like children playing giant-steps on a sandhill, and soon we were off the snow and back on to rock, and really out of the wind, so that there was an illusion of warmth. I stopped and looked back up towards the crests. The white wraiths were still swirling and dancing around them.

'How in the name of God did they get over that lot—with a *woman* with them?' I asked myself aloud and in English. And the answer came back aloud and also in English:

'Because we did it in the dark, Mr Wainwright. The turbulence starts at dawn and dies at sunset.'

Bowyer was sitting on a rock just above me.

Chapter Seventeen

'I'D HAVE THOUGHT that you'd have known that,' he went on conversationally. 'You've been pretty with it up to now.'

'Good of you to say so,' I said bitterly. I heard the soft scrunching of snow behind me, and two of the Chinese troops came up and slipped my rucksack off, then my quilted coat, and their questing hands went all over me, frisking me of everything and throwing gun, knife and moneybelt into a little heap in front of Bowyer. Looking sideways, I could see Tulsa getting the same treatment from the third soldier. Only when they stepped back from us and signed that we were now safe did the gun in Bowyer's hand drop.

'Better get your coat on again quickly,' he said. 'You were extremely lucky to get through that lot alive, if I may say so. The locals wouldn't dream of trying that in daylight.' He patted the rock at the side of him. 'Better sit down. You look just about all in. There'll be some tea shortly.'

I moved over to the rock wearily, shrugging myself into my coat, but my fingers were too numbed to do up the fastenings. He leaned forward and did it for me, and that was the final humiliation.

'All right,' I said. 'I've walked into it. Let's get it over— whatever it is.'

'Easier said than done, that,' he answered, and he looked genuinely troubled. 'If I knew more about you I'd probably just leave it to the troops. As it is, I don't know a damned thing about you, except that you've been dogging my heels. Care to elucidate?'

'Name of Wainwright,' I said. 'I like walking. You happened to be going the same way.'

'You're not making it any easier for me, are you?' He looked even more troubled. I had had time to study him by this. Close up, he was older than he had appeared through the glasses. The blondish hair had a lot of white in it. He was wearing a coat of skin-protectant grease on his face—something I hadn't had the sense to think of—and it picked out the deep creases each side of his nose and mouth, and the radiating wrinkles at the corners of his eyes. Like me, he had let his beard grow, and this increased the impression of age. His eyes were blue and direct. I've met Eurasians as fair as Swedes, but I've always been able to pick them as such. It's something about the bone formation; it's more finely chiselled than that of the pure European. But this man, whatever his papers might have stated to the contrary, was as English as warm beer and kippers. His voice was that of the normally educated middle class. We might have been discussing Arsenal's chances for the Cup in the saloon bar of a West End pub. A serious matter, even a worrying one—but certainly not cataclysmic.

'You've been very decent—on two occasions,' he went on. 'And that makes it rather more awkward for me.'

'Sorry about that,' I said, and tried to inject a little subtle irony into it. 'But what are you referring to?'

'Knocking off those Kampas for one thing, being civil to my memsahib in Rangoon for the other.'

'Both a duty—one a pleasure,' I answered. The 'memsahib' did nothing to place him. It's a term Englishmen use jocularly for their wives and sometimes their mistresses—Englishmen who have served in India and those who have never been further East than Tower Bridge, equally.

'Very kind of you,' he answered, as if I'd just picked up his umbrella for him. 'I must apologize for shooting at you on that occasion. I thought you were another of them at the time.'

'Think nothing of it,' I said, still trying to be subtly ironic, but sounding very hollowly facetious in my own ears. I was beginning to freeze. Then I saw one of the Chinese kick Tulsa in the ribs as he squatted in the snow. Tulsa rolled over and grinned up at the soldier—but it was a Gurkha grin that could have meant anything from polite acknowledgement to murderous intent. 'Would you mind asking that goon not to kick my chap?' I asked. 'He's just a paid employee—and rather a good one.'

'By all means,' he said, and cut loose with a magnificent spate of pure Hakka to the effect that if the son of a leprous body-louse did that again, he'd take his burp-gun from him and give the Gurkha his kukri back. The soldier scowled and spat, and his two pals giggled. That was loss of face, and I wondered without much hope whether I might have a chance of turning it to my advantage later—if there was to be a 'later'. I also wondered who had been kidding who, because Bhup Nath had said that Bowyer didn't speak Chinese.

But this was made clear by Bowyer himself, because he said, 'Blast! That's the first time I've used Chinese this trip. I learn a lot more by playing it dumb.'

He rose and stretched. 'Well, how about some tea and tsampa? I think my memsahib will have got it ready by now.' He preceded me through the soft snow round a bend in the crevasse wall—the bend that had led me into this in the first place, because it was snow-covered and had merged into the background so that I had not picked it up as a possible ambush spot through the glasses before we moved down the hill. It was a feeble bit of self-exculpation that gave me little comfort. Glancing back, I saw the Chinese motioning Tulsa to move forward with us, and I heard their burp-guns being unnecessarily uncocked and cocked again hintfully, but there was no more kicking.

She had her back to us, crouching over a spirit-lamp, and she looked round over her shoulder as Bowyer coughed politely. She was wearing grease too, but somehow it was not unbecoming. She looked tired, but the wonder to me was that she had got this far anyhow. At this moment she'd have been the highest madam in the world, unless someone had established a bordello on top of Everest.

'Mr Wainwright, my dear,' said Bowyer, sounding rather like a bishop ushering a visiting curate into the drawing-room. 'You've met before.'

She smiled and said, 'Find yourself a block of ice and sit down, Mr Wainwright. This is just ready. I'm afraid tea and tsampa is all we have.'

'I have a couple of cans of self-heating soup and some other odds and ends in my pack—even some coffee and sugar,' I answered. Bowyer chuckled a polite, 'Wouldn't dream of robbing you, my dear fellow,' but I saw the quick flash of sheer mouth-watering anticipation in her eyes.

'Robbing nothing,' I said. 'There's plenty there.' I turned and made back through the snow to where our packs still lay. They had searched us, but not the packs—and the rifle was in the one Tulsa had been carrying. I had it all doped out. I would sink down on my heels over it with my back towards them. I'd feign a little difficulty with the fastenings, and under cover of it get the two parts of the rifle together, and stuff a clip into the magazine. The soldier whom Bowyer had reprimanded was sulking by himself a few yards apart from the others, his burp-gun in the crook of his arm. I'd drop him first. The other two were squatting at a respectful distance from the spirit-lamp, licking their lips and swallowing their spit. Their guns were now slung across their backs, their two hands holding their wooden chow bowls in front of them. They would be easy while they struggled to get their guns round in front of them. Only Bowyer worried me. Bowyer and the girl, because she had a pistol too. Which first? If only I could rely on Tulsa taking his cue on the first shot and diving for Bowyer while I covered the girl——

206

But it was all to no avail. Bowyer barked an order at the nearest Chinese and he straightened and ploughed through the snow past me, picked up both packs and headed back to the camp. The sulky one, warned I think by a glance from Bowyer, now had his gun at the ready. Bowyer gestured politely to me to get what I required from the packs. I concentrated on my own, but the Chinese, unencumbered by Bowyer's nice manners, had now opened the other, and the rifle was discovered. If Bowyer suspected my intentions, he did not show it. He merely said: 'A Rigby? Beautiful weapon. I'll get one of my men to clean and re-oil it. This snow plays the devil with fine steel.' And that was it.

I handed the cans of soup and the coffee over to the girl, and she thanked me fulsomely but guiltily, as if she were a hostess and I a guest who had turned up with a contribution of caviar. As we gulped our tea and tsampa she heated the rest of the stuff, and then made coffee. It only amounted to a mouthful or so each, but she shared it scrupulously between us —including the Chinese in the bounty.

'Manna from heaven—ambrosia in the desert,' said Bowyer when we had finished and cleaned our bowls in the snow. 'But I'm afraid we are no nearer the solution of our problem.' He fished inside his quilted coat and produced some native cigarettes which he handed round to us.

'What *is* the problem?' I asked.

'You, my dear chap, obviously.'

'Why do I constitute a problem?'

He showed his first sign of impatience. 'You're either very obtuse or very naïve, Mr Wainwright,' he snapped. 'Of course you're a problem, and you very well know it. If I take you on with us you're due for an extremely unpleasant time—before dying. I don't know how much you know—but whatever it is, you'll tell it. Have no doubts on that score.'

'All right,' I said. 'So you're a good feller, and you don't take me forward—what then?'

'There's always the chance that you'll make it back to whoever sent you—and that, in turn, could make things awkward for me.'

I looked sideways at the girl. She was cleaning and repacking her few simple utensils and appeared unaware of what we were saying. The Chinese were squatting in a row, burping ruminatively over what to them had no doubt been a hell of a banquet. Tulsa leaned back against a rock looking up at the grey sky, his eyes closed.

'Nothing that I could tell about you is likely to make things awkward for you?' I said, and he laughed shortly.

'My whereabouts,' he said. 'That's all you were sent to find out, wasn't it?'

'Just confirmation, that's all,' I bluffed. 'Your general whereabouts are already known.'

'Only as far as Chamdo with any certainty,' he said. 'You have—*had*—an undercover radio link there. That's sprung, I'm afraid, Wainwright—and Rees was arrested there the day before yesterday.'

And that, oddly enough, held some slight grain of comfort for me. It's always an advantage to know when an opponent is lying. It helps in pitching one's own line in lies.

'Radio I wouldn't be knowing about,' I said. 'As for Rees being pinched, well, that's hard luck—for Rees—but it doesn't concern me.'

'You were on the same mission—travelling together,' he said accusingly.

'Travelling together certainly,' I agreed. 'That was for mutual convenience. He knows the ropes far better than I— and we split the not inconsiderable expenses. But he was up here on his own business, Mr Bowyer.'

'We're wasting each other's time,' he said angrily.

'Well, apparently *I've* got plenty of it—or not, according to what you intend doing with me,' I said. 'Suppose you come to the point.'

208

'That's damned impertinence,' he snapped. 'You don't seem to realize your position, Mr Wainwright.'

'Only too clearly,' I said. 'Yes, I've been following you. It would be useless to deny that—and I've been unpardonably clumsy and I've walked right into it, for which, if I ever do make it back, I'll undoubtedly be fired——'

'Fired by whom?' he shot at me quickly.

'My employers,' I answered sweetly.

'Wasting time again,' he growled. 'All right, then: there *is* a point, and I'll come to it. I'll offer you the nearest approach to a deal that I can go, and still remain persona grata with *my* employers.'

'Now we're talking,' I said. 'You open.'

'Who sent you—and why? Tell me that, truthfully, and I'll let you go back up that track.'

I'd been preparing for this. 'The International Monetary Fund,' I told him. 'We think you're ready to run gold into India, Mr Bowyer. Lots of gold—enough to make people in Basle, Zürich, London and New York very worried indeed.'

'What the hell would I be doing up here in these ghastly hills if that were my intention?' he demanded. 'Illicit gold only travels one road——'

'Hong Kong to Calcutta—ingots stuck under the deck of the freight compartment—pretty air stewardesses carry it in their girdles. Small stuff, Mr Bowyer—and with the new electronic detectors they've got, they're finding one shipment in three. Soon it will be one in two—then the lot.'

He raised his eyebrows. 'You surprise me,' he said.

'I don't think I do,' I told him. 'This is old stuff. It was old before you—er——'

'Were framed and put away—probably by your employers,' he interrupted. 'Go ahead—I'm not sensitive.'

'Thank you,' I said. 'Yes, it was old then. It was known— or to be strictly fair, suspected, that you were in process of organizing a regular route out of China into India—a route over which you could send it, not in ounces, but in tons, by the yak load. Gold that costs the People's Republic nothing in the first place, because they just take it from those who had it, and then sold for hard Western currency in the one place in the world where it sells for exactly double the International rate. Nice business for Chairman Mao, but absolute hell for the money market.'

'All right.' He nodded. 'So let's suppose that I was in the business, or was preparing to go into the business, before my untimely though temporary retirement. What the devil could I be doing now? What use would I be to anybody? Others would have taken up the "flick'ring torch that dropt from my nerveless fingers"—Newman.'

'We'd have been delighted to think so,' I said. 'Actually our information has been that you were kept fully in the picture, and in fact dictated a lot of the policy from jail, Mr Bowyer.'

'How could I possibly have done that?' he snorted.

'In England we'd have said by means of a bent screw,' I told him, and went on to explain. 'That's a corrupt warder or a——'

'You don't have to tell me that.' He grinned. 'You're talking to an expert. Yes, certainly I used bent screws—for such things as tobacco, whisky and getting uncensored mail in and out. But to run a project as big as the one you're suggesting—well, that's a bit of a tall order, isn't it?'

'It's been known,' I said knowledgeably. 'Putting a big boy away doesn't mean to say you're putting him out of business.'

He was silent for quite a time. I re-lit the butt of my cigarette and tried not to look anxious. But I *was* anxious— by God I was! If he took me on with him under guard the prospect would be very bleak indeed. I doubted whether they would have grade one interrogation centres up here in the hills; I'd probably therefore be sent down into the Chinese provinces proper—Kwangsi, and then on to Kwangtung—Canton. I shivered at the very thought of this. I'd undoubtedly be on *somebody's* files down there. There would be plenty ready to finger me for what I had done in the past—and hadn't done—and to testify at what passed with them for a trial—assuming anything was left of me after intensive interrogation. And this pathetic furbler I was putting up to Bowyer wouldn't do me the damnedest bit of good. They'd know bloody well who I worked for—and that it wasn't the International Monetary Fund. I stole a sideways glance at him, and past him at the girl. She had got everything packed now and was looking at him questioningly. He was nodding slowly to himself, as if weighing what we had been talking about, evaluating it and on the whole agreeing with it.

'I see,' he said slowly. 'Um—I wondered just who you were working for, Mr Wainwright. I don't wish to be offensive in any way, but I'd never heard of you before, and I know most, or know *of* most of the under-cover people in India. Um—it figures, as the Americans would say. But Rees —he's the wild joker. Now where would he fit into it, I wonder? Oh, of course, he's been around a very long time —too long, some say. Works for whoever pays him, but is as reasonably honest as anyone could be in his line of business. Who's paying him now, that's the question?'

Quite a question, I thought wryly. Quite an epitaph too. But I could see that he was fishing for an answer, so I made him work for this one. They value them more that way.

'I'm sorry,' I said. 'I couldn't discuss that—even if I knew. I've come clean with you, Mr Bowyer, as far as I myself am concerned—in fact, I've blown my whole assignment to you —purely because I've no wish to land in the hands of the Chinese. I'm fairly new in the business, as you have probably guessed, but I know what I could expect there.'

'You don't know,' he said with conviction. 'You don't know until it's actually happening to you—and then you can hardly believe it. They do some terrible things when they think you know something and you're holding out on them.'

I shivered again, and I wasn't putting on an act either.

'Don't let's talk about it,' I begged.

'I quite agree. Horrible—horrible. But to come back to Rees——'

'I'd rather not,' I said. 'I've come out of this pretty cravenly already. I don't want to blow him too—even if I could——'

'I'm sorry,' he insisted, 'but I'll have to make that part of the bargain——'

'You can't do that,' I squawked indignantly. 'We had a deal. I've kept my part of it.'

'Rees comes into it. You were working together—therefore, *ipso facto*, he was employed by the International Monetary Fund also.' He was staring at me intently. 'Come on, you've told me so much already—admit it.'

But for some reason I suspected a trap. Somehow he knew something about Rees—and any definite admission by me would bounce. Of that I felt certain. I hedged further.

'What the hell does it matter, anyhow?' I asked him. 'You say he's been arrested, so he's out of it. He'll have told all he knows by this time.'

'I was merely testing you when I said that,' he told me calmly. 'We both know he wasn't arrested. Now come on, Wainwright, we're wasting time. I've got to get on—and whether you come with me or go back over that pass is entirely dependent on your answer to these two questions. I know, or think I know, the answer to one of them—but I want confirmation. A. Who employed Rees on this in the first instance? B. Where is he now?'

The girl had moved out of the crevasse and was some distance away, stamping her feet in the snow in an effort to keep the circulation going, so I played this one angrily and nobly.

'Get stuffed, you bastard,' I said. 'I thought I was dealing

212

with a gentleman. We made a bargain, and you're ratting on yours.'

'There's no time for schoolboy heroics,' he answered coldly. 'Tell me that and you can go. Refuse to tell me—or worse, invent something that I can contradict with certainty, and you come with us. As simple as that, Wainwright.'

I thought for a moment of telling the truth, at least about Rees's present whereabouts—under five hundred feet of snow, glacier ice and pulverized rock—because I thought that this was his test question, that he knew of the avalanche. But then, like the small boy who keeps the threat of his big brother as an ace up his sleeve, a fresh idea came to me. No, Rees had to stay alive.

'Come on, Wainwright,' he prompted. 'The time's running out.'

'Chatterjee actually briefed him,' I mumbled.

He looked puzzled for a moment. 'Chatterjee? You might as well say Smith of London. Which Chatterjee?'

'The detective assigned to watch you when you came out of Alipore,' I told him. 'You gave him the slip and dodged into the Majestic on Chowringhee.'

He smiled. 'Do you know—I think we're somewhere in the same parish as the truth. That could well be.'

'I wish I'd let those Kampas get you, you son-of-a-bitch,' I said waspishly.

'I'm sure you do, now,' he agreed. 'All right: to come back to the question then. Who was Rees working for? Yes, yes, yes—it's quite likely that his brief came through Chatterjee—but who was his real controller?'

'How the hell do I know?' I snarled. 'Rees wasn't the sort to scatter information of that sort——'

'No, but since you were working together——'

'Only in so far as our objective was the same. We both wanted to know where you were going and what your contacts were en route—that and nothing more. We certainly

213

weren't exchanging girlish confidences about our respective bosses.'

'Who's *your* boss, incidentally?'

'A bloke with only one head. Keeps a barber's shop in Marseille. That's no part of the deal. Play the white man, Bowyer, I'm getting cold.'

'Finally—where is Rees now?'

'I don't know. We parted company after we crossed from Burma.'

'Why? That seems a peculiar sort of thing to do in terrain where each could help the other.'

'Because we each had our own ideas. He wanted to get ahead of you each day, and that meant a night march. It seemed crazy to me. I preferred to trail you.'

'I see. As it turned out Rees was right. If you'd been in front this morning you wouldn't have blundered into us, would you?'

That one didn't even call for an answer. He stood up, and I stood up with him. I wondered for a moment whether he was going to offer to shake hands, and hoped that he wouldn't. There's something melodramatic about refusing a man's hand, even when you don't like him. But I needn't have worried.

He called out. 'Right—coming, my dear—all of us. We'll have to see if our Oriental friends can get the truth out of this dedicated liar.'

Chapter Eighteen

HE CALLED OUT a swift series of orders to the Chinese, who then hustled me out on to the track, pushing Tulsa after me, but placing us so that there was one of them between us. And the sixth member of the party slid down the crevasse wall—I'd been wondering about him. He was manhandling a small but seemingly heavy radio-set and complaining in Urdu that we were blanketed by the hill behind us, and that in any case his batteries were almost flat. So the bastard had been in touch with someone the whole time—and I'd been trying to bluff with cards that he knew. Or did he? Would he have gone through this elaborate interrogation if he already had the answers?

The girl had kept some of the food and tea for the other man. She handed it to him, and he squatted with his back towards us while he gulped it down. Hindus don't like people watching them eat. Bowyer cursed and rumbled impatiently. The careful politeness was slipping now, which increased my doubts about how much he really knew about us. The Indian finished his food and belched in appreciation, as good manners dictate, and we set out—Bowyer leading, then a soldier, then the girl followed by Tulsa, the Indian, grunting under the weight of his set, myself, and two soldiers bringing up the rear. Tulsa turned and looked a question at me, and I shook my head. I didn't know what the question was, but I was feeling in a distinctly negative mood at the moment.

Bowyer said, with cold dislike, 'Don't do anything foolish, Wainwright. It wouldn't avail you anything—although I don't think the warning is really necessary. I wouldn't put you down as the heroic type.' That stung. I thought I caught a sympathetic glance from the girl. That stung worse.

But I had every intention of trying something foolish that night. He'd have to sleep some time—and the Chinese troops struck me as distinctly second water, so that with luck they could be relied upon to sleep on guard. There was always the possibility that they'd tie us up, of course, but I was praying against this. Blocked circulation in these temperatures could easily result in the loss of a limb or two. If I could steal away back down the track, even for just a matter of a mile or so, I could hide somewhere. I was pretty certain that the search they'd make for us wouldn't be too rigorous—they were as tired as we were. I was thinking in terms of 'us' because the idea of making a break without Tulsa was unthinkable. I wondered if he had the same thought. Perhaps that was what he was trying to get over to me.

We trudged on and up as I mulled over this. We were carrying our own packs. There was a little food left in each even after my lavish gesture at the halt. We'd have to secure those, of course—even pinch some of theirs if the opportunity offered. I was banking heavily on the heavy, drugged sleep of sheer exhaustion that hits trekkers in the high places when they halt at night. I'd have to be on guard against that myself.

I think that it was only this planning that kept me from going completely nuts during that march, for now the sheer ineptitude of what I had done was hitting me for the first time. I had just gone blundering on without properly reconnoitring the track ahead. Rees would never have done that. Looking back, I was amazed that Tulsa had let me do it. I could only suppose that he was confused and dazed after the battering we had had in the dawn wind—in which case, I grudgingly conceded, there was some slight excuse for me. I even started to justify myself. It was that bloody wind that was to blame. Apart from that I hadn't done so badly. Anyhow, I was still alive—and Rees wasn't. Given something that remotely resembled a break and we'd be away tonight —*and* we'd get back—*and* I'd show the bastards on the map how far Bowyer had gone. What bloody good it would do them I wouldn't be knowing—but I'd done my whack, or as much as was humanly possible of it—*and* in these mountains. Good God Almighty! I'd never been higher before under my own steam than the top of Hong Kong Peak. Pretty good show if you ask me—and bugger whatever the Gaffer might have to say about it afterwards. I was really giving my morale a build-up. I wasn't going to be a chopping-block for any flat-faced interrogator. This time tomorrow we'd be going in the opposite direction like bats out of hell.

And then the whole edifice collapsed.

I think it was Tulsa who saw it first, and he turned and signalled to me, stopping an angry poke in the back from the Indian—but I had seen it myself by this time.

High above us on the crest of the range we were climbing, a light was winking against the sky—just a pinpoint that flickered in a series of dots and dashes that might have been Morse, but which I couldn't follow at first—then it stopped, and repeated.

Bowyer was yelling angrily at the Indian in Urdu. 'Get on to it, you fool! Read it!' And the Indian was complaining bitterly in baby's English, 'Heliograph, sahib! Old-fashioned! I am not being taught these things at Calcutta Marconi School.'

I got it on the second transmission: Dot-dot-dot-dot—dot-dash—dot-dash-dot-dot—dash, and I decided to be helpful since it might mean shortening the journey back.

'They're signalling "Halt",' I told him. 'And now they're telling you to acknowledge.'

'In English?' he said suspiciously.

'Chinese and Japanese always Morse in English,' I said—

being superior as well as helpful. 'You can't send bloody ideographs over the air.'

He grunted, then yelled at the Indian again, 'All right, acknowledge it—don't just stand there gaping.'

'Acknowledge with what?' wailed the Indian. 'Bloody batteries finish on wireless, and not have got heliograph. What to do?'

'You'd better do *something*,' I told him. 'They're saying now that they'll open fire if you don't.' And that was the poor sod's death warrant, although I didn't mean it as such. He went a pale green, dumped his set, turned and took to his heels downhill—and the Chinese who had been ticked off unslung his burp-gun and let him have a short burst in the back, then looked round at us all for approval, like a gundog that has been really smart. The girl shrieked her horror and ran clumsily through the snow to where the Indian was spreadeagled in a bloody mess, but there was nothing she or anybody else could do for him now. She came back, sobbing quietly, and buried her face in Bowyer's chest. Even madams have their softer spots, apparently.

And then there was a faint coughing boom from the direction of the crest, and I started instinctively to count as I threw myself flat. I got to four before the shell burst—far to the right and well over us, but not so far off that any reasonable gunner couldn't correct for it in his next shot—and we were on a completely open slope here with not a vestige of cover. The others were now lying flat also. It was probably nothing heavier than a two-pounder, but it would be more than sufficient to do the lot of us if the next one landed within ten yards.

I called to Bowyer, 'Have you got a shaving-mirror or something?' but he didn't appear to hear me. He was cursing and yelling, 'Damn them! They know bloody well who we are. I've talked to the bastards on the air. They're *expecting* us.'

And then there was another boom, and just at that moment the girl got up and ran towards me, fumbling inside her quilted coat. 'I've got a mirror,' she began. 'Only a small one——'

I grabbed her and pulled her down beside me, pressing her into the snow. This one was much closer and it dazed and deafened us, but looking round I couldn't see that anybody was obviously hit, although, by the normal rules of bracketing, the next one would be *it*. I grabbed the mirror from her. It was only a small vanity-case thing but it was that or nothing. I lined it roughly on where I judged their signal to have come from, twisted it until I thought I had it more or less slanted towards the weak sun, and masked it with my hand and hoped for the best.

'A-C-K,' I flashed frantically, and kept on repeating. And apparently they saw it, because there was no more shooting, but the light started flashing again.

'Interrogative numeral eight,' I read, and translated to Bowyer. 'They're asking you why there's eight of us.'

'You can tell 'em that there's only seven now,' he said grimly, 'and two of those are prisoners. Explain later.' Which I thought was in pretty poor taste, but I sent it nevertheless, since it seemed that or be shot up again. They told us to advance then. I just sat on my ass and the gent who had rubbed the Indian out started to kick me in the ribs. He had his gun on full-cock and was looking really anxious for more applause.

I said, 'Fair shakes, Bowyer. I've pulled your chestnuts out of the fire twice now. Are you going to hand me over to those bastards up there? What have I ever done to you?'

'Get on your feet and start walking, Wainwright,' he answered. 'Or that particular bastard will drop you right where you sit. If you had an ounce of perception you'd realize that I'm as much a prisoner of these gorillas as you are. You saw what he did to Bapu—without any order from me.'

The girl said, with a sudden hiss of indrawn breath, 'No, no, you can't——' but he ignored her and went on.

'Believe it or not, but if we'd made another camp tonight before getting to where we're going, I'd have turned a blind eye in a hope that you'd get the hell out of it—and I'd have blamed these goons for it. But it's too late now. They've counted heads up there—and they'll want that number of heads on arrival—in one form or another. Look for yourself.' He pointed.

I did, and nearly vomited. One of the other Chinese had just finished decapitating the corpse of the Indian, and was playfully flicking the head at his pal. The gent who was covering me was giggling like a schoolgirl. Bowyer swore suddenly and lunged past me in time to catch the girl before she slumped. She recovered quickly, but I could see that under her tan and the face-grease she was white to the lips. I don't suppose she would ever have been called upon to witness anything quite as horrible as this before, but somehow I would have thought that in her line of business she would have been tougher.

They were flashing again now. 'What are they saying?' Bowyer asked wearily.

'Expedite movement,' I spelt out.

'We'd better expedite, then,' he said, and gave the signal to march. He walked on ahead with his arm round the girl protectively. The Chinese, within spitting distance of what they regarded no doubt as home, were full of fun, lumbering like puppies behind us and tossing that ghastly head from one to another like a football. I wondered if I could make use of this relaxation of guard, but I knew it was hopeless. There was no cover here at all, and they could have dropped us the moment we stepped out of line, puppy-dog gambolling notwithstanding.

It did, however, give me the opportunity to walk beside Tulsa, who had now been burdened with the radio set.

He was seething with anger—not out of sympathy with the Indian's demise—that, in his simple lexicon, was just another of these things—but because the *bandoowala*, which is their very rude term for the Chinese, had had the infernal impudence to use *his* sacred kukri to do it with, and very clumsily at that.

'I get it back, sahib,' he swore. 'Then *his* bloody head come off *ek dum*—one snick-click—tsss!'

I wished him every success, but didn't hope a lot.

We got up to the guardpost after an hour's fairly hard going, although the distance in a straight line down the slope could only have been a mile or so. Just before we arrived there, Bowyer turned and said over his shoulder, 'I'll do what I can for you, Wainwright. Stick to the gold story you told me—detail for detail. We both know it's bullshit, but at least it's feasible bullshit. They might even try to use you. It has been known.'

And you can say *that* again, I thought wryly.

The post was an expertly done job—white concrete built into a natural feature of the rock, and faced, igloo-fashion, with properly cut snow-blocks. Long before we got up to it I thought I could hear the faint whirring of electric bells, and then I realized that we ourselves were the cause, because the path was criss-crossed with trip-wires.

We filed in past white-overalled sentries and found ourselves in a large caserne that ran back into a natural cave. There were four gun emplacements—two looking down the trail we had come up, and two the other way, and I saw the breeches of four Czech 25 mm. Bringens. The term 'two resolute men could have held this pass against an army' probably died with Napoleon, but I thought it could have been revived here with some justification. No attacker could have brought mobile artillery up here without their knowing it, and it would have taken very expert pinpoint bombing indeed to winkle them out from the air, because they were both hidden and protected by the overhanging loom of the cliff above them.

The caserne was reasonably clean, though it stank of sour rice, dried fish and too infrequently washed bodies, not to mention the all-pervading stench of faeces one always gets when Chinese peasantry are herded together, even in these enlightened days of Chairman Mao. It accommodated, I should have said, about a half-company, which with them is a hundred men, and was commanded by a lieutenant whom I didn't take to at all. He was a young man with a pock-pitted face and a disconcerting squint, which caused him to look past one when no doubt he was under the impression that he was fixing one with a steely glare. He disregarded us and walked up to the three soldiers, whom he booted in the shins by way of a welcome home. Even that didn't endear him to me. The sulky one timidly proffered the head to him, no doubt as a peace offering. The lieutenant took it by the hair and belted the donor in the face with it, then threw it out into the snow. Having thus established just who was who in this outfit, he turned his attention to us. I had decided to play this one dumb, and to pretend to no knowledge of Chinese, whatever the consequences might be. I was relieved when he passed me with hardly a glance and confronted Bowyer, who was trying to block the girl's view of the un-pleasantness that had just occurred.

He barked in Cantonese, 'Why have you departed from instructions?'

'I haven't,' Bowyer barked back. 'I was told to come. I came.'

'Why the woman?'

'She is my wife. If I had left her behind they would have arrested her.'

'There have been no whores in China since the Cultural Revolution. It is against the wishes of the Chairman to import more.' Which was closer to the knuckle than even he

222

thought. I glanced quickly at the girl, but quite obviously she didn't understand, though I thought for a moment that Bowyer was going to lose his grip and hit him, and hunched myself for the consequences that would have followed for us all. But fortunately Bowyer just took a deep breath and got a bit pinched round the nostrils.

'We have come a long way,' he said. 'We require food and rest.'

'There are questions first. Who are these others?'

'Two who followed. The Englishman is an expert in gold currency.'

'Why were they not dealt with further down?'

'Because I only discovered them today. Ask your soldiers.'

'I am asking you. Answer.'

And then Bowyer showed his knowledge of the Chinese—or more particularly the Cantonese. It's like judo—there is a point in any altercation, if you can recognize it, where you can turn the heat back on the aggressor. But you really *have* to be able to recognize it, and then be bloody quick. This, Bowyer obviously decided, was that point. He didn't make the cardinal error of yelling and thereby causing this little jerk to lose face before his men. He just leaned forward and said between set teeth, 'I said an expert in gold currency—and I think a dishonest one. He could therefore be of use to you-know-who. If I am wrong in this, then you-know-who can deal with him—as he can deal with *you* if I have to endure more of this indignity. Cease now, small flier of even smaller kites, and give instructions for food and a place to rest that doesn't stink too vilely. I am weary.'

For a moment it seemed balanced on a razor's edge. 'A flier of small kites' is untranslatable into any Western language, but in Chinese it has sexual connotations of a peculiarly humiliating nature. I've heard it said that Chinese don't go red in the face when embarrassed. It's not true. This fellow went crimson-puce, and changed the subject quickly.

'Why did you kill the radio mechanic you were told to bring from India?' he mumbled. 'He is badly needed here.'

'I didn't kill him,' Bowyer snapped. 'That pig-dung did—without orders.' He pointed to the sulky one.

This gave the lieutenant a heaven-sent opportunity to get back on his perch. He strode across to the three troops who were standing to a travesty of attention, kicked the sulky one again and placed him under arrest. Then he yelled to someone in the gloom of the cave behind us, where the off-duty troops were crouching round a minuscule fire, and told him to get food for us and to clear out one of the disused ammunition magazines. Then, thank God, he stalked away.

A soldier came up and motioned to us to follow him.

'Did you get any of that?' Bowyer asked me.

'I'm afraid not,' I lied solemnly.

'A little shit—but a dangerous one. Lieutenant practising hard for full General. I've met him before—when he was a sergeant.'

'I saw him looking at me sideways,' I said.

'The cock-eyed bastard always looks sideways,' growled Bowyer. 'I've told him that you're a gold expert, and a crook, and as such you may be useful to somebody.'

'Somebody like who?' I asked.

'Don't push it, Wainwright,' he said. 'I still don't know who you're working for. Not that I think you'll get out of here with anything. I'm just letting you know that I haven't put any knocks in against you—and that I'm doing my best for you—such as it is.'

'Much obliged,' I said drily.

We arrived at a small concrete emplacement which had empty ammunition racks round it. The soldier went in and lit a smoky oil-lamp, then left us. It was deathly cold—worse than outside, because here there was a chilling dampness with it also. I noticed the girl then. She appeared hardly conscious, and Bowyer had opened his quilted coat and was trying to snuggle her inside it, and the hand that was holding her was patting her, like someone gentling a child. They were an oddly assorted pair, but there was obviously a deep bond of affection between them. I pushed a couple of ammunition boxes up against the wall, and it was only then that I realized that we were all still humping our packs.

I said, 'Better get our sleeping-bags and blankets out and make some sort of cover for the lady, or she'll freeze. Thank the Lord we've got a spot of food left, Tulsa and I, but there's no way of heating it.'

'They're getting us some,' Bowyer told me. 'But thanks all the same. Edna has held up very well until now, bless her, but seeing poor old Bapu get the chop—well, enough to upset any girl. Come on, lovely.' He guided her to the boxes.

Edna? I thought. It was Paola last time we met. Then I remembered Rees saying that the more exotic one was probably assumed for business purposes. Edna didn't suit her either.

The soldier came back with a pan of some godawful sludge of rice, millet and dried fish, but it was at least filling, and Bowyer, Tulsa and I shovelled it down without criticism, but the girl had difficulty in swallowing in spite of Bowyer's gentle coaxing. She was very obviously in a state of shock.

Bowyer said savagely, 'I'm going to twist that little get's tail for him, properly this time. If we don't get some warmth in here she'll be really sick.'

He strode to the steel door, but someone had closed it and fastened it the other side. He kicked and pounded on it and after a moment or so it was opened and the soldier looked in. Bowyer tore strips off him and demanded to be taken to the officer. The soldier wouldn't do that, but he went away and came back after a time with another one, carrying a charcoal brazier between them on two iron bars. It threw out a magnificent heat, but it worried me. Charcoal can be tricky stuff in a confined space. I mentioned this to Bowyer and he told the troops to leave the door open, and got a flat refusal, so the steel claw came out of the velvet glove again, fast. He kicked them both in the shins, which seemed in this army to be the normal means of securing instant discipline, and wedged an ammunition box in the doorway. That prevented its being shut completely and gave us some ventilation.

We pulled the girl's boots off and Bowyer loosened her clothing, then we chafed her hands and feet and got her bedded down, and finally she went off into a deep sleep, and it was not long before the philosophical Tulsa followed suit, leaving Bowyer and me sitting and smoking, each with his own thoughts.

He broke a long silence. 'I wish to Christ I could trust you, Wainwright,' he said. 'And even more—I wish you could trust me. We're in a jam—a bloody nasty one.'

'If trusting each other is going to get us out of it, suppose we start,' I answered. 'You open.'

'You know about me.'

'Very little, actually. You came out of jail and came up here to meet somebody, and it appears to have got unstuck somewhere. My orders were merely to see where the place was—and if possible who the other party was.'

He snorted. 'Are you trying to kid me that that's all the briefing you got?'

'More or less.'

'Nothing about my background?'

'Very little. I know you got done for gold-smuggling.'

'I was framed.'

I made a noise that was meant to sound non-committal and he said angrily, 'I tell you I was—and if you're working for whom I think you are, you know that's the truth.'

'All right, then,' I said. 'Who do you think I'm working for?'

'That bastard Barry.'

'Who's Barry?'

'Oh, well.' He sighed resignedly. 'If we're going to play silly buggers with each other we may as well drop it and get some sleep.'

But this was interesting. Very interesting indeed. Next to the Gaffer, I thought Barry was just about the best covered of the upper brass that we were fielding.

'No—go ahead,' I said. 'Just think aloud for a bit. I'll do the same. Maybe we'll finish up holding hands and telling all. For my part, all I want is out. If I thought that tipping a little bit of my hand would help, I'd do just that. So—again—who's Barry?'

'Fellow in Hong Kong,' he answered. 'Runs the British Far Eastern Bureau. Everybody knows that. What I'm interested in knowing, though, is whether you're just working for him—or for his boss, Kowalski.'

Chapter Nineteen

IT WOULD SIMPLIFY matters enormously in this racket if one could accept statements like that at face value—but unfortunately one can't. Spying and whoring, two methods of earning one's coffee and sinkers which have much in common, are neurotic businesses distinguished by a high content of bitchiness, particularly in the lower strata. We delight in taking each other's characters away—like schoolboys accusing their masters of secret drinking and queerness. It's the only redress against authority we've got. I'd have loved to have accepted this one against Barry without question. It would have explained everything—or nearly everything. Barry and Kowalski in cahoots. Kowalski ready to come in from the cold, but Barry deciding that he was hot enough already. I'm detailed for the pick-up. The tip goes across to the Comrades. Kowalski is liquidated, and Kam Foo and I get out of it—just—with singed asses—and the suspicion rests on Wainwright, the notorious bungler. It fitted perfectly. Hadn't that thought occurred to me at the time?

Bowyer was watching me quizzically. 'Not so far off the beam, am I? Just a matter of which one is controlling *you*. I'll have to insist on that.' But I had to test it.

'What difference would it make?' I asked. 'I'm not saying it's either—but you just pick which one you'd prefer, and carry on.'

He shook his head decisively. 'No good,' he said. 'There's always the chance that one, or even both of us, might make it back—and I'm not risking handing Kowalski everything he's ever wanted on a plate. I'd see all our heads on poles before I'd let that happen.'

'Including hers?' I said, nodding towards the sleeping Edna.

'If necessary,' he said solemnly.

'You're a liar,' I told him. 'If it comes to that, so am I— but I can still recognize the truth on occasion. You wouldn't willingly see anything happen to her. All right, if it will make you any happier, I'm working for Barry. I couldn't be working for Kowalski.'

'Why not?'

'He's dead.'

'I wish I could be absolutely certain of that,' he said. 'I'd come clean then—cards on the table, face up.'

It was a moment for Napoleonic decisions. I took a deep breath and shot the lot. 'He died on the night of April 14th last,' I told him. 'I may have killed him myself—there was enough stuff flying around—theirs and ours.'

'A pick-up job that went sour—up the Canton River?' It was a statement more than a question.

I shrugged. Nothing more in this conversation would surprise me now. 'You seem to know all about it,' I said.

He chuckled dryly. 'You'd be surprised,' he said, 'although you shouldn't be. You said it yourself—"putting a big boy inside doesn't necessarily mean you're putting him out of business." So you were the patsy who got away, were you? One of the two—the other was a Chink. It figures. "A pair of expendables," I heard. Well, if you're really telling the truth, that ought to put your Mister Bloody Barry in focus for you. *He* put the rub-a-dub on Kowalski—and I'll even tell you who to. Their Commandant there—fellow by the name of Hang Li. That mean anything to you?'

'No.'

'Pity. If you knew him you'd find the rest of it easier to believe. He was one of several that Kowalski had a bloody big sharp Damocles hanging over—usual thing—photos, letters, tape-recordings all neatly filed on the Hong Kong side. Anything happened suddenly to Kowalski, the purge that would have followed would have made Joe Stalin's knock-off parties look like Dorcas sewing circles. That's why he's lasted so long. But you probably know all about that.'

'Some of it,' I said dully. I was feeling very depressed indeed.

'So he naturally passed the tip on to Kowalski. Sorry to disappoint you. I assume they set up a stalking-horse for you. Anyhow, I can assure you that Kowalski was nowhere near that pick-up spot that night. There have been rumours, more rumours and counter-rumours since. He *has* been knocked off—he hasn't been—he's made his way back to your side under his own steam—he's in London—the CIA have got him pinned down in Tokyo. Unfortunately the Tokyo one seemed the most feasible, and that is what I was counting on when I came out. It may still be true—I hope to God it is. The one thing I'm really pissing my pants over is the possibility of his being up here. The reception I got today from this little louse makes me very worried indeed.'

He turned and regarded me closely. 'You're not looking so chipper,' he said.

'I'm not feeling it,' I told him truthfully. I despaired of ever becoming sensibly case-hardened. Every time anything really dirty-nasty like this came up—things involving our own side —it reacted on me the same way. Like the stench of this place. He seemed to guess my thoughts.

'Hell of a game, yours,' he said sympathetically. 'For the straight singler, I mean. You stick your neck out for peanuts, and you're just as likely to get it in the back from one of your own mob as not. Thank Pete that's one thing I've never been forced to do—touch espionage in any shape or form.'

The sheer inconsistency of this jerked me out of myself.

'What the hell are you doing now?' I asked.

'What I always do—or try to do. Playing my own hand,'

he answered. 'Oh, I know all about you people—I've used some of you—lots of you. Some of you have used me—or thought you have—but I've never been on a government payroll in my life. Good clean orthodox crime for Bowyer.'

'Well, I'll be f——' I began, the breath taken right out of me.

'Sh-h!' he said primly, and turned and looked anxiously towards the sleeping Edna. 'She might hear you.'

And that did it. I laughed. I laughed until I was sick, while he chattered angrily in case I woke her.

'All right, you win,' I said, wiping my eyes. 'What *are* you on up here? After the Chinese Crown Jewels? Come on, I won't tell the cops, spy's honour.'

'Bloody funny, aren't you,' he said waspishly. 'All right then, I'll tell you. I'm after the better part of eight million pounds sterling. Put that in your pipe and smoke it, you two-bit imitation James Bond.'

'Gold—like I said. Many a true word spoken in jest.' I grinned.

'Spare me the clichés, Wainwright.' He was really on his dignity now. 'Gold be damned. Do you realize what that amount would mean in terms of sheer weight? No, not gold. The new currency. Snow.'

'What are you going to do with it? Corner the ice cream market?' I began—then I realized what he meant. 'Good God—you mean heroin?'

'Exactly. Less than a fiftieth of the weight of gold—and a hundred times its value—ounce for ounce.'

'Good clean orthodox crime,' I quoted. 'Accent on clean.'

'Don't get on your high horse—ha, "horse"—good, that—that's another name for it. It's your people who put a lot of it in the pipeline, don't forget.' And he had me cold there.

'But that's round Hong Kong,' I said. 'Why come up here after it?'

'Hong Kong is where it starts—at least that's one of the

places,' he told me. 'But this is where it's collected in bulk—before being shipped along to the Break.'

I managed to repress a start, but only just. 'Why send it to the Break?' I asked, trying to sound a little bored. I think I even yawned.

'Oh God!' he said, pained. 'I began by feeling rather sorry for you, Wainwright. I'm feeling sorry for your wretched employers now. Are you really that dumb—or are you trying to pull my leg? I just told you—the new currency. That's what they're paying in now. Don't you realize that Albania is the dope centre of the world? That Tirana has ousted both Cairo and Istanbul and is ten times bigger than both of them combined ever were? A biscuit-throw from their coast across to Sicily—and the main distributors, the Mafia. Diplomatic bags, immune from search, going to every part of the world. It's the biggest business that ever was—bigger than the arms industry, which it largely finances anyway. Surely you've heard of the new Chinese heroin?'

'I see,' I said slowly. 'And you're going to cut yourself an eight million hunk off all this, are you?'

'I *have* cut off the hunk,' he said succinctly. 'Or rather siphoned it off. Kowalski put the proposition to me in Hong Kong, four years ago. That was when it was being set up, and he was the go-between with the People's Republic and the Albanians. He took me into Communist China as his assistant—vouched for me as a non-political. I came up to these parts as sort of depot manager. The stuff used to come up the passes by the hundredweight at first, then by the ton. It was sorted and graded here, then shipped along to the Break——'

'The Break being where in those days?' I asked casually.

'Where it's always been, for Christ's sake,' he said impatiently. 'Twenty miles on from here——' Then he realized he'd fallen for it.

'Doing your bloody job for you, am I?' he snarled. 'What

the hell does it matter, anyway? You'll never get back with it. I think I'm just talking for the sake of talking now. Where was I? Oh yes, this was the main receiving post. The fellow in command was as bent as they come—not only bent, but hooked as well—Kowalski always got them on it. Tried to get me on it—*me*—the filthy bastard. Anyhow, he was easy. It was just a matter of slipping a percentage of the top-grade stuff to one side here. It's in brick form, as you probably know. I got over three tons of it put away before I was put away myself.'

'But where the hell did you hide it?' I asked.

'Here, you bloody fool,' he snapped. 'Aren't I telling you? Do stop interrupting, will you? This place is a cave, half natural, half excavated, as you probably saw when we came in. The top end is all ammunition magazines. The stuff is in air-tight containers laid on the floors and thinly concreted over.' He bent forward, his head between his hands, and stared at the floor.

'Christ! I'm giving my guts away,' he said. 'Not even Kowalski—not *anybody*—knew that before this minute. I did it all myself while Kowalski was away—I used to make the commander take all the troops out of the post on the pretext of training—then I'd get down to it. There was a concrete-mixer here and all the material I needed.'

There was silence for a long time, and I thought he had gone to sleep, but then he resumed, talking in a flat monotone.

'It was that which put Kowalski's back up. I wouldn't tell him where it was—not until I had an absolute guarantee—and was out of the country with it. We were going to take it into India, through Burma, the way we came in now. Up here he could have double-crossed me without difficulty. Down there we'd have had a Damocles on each other. We went out to arrange a deal with a Syrian syndicate in Calcutta. Kowalski was on a spying mission for these people—looking at the Indian frontier posts. He said he needed me with him, and they let us go. And then the bastard planted this gold on me at Calcutta airport—just like that.'

He raised his head and stared at me wildly. 'That's the only bright spot in this whole lousy set-up,' he said. 'That is what I went to sleep on every night, laughing, in that damned jail. He put it to me reasonably, said this was absurd, we were in it together, it was too big for one to handle, and surely to God there was enough dough in it that we didn't need to fear a double-cross from each other, and so on, and so on. And I was just as reasonable. Sure—now we were out of China I'd tell him. And I did. I said I'd stashed it in a gun redoubt a couple of miles from here. Actually I *had* done some concreting work there and made sure the commandant knew of it. And Kowalski fell for it—because that's when he had me pinched. I like to think of him digging that dump over. It must have needled the balls off him.'

'How do you know that he, or somebody else, hasn't found the real place since?' I asked him, and he grinned at me and tapped the side of his nose.

'Nobody has touched that stuff,' he said. 'I'd have heard—and a lot of other bastards would have heard too. Old Bowyer the craftsman—the *crafty* craftsman.'

'So now you've come back to collect it?' I said. 'Somehow I can't see them letting you dig their floors up, just like that.'

I expected him to fly off the handle again, but he didn't. He turned his mournful eyes on me and said, 'Neither can I, the way things look at the moment.' He drove his fist into the other palm. 'Damn it, Wainwright, it was fixed. It was all fixed to the last detail, weeks before I came out of stir. The fellow who was Commandant here has been promoted. He's military governor in Chamdo now. He got word down to me. "Come and get it," he said. "Kowalski's dead. Cut me in on it in his place—and I'll come back to India with you." That's what he said.'

'And you believed him? No guarantee—nothing?'

234

'Why shouldn't I have believed him? I knew him. He's no dedicated Chairman Mao-worshipping Marxist. He's a bent Chinaman who likes good living, and a junkie to boot —and I've got the dirt on him—and he'd been promised his cut by Kowalski originally, and that was bugging him like hell. Do you *know* anything about the Chinese, Wainwright?'

'A little.'

'Well, figure it out for yourself. Disappointing a Chinaman over a money deal is like taking a kill from a Bengal tiger just when he's got his teeth into it. Oh yes, I believed him all right, because then I was believing that Kowalski was dead— I'd heard that from other sources. The two things fitted.'

'When did you first have doubts about that?'

'In Chamdo. The son of a bitch was nervy, jumpy, twitchy. At first I thought it was just because he wasn't getting his fixes regularly down there—the stuff's all up here, and they watch it properly now. He didn't come across with all he'd promised me—a proper column, coolies, and a safe-conduct that even he couldn't monkey about with afterwards. It was the brush-off all right. He just wanted me off the premises as quickly as possible, without getting further involved himself. I'm beginning to see it now. And he certainly didn't say that this little jerk was in command up here. This one *is* a Mao man.'

'But you still came on,' I said. 'You walked right into it. That's what I can't understand.'

'Oh, you clever, far-sighted, clear-thinking young bastard, you,' he raged. 'You can see it all now, can't you—now that I'm telling you. I had no option but to come on. He shoved us in the guest house for a couple of days while we rested, then put us in the charge of these three monkeys and *sent* us on. Anyhow, although warning bells were starting to ring. I wasn't stone-cold certain that I was being handed the belt at that stage. It had all gone so smoothly up until then. The trip had been laid on properly—I'd been provided with Bapu and

235

a radio set—I'd been getting my instructions at the correct times. I'd even been warned of the possibility of you people being on our tails—but that wasn't worrying me too much. If you managed to get up here I knew the Chinks would deal with you.' He grinned mirthlessly. 'That part of it looks like coming true at least.'

'As a matter of interest, where did you get that particular tip-off from?' I asked.

'You've got your gall with you,' he said. 'Why the hell should I tell you?' Then he shrugged. 'Not that it matters much now. I got that from a two-bit crook who was supposed to have been masterminding my flit from Calcutta—and who made a balls of things.'

'Snaith?' I asked, and he snorted.

'I'll Snaith the bastard if I ever see him again. If it hadn't been for him I wouldn't have landed Edna in the mulligatawny here.'

'How did that come about?'

'Edna, bless her,' he answered, and his whole face softened, 'came out to be in Calcutta when I was released—but then I got the tip inside that Chatterjee had tabs on her, so I sent word out to Snaith to get her a false passport and to ship her on to Rangoon. It was either that or send her back to England, and I knew she'd jib at that. He pocketed the three thousand rupees the falsy was supposed to have cost, and pinched one from a whore in a Lower Circular Road knocking-shop, the dishonest sod——'

'Paola Alberghetti?' Illogically I was strangely relieved.

'That's right. You had to be in Burke's Landed Gentry to get into that at one time. She's down to a hundred chips a bump now—sailors half-price. Damn it all!' he went on indignantly. 'They're not even alike—but you know what passport photos are. It got Edna through, but every fool in the world knows that there's a mark on whores' passports out in these parts. She was subjected to all sorts of annoyances.'

'By whom?'

'The cops in Rangoon—who else? Randy lot of bastards. A superintendent and two inspectors round to the hotel the same night, after a free lay. The Burmese have got the morals of monkeys. Scared the hell out of the lass. And she's from a good family. Christ, her old man was a missionary in the Deccan.' He glared at me furiously. 'What the hell are you grinning at, you bloody ape?'

'Certainly not at Mrs. Bowyer,' I assured him.

'You'd better not,' he growled. 'Girl in a million that—fifty million. She knows the worst of me—or nearly, but she still sticks to me. Anyhow, I couldn't leave her in Burma then, so there was nothing for it but to send for her from Letpadam—and here she is. And all because of Snaith.'

'What had Chatterjee got tabs on her for?' I asked.

'Purely as a second lead to me. They knew damned well that I was going to make a flit, and she was insurance against my shaking them cold—which I did, in spite of Snaith.' He said this with some pride, then looked at me sheepishly. 'Yes, I know you managed to hang on—but you had Rees with you, and he's the better of any ten top cops East of Suez—the son of a bitch. I wish to God he was here now. I think he'd be a bit my way, if only because of Edna. Wainwright, where is he?' he finished desperately.

And I think in that moment I almost told him, because I was accepting him now at face value—a frightened man tortured by anxiety. But some forgotten vestige of my training came to the surface. Rees—even a dead Rees—was still the ace in the hole, an ace I might conceivably be very glad of at some time later.

'He's around somewhere,' I said vaguely.

'I'd trust him,' he said. 'He's a gentleman—which is more than some of you other buggers are. No offence meant to you personally,' he added hastily. 'But I'd be prepared to make a deal with him—with some hope of his sticking to his end of it.'

'What sort of a deal?'

'He could name his own terms. All I want is out for Edna. Out for me, too, if possible—but Edna for sure.'

'All right,' I said. 'Rees could name his own terms—*now*, when you're scared——'

'Who said I'm scared?' he demanded.

'Let's not kid each other, Bowyer,' I told him. 'You're scared all right. So am I. But suppose it turns out that there's no need for you to be scared, that Kowalski *is* dead, and that they let you out with this stuff. What about Rees, or me, then?'

'I'd cut you in for a piece, naturally. I said he could name his own terms, didn't I? So could you.'

'But Rees is a gentleman,' I said. 'Your own words. He mightn't want a piece. Some gentlemen have pretty narrow views on the heroin racket.'

'Well, that would be up to him, wouldn't it?' he said with a shade of uncertainty. 'Up to you too. It'd be there if you wanted it.'

'Don't talk cock,' I said. 'What I'm saying is, what good would a couple of tons of junk be to you down there if we were at large and knew about it?'

'You're not cops,' he mumbled.

'We're on that side of the fence. Personally I'd shop you— bing!—just like that. Like you said, I'm no gentleman——'

'I didn't say that——'

'——but I don't like heroin either. Incidentally, does she know about it?' I nodded towards the sleeping Edna.

'Good God, no!' he exploded, shocked to the core. 'She'd kill me.'

'Then what the hell does she think you're doing up here? Collecting butterflies?'

He looked sheepish again. 'A trade deal for the Chinese Government. Honest but illegal. She thinks that's what I was framed for—and she's on my side because of it.'

'Right!' I shot back at him. 'There's your deal. Call it a mutual aid pact if you like. If we get out of here we'll join forces and I'll help you back. But the junk stays where it is—or we refer the whole thing to Mrs Bowyer.'

'Er—thanks,' he said awkwardly, 'but—er—I'd feel more comfortable if Rees were in on it. I mean—well, he knows his way around up here. I don't know about you, but *I* wouldn't be able to make that trip back without guides and equipment and supplies and all that—and we wouldn't have the Chinks to help this time.'

'I'll answer for Rees,' I said. 'We've got to meet up with him first—and we won't do that in here. The first thing we've got to do is to get out. We've got a guide'—I jerked my head at the muffled form that was Tulsa—'and I don't know whether it's occurred to you, but your pal the commandant isn't up to his job. We've still got our packs and you've got my arms in yours, plus odds and ends of food.'

'Not enough to last us back,' he said anxiously.

'I've got contacts once we're over the pass,' I told him, and added, since it seemed to count so much with him, 'and, of course, a lot of our difficulties will be over once we meet Rees.'

'Where will that be?' he asked eagerly.

'Let's think about getting out first,' I said profoundly. 'That's going to be the biggest obstacle of the lot. What sort of guard do they keep at night here? Do you know?'

But that didn't seem to be worrying him. 'A couple of sloppy sentries, asleep most of the time. They rely on their trip-wires. A bloody mouse couldn't get down that track without starting a dozen alarms ringing. But there's still no problem there—I know a back way out. Don't forget I was here when they were constructing the place. It's what happens once they discover we've gone that worries me. There's only one way we can go, and that's the way we came—and they'll be after us like a pack of bloody wolves.'

239

'Any possibility of going the other way, and then circling round over the top?' I asked him, and he looked at me pityingly.

'I didn't seem to make myself clear,' he said. 'That's the way to the Break. God Almighty! Haven't you people any idea of it at all? It's a city, I tell you—a nuclear-proof city. That place will be their nerve-centre when the crap hits the fan in the future and their surface cities have been flattened. The Yanks and the Russians are digging the same sort of places, but here it's all been done for them already——'

'Caves?'

'That's over-simplifying it. A series of faults along the course of an underground river—the Yangtse itself before it comes to the surface. They've got everything they need there—in duplicate. A hell of a big nuclear reactor *and* hydro-electric power—top technicians—Czechs, Poles, Hungarians, Albanians—from every country that doesn't like Russia.'

'For a bloke who never touched espionage, you seem to have been doing all right,' I told him.

He shrugged. 'I was part of the fixings,' he said. 'I just kept my eyes and ears open and my mouth shut. They're used to Europeans being around—there must be three or four hundred of them permanently stationed there, plus a lot more coming and going. Of course there's a hell of a lot going on that even I never got a chance to look at—but I could make guesses. Don't forget I'm a pretty good technician myself, one way and another.' He finished on a note of pride.

'Do you realize what value this could have been to our own people if you'd only had the sense to talk when you got back?' I asked him. He stared at me.

'What do you mean by "our own people"?' he asked. '*I've* got no people—only her.'

'You know damned well what I mean,' I snapped. 'There

240

may be a few splinter factions, but when it all boils down there are only two sides in the world today—Them and Us——'

'So you're admitting me to your club, are you?' he said dryly. 'Thanks, but you can stuff it. I'm a loner, Wainwright—I have been ever since I pulled my way out of an Indian bazaar by my bootstraps—correction—by what *would* have been my bootstraps if I'd had any bloody boots. No, thanks—I'm not knocking on any doors. That way you don't get them slammed in your face——'

'Oh, stop being sorry for yourself,' I said. 'All right, you're a loner, but there's one question I'd like to ask——'

But I didn't have time to, because at that minute Kowalski arrived.

Chapter Twenty

JUST LIKE THAT. The door opened and he was standing there with two soldiers, one of them carrying a lamp. I'd never seen him before, not even a photo, but there was no mistaking him from a graphic word picture of him that the Gaffer had once given me. 'Happy-looking bastard—round-faced like a Glaxo baby—scowl masking a grin—looks at you very direct. Try describing Winston Churchill if you didn't like him.' That was him to the life. I heard Bowyer's sharp intake of breath that was almost a groan and he made a quick step to one side. I think he intended to go for one of the guns in the packs, but it was too late then. The soldiers had him by the arms and through the door.

Kowalski looked at me quizzically. He stood with his feet apart and his hands thrust into the pockets of his quilted coat, a karakul cap pushed to the back of his head.

'Wainwright, eh?' he said. 'One of the Gaffer's bright young men. I had a file on you back in Canton. Not so terribly bright at the moment, though—not that I'd say it was all your fault.' Except for the characteristic lengthening of the vowel sounds by the Shanghai Mig, his English was accentless. He might have been a kindly colonel gently criticizing a green subaltern after a training exercise. 'I never did agree with his system of throwing you youngsters in at the deep end and leaving you to drown if you didn't come up with something useful. Not sentiment—I'm not a sentimental man—just plain bad economics I'd call it.'

He felt in his pocket and fished out a packet of English

cigarettes, extracted two and flicked me one. I made no attempt to catch it, but my eyes followed it to where it rolled.

He lit his own and twinkled at me humorously over the flame because my sidelong glance had not escaped him.

'That's right.' He grinned. 'You can use it later—if they let you.' He blew out a cloud of smoke. 'No, not your fault,' he went on. 'This all started when you would have been sucking sugartits back in old Shanghai. Christ, it goes back to Chiang Kai-shek's days. *I* set it up and bought half a dozen of his Sling Dung Hi generals, and the stupid bastards thought they were buying *me*. Then I bought the Comrades, then the Japs, each with his own coin—junk when they wanted it, or the things junk could buy for them—and when I struck the very rare sea-green incorruptible, with information. Junk for info, info for junk, round and round the mulberry bush, with reliable old Kowalski always the man in the middle, too valuable for any of them to knock off, a safe deposit full of Damocles ready to open like Pandora's box if ever anything went wrong with my digestion.' He cupped his hand. 'I had 'em there—the bloody lot of them. I've still got 'em there. Then a tenth-rate little spieler like Bowyer tries to hijack me out of the real nest-egg I'd been building up for my old age, and nearly succeeds, the bastard. So what do I do? I stage my own bow-out when you people try to get me off the beach up the Canton River, because I know that Bowyer is due out from Alipore before long, and he wouldn't have the guts to come back up here to collect the boodle if there was a chance of my showing up. And it works —and the wily old Gaffer sends you in on his tail because neither he nor anybody else knows for certain whether I'm dead or alive, and this might be a lead. And while Bowyer's got his eye cocked over his shoulder watching you, I'm sitting up here all the time with the string in my hand, ready to pull it.' He shook his head sadly. 'You walked right into it.

243

I've got nothing against you, boy. I've got nothing against any professional trying to make a near-honest living. You're my type—a gentleman—and they're getting as rare as rocking-horse shit in this business nowadays. I'll be sorry to see you leave.'

And like a fool I asked, 'Leave for where?'

He looked surprised at the very naivety of the question. 'The Interrogation Centre at the Break—where else? There's a couple of makee-talks being sent up for your special benefit.'

'Wasted journey for somebody,' I said wearily. 'I know damn-all about anything, except that I was told to follow Bowyer.'

He clucked sympathetically. 'Yes, I kind of guessed that,' he said. 'But I had to embroider things a bit in my own interests. You're a very important man in the Gaffer's set-up, I told 'em. You know plenty. Only a matter of getting you to spill it. Great excitement. All the local brass is gathering there to get in on the act before the real heavy mob arrives over from Peking. While they're preoccupied there I hope to be out and over the passes with a bit of private baggage of my own. I'm afraid there's not much future in it for you, except for a bit of discomfort and the big chop at the end of it, but then, that's one of the contingent liabilities of this business, isn't it? Occupational hazard, as they say.' He smiled at me benignly. 'Well now,' he said. 'It's been nice talking to you. I hope I've been able to dot a few i's and cross a few t's for you, and generally put things in focus.'

'You've at least confirmed something I once heard the Gaffer say about you,' I answered.

'What was that?' he asked, interested.

'That if there was royalty in bastards you'd be the king, queen, and crown prince.'

He looked indignant. 'The lying old sod!' he exploded. 'He can't be honest, even in his insults. *I* said that about *him*—many long years ago.' Then he turned on his heel and went abruptly, and I could hear him chuckling as he went down the passage.

Tulsa was sitting up looking at me. Thank God, the girl still slept the sleep of deep exhaustion. I hoped she would stay that way for a long time. They had left the door ajar again fortunately, no doubt because their hands had been occupied with hustling Bowyer out.

I went and looked into the passageway. To the right it ran into the big caserne where I could dimly see soldiers sleeping in shelved bunks round the walls. The other way it ran past a series of steel doorways before turning a right-angled bend to the left. The lighting system seemed to be a hodge-podge of dim electric bulbs sparingly spaced throughout the whole place, and the smoky oil-lamps the troops carried. Out here, away from the charcoal *sigri*, the cold was intense, and so was the stench I had noticed as we came in.

I thought bitterly of the time Bowyer and I had wasted talking of what now seemed complete inconsequences. He knew of a back way out, he said. If only he'd told me more about it we might have had some faint chance. I noticed that all the steel doors except that to our chamber and the one next to it were heavily padlocked, and all were stencilled with the Chinese ideograph meaning danger, and rough pictures of men's heads with cigarettes in their mouths heavily overscored with red crosses, which is their conventional sign for 'No Smoking.' The lamps they were carrying and the charcoal sigri in our chamber seemed to be a typically Chinese dereliction of this.

I went back into the chamber and retrieved my gun from Bowyer's pack, tossing his to Tulsa. I don't know why I did it exactly, except that I might have had a half-formed hope that I wouldn't be searched before going into the interrogation room, and that there might be a chance of getting at it before the going got too rough.

I said, 'I'm sorry about this, Tulsa. I've brought you into trouble.'

His teeth flashed in a grin through the gloom as he stowed the gun away and patted it.

'That all right, sahib,' he said. 'Maybe I get bloody bandoowala who take my kukri.'

'Tell them you know nothing,' I advised him. 'Just that I hired you as a guide in Chamdo. I say the same.'

He nodded his understanding and told me not to worry about him.

'Bowyer sahib told me that there was a way out—back,' I told him. 'I go and have look-see. Stay with the mem-sahib.' I hadn't the faintest hope, but anything was better than sitting here just waiting.

I went back into the passage and then, because it was obviously not much good going into the caserne, I went the other way—up and round the right-angled bend. And I realized where the stench was coming from, because it ended at a square pit that was more than apparently the latrine for the whole place, and a couple of troops were squatting there companionably. How they could stand it I just wouldn't be knowing, but I suppose it was better than getting one's backside frostbitten outside. I beat a hasty retreat and explored our chamber thoroughly to see if any sort of cranny led out of it, but the walls were plain, unbroken concrete. I went into the one next door, but it was just a duplicate of our own.

There was nothing for it then but just to sit and wait, and think, madness notwithstanding, of what might have been but for my own stupidity, and, I thought savagely, Bowyer's as well. Then I went to sleep.

The clang of a door and the shuffling of feet outside woke me. I thought, with a chilling feeling round the pit of my guts, that they had come for me, but the noise was further down the passage. I looked at my watch. It showed just short of nine. I'd been asleep for over three hours. Tulsa was on his feet peering out into the passage. I got up and went across to him.

'Bowyer sahib,' he whispered. 'They put him in next room.'

The troops came out and shot the bolt on the door and then went off to the caserne. I waited until they were out of sight, then slipped out and went along to the other door and eased the bolt back. Light filtered dimly in from the passage and I could see Bowyer lying on the floor, face downwards. I went in and knelt beside him and tried to turn him over, but his agonized whimpering stopped me. He was stripped to the waist, and my hands slipped on his wet shoulders. They'd been working on him all right. I swallowed hard to fight back the nausea that nearly overcame me.

'Bowyer, it's me, Wainwright,' I whispered urgently.

'Get—her—out of it,' he croaked. 'Or—or shoot her—if you've got to. Promise me, Wainwright—promise me. He's —going to—give her to the troops——'

'One or the other—I promise,' I said. 'But for Christ's sake, why did you go through all this? Why didn't you tell the bastard and get it over?'

'Make time——' he gasped. 'I had to—see you again. There's a chance—back way.'

'Tell me quick,' I said.

'Top of passage—latrine—outfall pipe opens into pass lower down cliff. They can't use it—bloody fools—didn't realize it—would freeze up. On—right—of the pit——' His voice was fading.

I shook him gently. 'I'll get Tulsa,' I told him. 'We'll get each side of you——'

'Shut up and listen,' he answered. 'There'll be a delay now —I've told him where it is—but they'll have to clear one of— the magazines out first—dig up—floor. Get out now—and get as far from cliff face as possible—*Now*!'

'Come on,' I said, and added without conviction, 'If we

247

can do it, you can.' I tried to raise him again, but I could see it was hopeless.

'Don't be a bloody fool,' he said. 'You're wasting time. You promised, Wainwright—you promised.'

'What the hell is *she* going to say when she finds out that we left you?' I asked.

'Tell her—anything you like—just so as it isn't the truth.' His voice was fading again. I bent over him and just caught, '—girl in fifty million—good family——' Then I was conscious of Tulsa kneeling beside us and feeling Bowyer gently.

I said, 'We've got to get him on to his feet and out of here.'

'No good, sahib,' he answered. 'Feel leg.' And only then did I realize that the whole thing was twisted grotesquely outward from the hip down. Bowyer had rallied for a moment and was talking to Tulsa in Urdu too fast for me to follow.

The Gurkha nodded solemnly, stood up and touched me on the arm.

'Sahib right,' he said. 'We move fast. He no can do.'

'I'll leave you a gun,' I said miserably. 'In case they——' but I couldn't finish it.

'Nothing more they'll want to do,' he said. 'I've told 'em. I'd only get the works again if it wasn't the truth—and it *is*— my oath it is.'

I said, 'All right,' dully. I got up and moved to the door. I didn't say any more. What was there to say? 'Goodbye— good luck?' Bit stupid under the circumstances—and I'd seen what they'd done to his fingers by this time, so a firm manly handclasp was out of the question also. I just thought of the priggishly superior advice I'd given to Kam Foo in somewhat similar circumstances.

We just had time to get back to our own chamber before they came up the passage. Kowalski, the Commandant and four troops carrying picks and crowbars. Peering through the chink of the door, I saw them unlock a magazine three up from us and I thought that this finally had cut off our retreat, because we had to pass it on the way up the passage. They started to drag boxes out, and I felt pretty fluttery round the stomach as I saw the way they were doing it. There was gun ammunition, crates of hand-grenades and even some of that most volatile of stuff—phosphorous flares—all easily distinguishable because some of the cases were open and their contents just strewn around. God, I've never seen such a Fire Officer's nightmare in my life—and they were just chucking it out into the passage as if it was cheese. Then, when they'd got one corner of the place cleared, they all went inside, and I could hear the clanging of the picks on the concrete.

This appeared to be our moment. I stepped across to the girl. She had awakened but still seemed dazed. I pulled her to her feet, hissing at her to be quiet, and got her into her coat, while Tulsa sorted out the packs. I got my arm round her waist, and hers across my shoulders, and we slipped out into the passage and round the pile of ammunition, and scuttled up towards the thickening stink—and we ran straight into the sulky soldier who was coming away from the john, doing his belt up.

His mouth opened to yell, but Tulsa swung one of the packs into his belly, and was on to him like a terrier. I heard the hollow thump of his head on the concrete and a happy little grunt from Tulsa, but I was too busy steering and supporting the girl to look round.

We came up to the edge of that ghastly pit, and Tulsa, who had evidently received more detailed instructions from Bowyer than I, squeezed past me round to the right. I'll skip the details thereafter. My gorge still rises when I think of it—but we found the outlet. It was a sloping chute from the side of the pit about two feet in diameter. Thank God that which it contained was mostly frozen, but sliding down it still remains the experience of my life I would least like to

249

repeat. Tulsa, brave little bastard, went first—then I lowered the girl down—then I followed.

We came out about twenty-five feet down the cliff side, into a snowdrift. I never appreciated the clean feel of snow so much before. Above us I could see the loom of the cliff into which the caserne ran back, and my heart stood still as I heard a cough and somebody clearing his throat right above me.

These people wear white overalls over their quilting, and they merge into the snow. We, I knew, would stand out once we moved from the shadow of the cliff—but we had to, because this was where the path ran, with its trip-wires. I was taking it very gingerly for this reason, easing the girl forward a foot at a time, but some madness seemed to descend on Tulsa, and he was dragging us forward recklessly. I hissed at him to be careful of the wire, but he hissed back, 'Bugger wires, sahib—get away from cliff!' And then, of course, the inevitable happened and we must have hit a bunch of them under the snow, because I heard the muffled clamouring of bells above us and a startled challenge—and then a search-light came on and swept the path, and it held us even as we dropped flat.

There was a pounding of feet as the guard turned out, and then a ragged fusillade of rifle shots that came pretty close because I could hear the rounds hissing into the snow. But somebody must have joggled the searchlight, because it left us for a moment and I rolled to one side, pulling the girl with me.

The snow seemed to have revived her, because she suddenly became aware of the absence of Bowyer, and started to call for him frantically. There was nothing for it short of slugging her, so I pushed her face down into the snow and held it there. She struggled violently and broke free and started to run wildly back up the path. Tulsa dived at her and brought her down—and by this time the bells were really ringing.

I heard someone yell to stop firing and get down after :
and then the clang of the barrier as it swung open, and I was
weeping with sick resignation. We had been so close to it.

Then as they piled out there was a rumble and a blinding
flash from the caserne door that lit the whole scene as brightly
as the midday sun. I saw the guards frozen in the light for a
split second, then they vanished as another flash shot out and
the whole of the emplacement just seemed to crumble and
slide—and that was followed by a deafening roar, and I was
picked up like a leaf by the wind and swept downhill.

Blinded and deafened, I slid to a halt and picked myself
up shakily, then I saw movement to one side of me as Tulsa
emerged from the snow tugging at the girl. I gaped stupidly
back at the emplacement, but all I could see was a column of
smoke, black against the night sky, rising from a tumbled
heap of concrete. Beside me Tulsa chuckled throatily.

'Bowyer sahib say he fix proper,' he murmured. 'Hit
wrong place whole bloody lot go boom-bang.'

And then I understood. 'Old Bowyer—the crafty craftsman,' he had said. 'Nobody has touched that stuff or I'd
have heard—and a lot of other bastards would have heard
too.'

So that was why he had stood out against the treatment
for three whole bloody hours. To make time. To try and get
word to me. To get his Edna—the girl in a million—from a
good family—out of it.

The rest is almost anticlimax. We made it to the pass in
eight hours—with me lying steadily to Edna for the first four
of them. Bowyer had left ahead of us, I assured her, and
would be waiting for us at the pass. But it was no good. I
had to tell her in the end, as gently as I knew how, bowdler-
izing and glossing where I thought it necessary to spare her
feelings, but sticking to the truth where I could. I certainly
stuck to the truth as far as he was concerned. I think it was

the only time I ever used the words 'a very gallant gentle-man' without them sounding corny in my own ears. She took it very well indeed. She just screwed up her face—and then went dead. And she stayed that way, her face a blank mask, walking mechanically between us, all the way to Bhup Nath's place, and then beyond it, over the lower passes, skirting Chamdo, and so down again to Myitkyina and into the care of Puram Singh's excellent organization once more. I paid Tulsa off there—with five hundred rupees and a new kukri. He was delighted. I felt cheap.

Edna thanked me nicely, as a girl of good family should, when I put her on a London plane in Rangoon, this time on her own passport, which she had been carrying next to her skin, together with her marriage lines.

But she was still dead inside.

The debriefing was in London—by the Gaffer himself, in his filthy flat near Victoria. It wasn't any worse than usual, but very, very thorough. He sat back when it was over and picked his rotten teeth with a matchstick and grinned at me like an obscene goat.

'So you're fingering Barry this time, are you?' he asked.

'I'm telling it to you as it was told to me,' I said.

'By Bowyer?'

'By Bowyer.'

'And you believed him?'

'Yes. He had nothing to lie for then.'

'He wasn't. It was like he said. Hang Li passed the tip on. It was Kowalski who reneged on coming out. He had no intention of coming—not then. We know why now, don't we? Poor old Kowalski. There'll never be another real pro like him.' He grinned even wider. 'Sorry to disappoint you. I don't like Barry either. He's as queer as a four-dollar bill, but he ain't doubling for anybody—not as far as we know,' he added with his usual caution. He rose and stretched. 'Oh, well, no more of a bollocks-up than usual. You haven't brought back anything we didn't know—but confirmation is always a good thing. At least we'll know where to put the ferrets in, won't we? Maybe a ferret like you—you never know your luck.'

'I do,' I said. 'And I'm not pushing it. *I'm* quitting this time. I'm sick of being fired, and then re-hired without being consulted.'

'You want to bet?' He twinkled at me. 'Quitting be damned. They think well of you up top. Christ, you've just had a raise. Two hundred a year—less tax, of course. That'll put you up twenty-five bob a week, net. The things the British taxpayer does for some of you geniuses. Cor!'

'I'm still quitting,' I said firmly.

'Enjoy your leave and come back refreshed,' he said. 'Have a bit of fun—you could do with it. Talking about fun, not a bad bit of stuff that Mrs Bowyer, is she? I bet the trip back was warmer than the one out, eh?'

I leaned across the table. 'You're an old man, Gaffer,' I said. 'But make a crack like that again and I'll beat the crap out of you.'

'You could always try.' He grinned. 'I'd have you on your back, twitching slightly and moaning for your Ma while you were still making your mind up.'

You could never get the last word with the filthy old swine. He yawned. 'Well, that's the lot from me. Any questions?'

'Only one,' I answered. 'You had somebody waiting for me at Chamdo. How did you know I'd make it?'

'Wainwright,' he said solemnly, 'a man who would push on towards his objective as you did, alone and without supplies, would be bound to make it. We never had a moment's doubt about you, lad.'

And believe it or not I had to swallow hard before I could go on. *This*, from the *Gaffer*.

'Good of you,' I mumbled modestly. 'But I still don't

understand how you *knew* I'd gone on alone—that the others were no longer with me.'

'Rees told us, for God's sake,' he said, staring at me. 'Who else?'

'But Rees was *dead*,' I squeaked.

'Dead my foot,' he said. 'He and his Pathan dug themselves out of the snow three-quarters of a mile down the valley—a broken arm and five busted ribs between them. They were watching you through the glasses, but they couldn't do anything to help you.'

I thought my heart would burst. 'That's the best news that's come out of the whole rotten show,' I said enthusiastically. 'Can you put me in touch with him when I go back? I'd like to thank him.'

He grinned again. 'I wouldn't bother if I were you,' he told me. 'Actually he was a bit sour about it. He reckoned if you'd had the sense of a louse you'd have found the one line of retreat out of that valley—and that if you'd found it you'd have taken it like a bat out of hell. You were looking hard enough apparently, but in all the wrong places—as bloody usual.'

O, blessed is he who expects nothing but whips and scorpions from the Gaffers and Reeses of this business, because that shall be his portion.